On a Blanket with My Baby

♦ ♦ ♦ ♦ ♦

ALSO BY BILL KENT

Under the Boardwalk
Down by the Sea

On a Blanket with My Baby

♦ ♦ ♦ ♦ ♦

A novel of Atlantic City

BILL KENT

ST. MARTIN'S PRESS
NEW YORK

This novel is fiction. The people, places, procedures, organizations, and geographic locations are imaginary. Any resemblances to existing items, elements, and personalities are coincidental and unintended.

Library of Congress Cataloging-in-Publication Data

Kent, Bill.
    On a blanket with my baby / Bill Kent.
        p.   cm.
    "A Thomas Dunne book."
    ISBN 0-312-11870-8
    I. Title.
PS3561.E51605   1995
813'.54—dc20   94-46274
                                                         CIP

First edition: April 1995

10   9   8   7   6   5   4   3   2   1

For Elaine,
of course,
and for Stephen Leo,
who has learned to turn his blanket into amazing things.

Acknowledgments

♦ ♦ ♦ ♦ ♦

VIP List: Robin Rue, Ruth Cavin, Ross Thomas, Peter Blauner, Art Bourgeau, and members of the Atlantic City Police Department and the Atlantic City casino industry for taking me back-of-the-house.

Contents

♦ ♦ ♦ ♦ ♦

On a Blanket with My Baby

◆ ◆ ◆ ◆ ◆

Chapter One

♦ ♦ ♦ ♦ ♦

Harry the Toad

He dreamed of the ocean. He could smell it and he could hear the ratcheting snap of the handcuffs going around his wrists. He felt the cuffs bite into his arms as he was lifted and the cuffs hung from a corroding hook beneath Brighton Pier. His arms hurt. He wanted to shout for help but the ocean would drown out his cries. He was aware that he was just out of view of the Boardwalk.

He felt the water swirl around his legs and shuddered as the garden hose whipped across his chest, his arms, his face. Then came the baseball bat.

Faces floated into his vision. He heard laughter of men enjoying themselves. Then he heard his gun discharging. When he heard the gun he woke, the sound becoming a question:

Had he killed someone?

He couldn't move. He opened the eye that would open and saw a man looking at him. The man had a round, flat moon face, with a nose that had been broken many times.

"Uh, hi," Louis Monroe said.

The man asked him if he knew who he was.

"Gant," Monroe said, his throat constricted, his mouth dry. "Captain Marty Gant. You're in charge of the vice squad."

"Was," in a low voice.

"I retired," Gant said. "This gentleman to my right is Harry the—I mean to say, Councilman-at-Large Harry

1

Todesco. Councilman Todesco sits on the Public Safety Commission, which supervises the police budget—"

"Safety first," Councilman Todesco said, "That's my motto." He had a broad, wide beak, fluffy white hair, square, tortoiseshell glasses and a wide, jowly mouth, tensed now as he looked at Monroe.

"There's an election coming up," Gant concluded. "Councilman Todesco is visiting all fifteen-LODs. Get his picture taken showing his support for the troops."

A 15-LOD was a radio code for an officer injured in the line of duty.

"Take my picture, take my hand, just don't take my wife, she's dead," Councilman Todesco said. He tilted his head when he looked at Monroe. "Why is this man isolated?"

Gant said, "You know why."

"We don't want you talking in your sleep, do we?" Todesco said. He winked at Monroe. "Nice setup. If it were me, I'd watch smutty movies and feel up the nurses all day." He turned to Gant. "This is the one you told me about? The one who'd turn his own wife in if he caught her hands in the cookie jar."

"I'd rather not have him do that, but, yes, Lou here is a regular Boy Scout. Honest as they come. Respects the law. Follows it to the letter," Gant said.

The councilman turned around and called, "I'll only be a minute in here. Tell the, umm, *ex*tinguished members of the media that I'll meet them in the lobby? Heh." He closed the door to Monroe's room, approached the bed, folded his hands, raised them to his face, stuck his thumbs in his ears, and wiggled his fingers at Monroe.

"Gotcha!" he said.

"What I'm suggesting, Councilman," Gant continued, "is for an administrative order, to come down on your say-so, requiring Detective Monroe to maintain silence about events leading up to his injuries. I assure you, sir, he would do exactly that."

Todesco came close, stuck his face into Monroe's vision. "Son, how you feel on the subject of revenge?"

"It's wrong, sir."

"Can you think of a time when it's justified?"

Monroe tried to think. "No, sir. Revenge can never be justified."

Todesco nodded, apparently impressed. "Now, son, how'd you like to make a deal with me?"

"I'm sorry, sir. I don't make deals."

"I run a car lot up on Route Thirty, son. Todesco Luxury Motors. New and used. Imports, too. You'd be surprised how many imports on the road are used. Better than new. A few knocks, a few years on the road, toughens a car. Now, you'd think that would be enough, but everybody who comes on my lot wants a deal. I want to give you a deal, son."

"If I came on your lot," Monroe said with difficulty, "all I'd want is a car."

Todesco stood, backed off. "Gant, this guy is poison. I know the type. He's the kind that would come into my lot with *Consumer Reports* under his arm, tell me how much I paid for a car, and say he'd take a car for that plus two hundred bucks."

"I told you, Councilman," Gant repeated, "he's as honest as they come."

"That's even more reason for me to throw a blanket on this baby. I want him declared physically and mentally incompetent."

Gant was shocked. "You can't do that, Councilman."

"I'm not doing a thing. But it'll get done. The order will come down."

"Sir, I brought you here—"

"To show me some poor fifteen who was found beaten half to death under Brighton Pier on the same night that a state police special investigator, an Atlantic City patrolman in the state witness protection program, and the head of the department's Internal Affairs Division conveniently disappeared. Do I have to tell you *again* that it's in the mayor's interest, as well as my own, that they stay disappeared?"

Gant pulled Todesco aside. "This is one of the best we got. You declare him incompetent and you'll have to retire him."

"Then we'll retire him. Didn't you say there was some doubt about him being injured LOD? If he wasn't in the line of duty, and we can prove negligence, we can get out of giving him his disability benefits."

"Councilman, you can't do that to this boy. At least make it physical," Gant pleaded. "We can put him on the desk."

"I can do anything I want to this boy and I'm doing what I want to this boy because I don't like his kind. They have no respect for the way business is done around here. They have attitude problems. They think everything'd be better if it were out in the open. I throw a blanket on him, and he's out of the picture. For good."

"Councilman—" Gant began to protest.

"There's a half-a-billion-dollar redevelopment project riding on the mayor getting reelected. Any kind of inquiry or publicity into what happened to your boy, here, might raise some questions that we don't want raised, let alone answered."

"Dammit, Harry," Gant sputtered, "Mayor Tilton *will* be reelected."

"We just have to make sure it looks like he deserved it." Todesco smiled at Monroe. "The hospital folks treating you well here? They're all good friends of mine. Any special treatment you want, you say the word. And make sure you cast your absentee ballot for Mayor Bernard Tilton," Todesco said.

Gant muttered, "If he's *mentally* incompetent, it's illegal for him to fill out a ballot for Sunburn Bernie or anybody else."

"A few screws loose never stopped anyone," Todesco beamed. "Ta-tah for now."

Gant waited until he was gone. "I had hopes."

"Of what, sir?"

"Of keeping you on."

"He can't make me retire."

"He can do things you don't want to hear about."

"Not if I don't let him."

Gant sat down, his head in his hands. He looked up for a while. "Lou, you're not crazy, are you?"

"Sir?"

"The quacks here have informed me that the kind of injuries you've sustained can cause memory loss, especially of the incident during which the injuries took place, and that some of this loss could be permanent. You'll recover physically, but we can't be sure when, and you can't be sure how complete it's going to be. They say there's a chance of recurrent psychological episodes, visions, hallucinations. You don't have any of those, do you?"

Monroe said, "No," as the sea rushed around him.

Gant got up, made sure the door was closed. Then he pulled up a chair until he was close to the bed. "Can you see me from here?"

"Yes, sir." Monroe saw that Gant wasn't wearing the blue jeans, loud checked shirt, string tie, pigskin suede coat, and other western regalia in which he typically indulged. The man looked almost elegant in a pale blue shirt, solid navy neck tie, and somber, dark brown suit that draped gently over his paunch.

"How much you remember what happened to you?"

"I don't know, sir."

"I was present when they strung you up. And your wife was there with the baby. We were being forced to watch what was being done to you."

"Sere," Monroe said, his voice rising. "How's Sere?"

"Just as fine as she can be. Ellie's been around to see you,

5

and she's brought her along, but she says she hasn't gotten much of a reaction out of you."

"I want to see Sere," Monroe said.

"Ellie'll come around again as soon as she gets done at the casino."

"Casino . . ."

"She's got a job with the Alcazar. She's going to be in marketing. Handle the high rollers, dream up excuses for them to come down, player parties, that whole thing. You must've heard—"

Monroe tried to shout. "I don't want her working for a casino."

"You will when you see her paycheck."

"Sir, how long will it be before I get back on active duty?"

"You been using those ears? You can't go out on the street again, as bad as you've had it, and expect you're going to perform like your usual self. Look at what happened to Darrell Pratt. I used to get a stack of brutality citations on him every month when he was in Vice. Then he takes three rounds below the belt, takes the sergeants' exam in the very room you're in, puts on a hundred pounds, and is polishing his ass to be the next public information officer. Wouldn't be surprised if he gets it."

"I'm going off the painkillers. I'll take physical therapy. I'll be okay," Monroe said. He tried to pull himself up but his left side was dead from his neck down. He felt an odd, dull throbbing in his chest along his right side. He couldn't take a complete breath, and when he did, it sounded as if men were laughing at him.

"Lou, you remember why you were beaten?"

"Something about . . . someone wanted to know about some link between the mayor and some drug dealer, I think it was Pieto Soladias. There was no link. They didn't have any evidence but they wanted me to say they did."

"They wanted you to cooperate so the mayor wouldn't

get reelected," Gant said. "But they're off the map now, and it's in the interest of a lot of people, from the mayor on down, if what happened to you fades into the sunset, especially Harry the Toad, who is pushing this Miracle Mile project. They want to raise a half a billion to rebuild the center of town, put in some kind of entertainment complex, theme park, shopping mall, some such nonsense. Problem is they need some big investor to pony up the seed money, and everybody's sitting tight until the election.

"Now, if you go along with things, you're going to have some pretty grateful people in your corner. I'm going to get some paper made up, say you were on duty when you were hit. The department's picking up your medical bills to the end of December. By then you'll be retired. I'm going to get you full disability with a prorated pension. Long as you're going to fade off into the sunset, you can at least go out in style."

"I'm not retiring," Monroe said. "As long as there are people out there who did this to me, there should be people like me going after them."

Gant put his head down again. "Dammit, Lou, I feel so bad now, what I did, getting the Toad involved. You can be so certain, so sure of how something's going to go, and . . ."

One of Monroe's eyes was under gauze. The eye itself was okay. It was just the socket that had been fractured. He closed his good eye.

"Well, I guess that's what a father-in-law is for, to mess up his son-in-law's life."

Monroe opened his eye. "At least you tried, sir. When I get out, I'll do something to show them. You'll see."

"I'd prefer not to. And I'd prefer if you kept mum about me being your real father-in-law on account that Ellie's got a casino license now. There's a hell of a lot nobody has the right to know about her, and it should stay that way."

Gant stood. "One more thing. Civilians get their handkerchiefs out when a cop gets hurt or killed in the line of duty, or a prick like the Toad, who hates us, wouldn't be here grabbing a photo opportunity.

"But if a cop's beaten half to death because he happened to run into a bunch of law enforcement scumbags who, when they didn't have evidence to ruin the mayor, decided to torture it out of you in front of your family—people don't want to hear about that. If they do hear about it, they assume whatever happened happened because the cop did something he shouldn't've done, and he got what he deserved."

"You're saying that, what happened to me, I didn't deserve, sir?"

"Just keep your mouth shut," Gant said, gathering his hat and coat. "You're being formally deprived of your sidearm."

At the mention of his gun, Monroe felt the ocean spilling into his throat, though his mouth was so dry he could barely speak. "Did I kill anybody, sir?"

Gant was almost out the door when he said, "Nobody that mattered."

◆

"I got the job."

Monroe had been wondering why it hurt when he slept. He had been having two kinds of dreams. One left him weary and used, the odor of seawater in his nose, the sight of the foam churning around his legs, his mouth filled with the salty taste of his blood.

In the other he was effortlessly gliding through the Pine Barrens in his robin's-egg blue Datsun 280Z. After having that dream, he could feel every ache in his slowly knitting bones, the tightness from swollen joints, and the chafed places in his skin where the casts had rubbed him raw.

She repeated, "I got the job. I really did. It won't be official for another two weeks, but it's just amazing. Executive casino marketing representative. It's part-time, with benefits. They want me to handle some of the special events and the VIP marketing. It's mostly nights, some days, too. I might have to travel a little, but that's down the line."

He saw his wife's face hovering over him. She was thinner, wearing makeup, her brown hair cut straight and swept back in a way he had never seen.

"The money is *wonderful*," she continued. "Take your salary. Multiply it times three. Then add twenty thousand."

Then he heard a squeaking sound.

"Is that my girl?" Monroe said. "Let me see my girl. I want to see my girl."

Ellie lowered her eyebrows, but only for a moment as she shifted her arm to show a small, chubby pink face with a fuzzy red hat on her head.

"Sere, say hello to Louis," Ellie said.

Sere stared at him with slate gray eyes.

"How about a hello for your dad," Monroe coaxed weakly.

Ellie's lips went flat. "Don't say that."

"Say what?"

"That you're her father."

"But I am. Not biologically, but—"

"It's important that we don't hide it from her," Ellie said. "Not the way it was hidden from me."

Monroe paused for a while. "Does this mean you don't want me to say she's my girl?"

"She doesn't belong to you," Ellie said. "She belongs to herself."

"But her father's dead. What difference does it make if she calls me her father?"

"It makes a difference to me," Ellie said. "And it will make a difference for her."

"Hi, kid," Monroe said. He looked at Sere's fat face with his good eye.

"Aren't you going to congratulate me about the job?" Ellie asked.

Monroe chose his words carefully. "What do you know about marketing?"

"A *lot*," Ellie said, smirking. "Besides, it doesn't matter what you know. It's who you know. When I was a whore—"

"Ellie! Do you want her to know that, too?"

"I've socialized with some of the biggest high rollers this town has ever had. I know them. They know me. When I pick up that phone, they're going to listen."

"They'll have expectations," Monroe said.

"They can expect what they want, but if they want to see me, they'll have to gamble in the casino."

"Ellie, we don't need you working this way—"

"You need me more than you think. Who's going to earn a living after your disability pay runs out? Who's going to pay for the nurse who'll look after you *and* Sere? Who's going to get us a decent car to drive and a decent place to live? Who's going to pay for Sere's private school?"

Monroe took a long, deep breath, and the sound of the air rushing in and out of his lungs made him think of waves tumbling in. He saw briny foam scudding over the waves and felt the water and the blood coursing through his nose.

He said, "I'm going to get fixed up, and when I get fixed up, I'll go back to work."

"Louis, I saw what they did to you. . . ."

"What they did doesn't matter—"

"It does now." Ellie shifted Sere so the baby rode on her other hip. "I have an opportunity to change the way this city is perceived. We have to make that change now. Sooner than you think, every state in the Union's going to have some kind of casino gambling. We need to fix the city's image, fast. I want your help, Louis."

"I can't help you make people lose money," Monroe said. "People who lose money don't have good opinions about the place that took the money from them."

"This job," Ellie said, "is going to give us the money to make our lives better."

"Our lives are okay," Monroe replied, trying not to think about the itching under his leg cast.

"Not anymore. We're moving to the mainland, and we're getting a better car. That junker you drive stalls out all the time. The guys down in valet parking can make it disappear and we can put the insurance money toward Sere's college education."

"That's committing fraud," Monroe said.

Ellie changed her tone. "It's taking advantage of an opportunity. I can lease a company car through the casino. Nothing's going to hold me back from what is rightfully mine."

Monroe felt the water touching him, burning him. "Why do we need all these things?" Monroe asked. "We have each other. Isn't that supposed to be enough?"

"Not anymore," she said, wiping Sere's chin.

He watched her go, the painkillers preventing him from feeling.

♦

That night he got a phone call. He groped for it in the dark. He heard a strong, sharp female voice. "Is this Detective Louis Monroe?"

"Uh, hi."

"You the owner of a light blue Datsun two-eightyZ New Jersey plate number SLK T2Z?"

"Uh, I think so."

"This is Officer Elizabeth Todesco, Traffic Safety Division. I normally wouldn't have bothered you in the hospital, sir, but while on patrol this evening I identified your vehicle as illegally parked on Nevada Avenue beach block. We keep the plate numbers of all departmental personnel and, if there's a violation situation, we call the owner first, as a courtesy. Did you park your car on Nevada Avenue in front of that goddamn pisshead drug dealer Pieto Soladias's grocery store?"

"I . . . no. I haven't been able to . . . are you related to the councilman?"

"Harry the Toad is my father, but I didn't get my job because of him and I think he's a corrupt scum and I'm not voting for the mayor and I hope the whole Miracle Mile goes belly-up."

"I didn't mean to—"

"No problem."

"I, uh, didn't put my car there."

"Do you have any idea how it got there? Nevada Avenue has become a high-crime zone and we've had reports of vehicles being broken into and stolen by Soladias's scumbag junkie fucks."

He recalled a narrow, quiet street of two-story wooden guest houses and a few small shops, inhabited mostly by Italian, Jewish, and Chinese senior citizens who had stubbornly held on to their homes when the Alcazar Casino Hotel went up two blocks away.

"Since when are there junkies on Nevada Avenue?"

"Since the end of the summer. Labor Day Weekend they moved in."

He had been in the hospital since . . . "What month is this?"

"October, Detective Monroe. You going out for trick-or-treat?"

Monroe took a breath. He had been injured in September.

"There's been a significant junkie population for at least three months," Officer Todesco said. "Right after the low-income housing went up in the Inlet, Soladias moved his entire operation to Nevada Avenue. Overnight, it's become a slum. Crack houses, shooting galleries, stabbings, reports of gunfire, arson, looting. Vehicles parked there that are not part of Soladias's crew don't stay there for long."

"I'm not part of his crew," Monroe said.

"Makes sense. I heard Soladias tried to kill you while you and Sergeant Almagro had him under surveillance last summer. Anybody a prick like Soladias wants to kill is okay in my book."

Monroe was still absorbing the shock about Nevada Avenue. The street had been one of the last beach-block neighborhoods that hadn't been touched by the casino boom. During his first year working the Boardwalk beat he would wander down and imagine himself buying and renovating one of the guest houses. Then, a few months later, after a nor'easter blew in on a lunar high tide, he saw Nevada Avenue under two and a half feet of water. It was possible to repair the flooding damage to the guest houses, but any cars that had been parked on the street were ruined by the corrosive brine.

Even then, five years back, Monroe had wanted his rusting 280Z to last.

"I—I have no idea how my car got there."

"Wouldn't surprise me if Soladias had it stolen, just so his people could trash it. Sometimes the parking attendants at the casino abandon vehicles on Nevada Avenue in exchange for drugs. The vehicles aren't on the street more than an hour before they're ripped and stripped and all that's left is a carcass for the insurance adjuster. It's good luck that I was in the area and identified it. Can you come out and take possession of the vehicle?"

"Not right away."

"Then on your consent I'll tow it back to your residence on Clam Creek. I recommend you inform your neighbors to keep a better watch on your property."

"Yes," Monroe said, amazed at how the painkillers made it impossible for him to get mad. "I'll tell my wife."

"All of the good ones are taken. Anything else I can do for you?"

"Sure," Monroe said as the ocean rose around his neck. "Get me out of here."

Chapter Two

◆ ◆ ◆ ◆ ◆

Gals with Clout

In November, Mayor Bernard "Sunburn Bernie" Tilton was reelected. His victory party had been in the Alcazar Casino Hotel and Ellie told him how she had set it up, agonized over the hors d'oeuvres, fretted over which lounge band to get to play. She was also doing the Friday night high-roller parties, and other special events.

"Sounds like fun," Monroe said flatly.

"I can't wait to bring you to one. Just think, every week another party."

"I work nights."

"Not anymore."

He was finally released in December. He didn't look out the window of the Mercedes as Ellie drove him from the hospital. He was doped up rather heavily. On the way, Ellie had told him that Sere was at home with the landlady, Mrs. Pasecki, who lived in the ground-floor apartment and offered to come upstairs to baby-sit.

Before he'd met Ellie, he had lived in a one-bedroom apartment on the second floor of an illegally subdivided house at the northwestern edge of Atlantic City's Inlet section. Ellie had moved in and now couldn't wait to move out.

She said she would pay Mrs. Pasecki with a comp slip for free meals and free tickets to the shows at the Alcazar, and they had a fight about that. Monroe felt that they should pay Mrs. Pasecki cash, and, if it was more than so many dollars a week, they'd have to pay taxes and Social Security. Ellie had said it was Mrs. Pasecki who wanted the comps. Mrs. Pasecki told her that when she was Ellie's age, she would get paid in free booze when she baby-sat for Atlantic City Mob boss Paulie Marandola's kids. The fight ended with Monroe wondering why it was that in the six years he'd known Mrs. Pasecki, she'd never told him she baby-sat Paulie Marandola's kids.

They almost started up again when Ellie told her husband how bad her new midnight blue Mercedes sedan looked parked next to Monroe's grimy, rust-pocked 280Z. Monroe told his wife that she had better not try to get his car stolen again. She said she had been running an errand for Carl Cayleen, the Alcazar's CEO, and—

"What kind of errand you have to run near Nevada Avenue?"

"I had to drop off some papers. The Alcazar is negotiating the purchase of some property for a new hotel tower and one of the landowners said to drop the papers off at this place on Nevada Avenue."

"Who would have an office on Nevada Avenue with all the junkies around?"

"I don't care who they are. We want the land. They have it. I get the order to drop off the papers. I drop them off."

"But you're a marketing exec—"

"As long as they pay me six figures, I'll clean the toilets if they ask me."

"This place you dropped the papers off? You see anybody that looked like a criminal type?"

"Lou, I don't want to get into this. . . ."

"You see, the reason they'd ask you to drop the papers is that if a full-time casino exec is seen associating with a known member of organized crime, the execs lose their license, automatic. With independent contractors, there has to be a pattern of association."

She stopped the car. "Lou, did it ever occur to you that

the reason they asked me could have to do with the fact that I am famous?"

"You're *what*?"

"I'm profiled in the December issue of *Rolling Chair* magazine as one of the—can you believe this?—top ten girls with clout. They took my picture in front of a craps pit."

"Why do you think that has anything to do with it?"

She smiled at herself in the rearview mirror. "I have a *reputation*. I can impress people. I was sent to underscore how important this land acquisition is. We have to expand if we're going to get serious about convention business, and this new tower will put us close enough to link up to the Miracle Mile. And I'm up there, where it's happening."

"You were always important to me," Monroe said.

She started the car. "This is different."

He took a breath. "So how did my car get stolen?"

"It *wasn't* stolen." She said she'd parked the car and came back and found it missing but her contacts in the department informed her that the car had been towed by the police back to Clam Creek.

"I rode home in this Mercedes that very night, and, believe me, if your car had been stolen, I wouldn't've missed it."

She told him she was only part-time. She defined part-time as being at the Alcazar Casino Hotel seven nights a week, usually from five P.M. on, coming back as late as two or three A.M. "There could be nights I won't come back, when I'll have to stay over at the hotel to be at a breakfast meeting or whatever. You're going to have to get used to being without me."

When she wasn't at the casino she was out shopping, or home, on the phone, talking business. She didn't tell him what she was doing and he didn't ask. The landlady, Mrs. Pasecki, came in when Ellie was at work. Mrs. Pasecki was supposed to look after both Sere and Monroe but Monroe had gone off painkillers and had become angry at everything and wanted to do nothing more than play with his daughter, with whom he had fallen hopelessly in love. They had something in common. They were both helpless.

One morning after helping him in and out of the bathtub, Ellie mentioned that her job was riding on what she could pull off for Christmas, in which most players stayed home to celebrate the holidays with their families and casino business died. She had to come up with something to bring them in, or go after the Oriental players who didn't celebrate Christmas.

"But everything you can think of that's been done for Oriental players has been done. Singers from Hong Kong, cultural shows, theme parties. We need a fresh angle bad. Any suggestions?"

"How about local people? Spotlight somebody local who's doing something decent," Monroe said.

"Gamblers don't like people who are decent," Ellie said. "To a gambler, a hero isn't afraid to put it all on the line—"

"I know a lot of people like that."

"And fight a losing battle—"

"That narrows the field a little."

"And wins anyway."

Monroe paused. "They have to win?"

"*Have* to."

Monroe thought hard. "But it's not that simple."

"It never is."

♦

Then there was the night the casino had an investors' party for the Miracle Mile project. She brought home a stack of glossy promotional brochures, glittering renderings, and a picture of Councilman Todesco shaking hands with Sunburn Bernie and Carl Cayleen, CEO of the Alcazar Casino Hotel, Inc.

Monroe couldn't understand why anyone was getting

excited. If you live long enough in Atlantic City, you grow numb to these plans. The people behind them always promised that if they were only given the time, the money, the land, a stack of zoning variances, tax credits, and numerous other gifts from the taxpayers, their plan would solve the city's problems and turn Atlantic City into the paradise that the legalization of casino gambling had intended it to be.

You work the Boardwalk, as Monroe had done, and you grow to understand that these plans are scams designed to make people part with money. Why else, months later, do you hear about the backers of these plans going bankrupt, or skipping out of town, leaving hundreds of local contractors, architects, printers, caterers, and other local businesses holding bills that would never be paid?

Monroe had always believed that the city didn't need grand, flashy plans, but slow, steady, dependable effort. It needed people like him and his wife.

It was strange: only on the nights when Ellie didn't come home would Sere sleep through the night. The silence, and the agony in his slowly mending body, would keep Monroe awake. On some nights he would hobble out to the living room and watch his daughter asleep in her crib.

It was on such a night that he discovered he could go down the stairs by himself. He had been looking at Sere, his right hand on the crib, wondering, again, how her coming into his life had changed him, when he heard the doorbell ring and jumped so high he thought he'd hit the ceiling.

Sere didn't stir.

He put his right hand against the wall and hopped toward the stairwell that led down to the front door.

Under the single bulb, the stairs seemed impossibly steep. He used to go up them three at a time. Now, as he gripped the edge of the railing and the doorbell rang a second time, he told himself that it was late and maybe he should just ignore the bell.

Then he remembered when he'd been hurt in a fight, and, the very next day, he'd put on his running shoes and sweat-pants and run the Boardwalk. The first mile had been ex-cruciating. The second mile was difficult. The third was not so difficult. By the fourth he was flying.

He didn't want to fly down the stairs, but, when the bell rang even more insistently and he heard a female voice cry, "Ellie!" he decided it was worth a try. He swung out his stiff left leg, grabbed the banister, and jumped.

The shock of his ankle hitting the hard wood went up through his spine and rattled his teeth. He tried not to tense on the third step.

By the tenth step he felt as if he were on a pogo stick. It was almost fun.

He unlocked the front door and a woman collapsed in his arms. She nearly knocked him backward before she said, "You're not Ellie."

"Uh, hi."

She glanced at his face and looked away.

"I'm Ellie's husband. Louis."

Nobody looks good under the light of a single bare bulb. This woman had a broad, wide face narrowing to blunt, thick lips and an oddly pointed chin. Her nose had been broken a long time ago and there were scars on her cheeks beneath streaks of black mascara, where she had been cry-ing. Her muddy brown hair was awry and a dark bruise was forming under her left eye.

"Who hit you?" Monroe said.

"Who hit *you*?" she asked him.

He awkwardly closed the door. "Somebody bigger than me."

"You hit him back?"

He put his hand against the door as the ocean came up and he heard the shots being fired. "I don't want to talk about it."

That set off the tears again. She covered her face, slid

down, and sat on the first step. "I want to see Ellie."

"She's not here," Monroe said. "You're a friend of hers?"

"She . . . helped me."

Monroe nodded. When he had met her, Ellie had quit the high-class call-girl service that had employed her. She had been pregnant and Marty Gant had put her on the police department payroll as a counselor for teenaged prostitutes and runaways.

Monroe regarded the woman in front of him. She was in her midtwenties. The clothes he could see under her coat were modest: a dark brown suit, gray blouse—the kind of uniform midlevel secretaries and office workers wear. There was nothing to indicate that she had ever needed Ellie to counsel her.

Which meant that she might have been one of Ellie's successes.

"I'd invite you up," Monroe said, "but we have a baby upstairs and—"

"She had her baby!" the woman exclaimed.

"Uh, yeah."

"Can I see?"

Monroe warned her that Sere was sleeping. The woman started up the stairs, then paused, halfway up.

He was trying to figure out how to come back up. Then he was trying to figure out how to tell her that he had never climbed steps unassisted since he'd been out of the hospital.

But the sick, the wounded, the injured, and the impaired sometimes share a common understanding. The woman merely came back down the stairs, threw his right arm over her shoulder, and helped him up.

She spent a few minutes in that motionless fascination that people—some people—have with infants. Then whatever had been bothering her came back, and she covered her eyes and went to the couch and cried silently in the dark.

He waited for her to stop.

Monroe gave her the nearest thing—a cloth diaper—so she could wipe her face. After a while she asked if Ellie was going to be home soon.

Monroe said he couldn't be sure.

In the silence they heard Sere breathing. It was like the ocean waves, coming in and out, but faster, lighter.

After a while Monroe said, "I look at her and I can't understand why anything bad has to happen."

The woman gripped the diaper tightly and sat still for a few minutes. Then she went to the stairwell and hesitated.

Monroe followed her. He lowered himself, his left leg straight out, his right bent under the banister.

He said, "Ellie told me what she used to do. She didn't mention names."

She remained standing, her eyes on the dusty, beige enamel walls.

"So somebody hit you."

She nodded. "But that's not the problem."

"That's enough of a problem."

"It's my boyfriend. He hit me."

"When I was a cop, my partner and I, Darrell Pratt, would go after pimps that hit their women. They used to call Darrell "Bad Day," because he'd make sure those guys were having a bad day when he left." He paused, ran his hand along his leg. "I don't think we can do that right now."

"My boyfriend had a reason to hit me."

"Reasons have nothing to do with it," Monroe said. "If I was a cop, I'd lock him up."

"He hit me because, well, I work for someone, in his office, and he, well, I don't know how he found out what I used to do—I mean, Ellie got me to give it up, and I did everything to give it up. I got this job, and, this man I work for found out what I used to do. I didn't tell him, but he found out, and ever since he's been saying things, and touching me, and saying things about what he wants me to

22

do for him, and I've got a job review coming up and—"

"You told your boyfriend and he hit you?"

She nodded.

"Can you leave him? Can you move in with somebody he wouldn't know about and just not come home?"

"My clothes and my checkbook are there, but, I can move in with a friend."

"You can come back when he's not around and clean your stuff out. But don't go back to that guy. Don't talk to him on the phone. End it right now."

"But . . ."

"What?"

"I want my job. I want it because it's the only thing I have and . . ." She started to cry again. "I wish Ellie was here."

"Me, too," Monroe said.

"Can I go to where she is now?"

Monroe didn't want to tell her that he doubted if his wife would have the time. "We can talk here for a while." He thought. "Is this guy, the guy who is doing this to you, is he in a powerful position?"

She nodded.

"Can he fire you?"

"I don't know. I think so. They say he can make you resign."

"Then you have to fight him."

"But I'll lose. That's what they say. They say unless you have a lot of money for a lawyer, or you get into the media, you lose everything."

"Some lawyers might take it on a contingency basis. But what you need to win isn't important. Some fights, the only thing you can do is . . ." He didn't want to say lose, but that was how he felt. "But you have to fight, you have to stand up to it."

"Why? I know somebody, she does her boss and he gave her a promotion and a raise. I know somebody else, the boss divorced his wife and married her. I mean, they say if you just accept it and go with it, it might turn out okay."

"You can accept it but if you don't do anything, then you *know* you're going to die," Monroe said, the ocean rising in his mind. "I mean, not die. Lose."

"What happened to you? Did you fight it?"

Monroe nodded.

"What did it get you?"

"Everything changed," Monroe said. "Rapidly. Too rapidly. I want it back the way it was. All of it. But that's impossible. I've been told . . . I've been told to accept it, not do anything more, just go along with it."

"Is that what you're going to do?"

Monroe fell silent. "I don't know what I'm going to do."

She stood beside him for a while. Then she went quietly down the steps.

The next morning, he told his wife about the visit.

"She was in the same room with my baby?" Ellie said, wrinkling her nose.

"Looking at Sere calmed her down," Monroe added. "She didn't give her name. I thought maybe, from her description, you could figure out who she is and we could do a follow-up."

"I don't care who she is. I don't want her in this apartment again."

"But she needed you," Monroe said.

"Not me," Ellie said. "Not anymore."

♦

When it no longer took Monroe twenty minutes to climb the stairs, Darrell Pratt called him and told him that Gant was going to work something out with Harry the Toad and the mayor, and that he should put on his old uniform, and bring a crutch.

"But I don't use the crutch anymore," Monroe said.

"For the emotional impact," Pratt said. "Bring a tear to the Toad's eye."

Monroe awkwardly removed his uniform from the closet. He hadn't worn it since he'd gone into plainclothes, which was less than a year ago. So why did it feel so tight?

He looked at himself in the mirror. He tried to see past his left arm, which, out of the sling, hung at an odd angle, resembling more a chicken wing. His tie didn't look right, but it never did. He had tied his shoelaces one-handed and they looked like a tangle of black string licorice.

But under his deep blue pants with their bright yellow stripe you couldn't see his leg, still stiff and swollen, with scars in the skin where pins that held shattered bone together had been inserted, then removed.

The multicolored blotches on his face had faded. There were still lumps on his face, around his left eye and jaw. His left shoulder seemed a little higher than his right. He pulled down the cloth of his blue blouse until his shoulders appeared even.

He decided he looked pretty damned good, even if, at five feet two inches tall, he lacked the imposing presence that people expected from a cop. What would he have become if the department hadn't eliminated height restrictions to encourage female enrollment?

In Atlantic City, most people either worked in the casino industry or worked for someone who worked in the casino industry. As a cop, Monroe had told himself he didn't have to specialize.

He had found precious few of those people in Atlantic City. But he had found his wife, when she had quit working as a high-class call girl. She, too, felt that she was working for people who wanted to have a decent life. She was certain that she could make the city better, just by being in it and doing what she thought was right.

He was never more certain than on the day he married

her. He was never more astonished than when he watched her give birth.

Now he stood in front of his apartment house in a black police-issue slicker, feeling the slushy, freezing rain spill around him. His left arm was in a sling. The crutch pushed too high into his right armpit.

"The wounded hero returns from the front," Pratt said to Monroe, using his cane to trip the latch and open the passenger-side door of the navy blue "official business" Buick that was normally used to chauffeur the department's administrative inspectors.

Monroe made a show of getting into the car, to hide his surprise at how fat his former partner had grown. "Can't I just leave this at home?" he groaned.

"Gant wants to do it the old way, then we do it the old way," Pratt said as he put the car in gear and glided off into the Inlet. "I told him, the old way don't mean shit around city hall, except for old farts like him, but Gant don't ask my opinion."

Monroe slammed against the side of the car as Pratt skidded and slipped down the gray streets. Pratt had always had a heavy foot when driving unmarked police vehicles up and down Pacific Avenue. Some things don't change.

But the city had. Monroe had grown up on the mainland near Atlantic City and then had lived in Atlantic City for six years, and he found himself not recognizing the streets. Entire blocks that had been jammed with corroding row houses and sagging slum housing were now flat, naked, open to the wind and the rain, which turned the recently disturbed sandy dirt to a muddy, angry burnt umber.

In their place were squat, tight little rows of low- and middle-income housing nestled on streets lined with new white sidewalks and streetlamps. The town was finally cleaning up its act, he said to himself. The money from the casinos was doing what it was supposed to do: make the town new again.

But there still were plenty of vacant lots, burned-out shops, and woefully forlorn, abandoned slum housing. Atlantic Avenue was still marred by graffiti-scarred ruins. Despite the new housing going up in the Inlet, along Atlantic City's Grand Boulevard, the tired, boarded-up, and tumbledown remained the rule rather than the exception.

"You're looking at the future, right here," Pratt said. "I got an inside track that the Miracle Mile is going under. Harry the Toad thought he had an investor for the seed money, some guy owns a lot of the land the project would be built on, but he won't commit the money. Harry is trying to cut a deal with the casinos, but they're already putting out too much. The plan is for ourselves to be there right where he don't want us."

"How's that going to help?"

"Only way he'll get rid of us is to give us what we want."

"What's that?"

"Power and glory, Lou boy."

He put the car in a space reserved for administrative sergeants and accompanied Monroe into the lobby and toward the elevator, nodding at the lumpy woman at the sign-in desk.

"Aren't you going to sign me in?" Monroe asked Pratt under his breath.

"Why should I?"

"I had to turn in my badge. Until I get reassigned to active duty, I'm technically a civilian and civilians on police business have to be signed in."

"With me you don't need to," Pratt said as they neared the elevator. "Besides, if nothing happens, you might not want it known you were in the building."

"What's supposed to happen?"

Pratt held a finger to his lips. "Down, boy. Time for you to start thinking like a lawyer," Pratt said as the elevator doors opened and Monroe entered the elevator. "Don't ask about anything you don't want to know."

They got out on the fifth floor, known as Foambuttville, Foambuttonia, Foambuttboro, because it held the office space of the department's administrative inspectors who were famous for the size of their behinds.

The fifth floor also held the most opulent men's lavatory ever installed in a public building. According to legend, it was the gift of a Mob-linked plumbing contractor who had done work on a Mob-financed condo overlooking the Intracoastal Waterway in Upper Chelsea. Shortly after the condo passed inspection, a local environmental group sued the developer and the city over the raw sewage leaking from the condo into the waterway. Under a peculiar out-of-court settlement, the city, not the developer, paid $500,000 to the same Mob-linked plumbing contractor to attach the condo to the city's septic system.

As per unwritten regulations governing the old ways of doing business in Atlantic City, ten percent was returned in the form of an expanded lavatory to the fifth floor of city hall. It was not known if additional compensation went to the foambutt who had jurisdiction over the Bureau of Licenses and Inspections.

Still, $50,000 bought one hell of a men's room. The facility became symbolic of the old ways because, during the city's wild and woolly past, the most confidential business was traditionally conducted in lavatories, where the cacophany of plumbing noises frustrated the FBI's most sophisticated listening devices.

Almost as quickly as it was installed, the fifth floor foambutt men's lavatory became dated: improvements had not extended to the women's lav. Though the police department did not have female administrative inspectors, it did have the twice widowed and once divorced "Dangerous" Delores LiPatti, the Foambutts' administrative assistant, commanding the police department's computer in a glass cubicle behind the fifth-floor reception desk. As soon as the contractor indicated that he would not so much as polish a fitting in the women's lav, several warrants were issued for his arrest in connection with failures to pay city taxes on business income. These warrants were later found to have been the result of a computer error, but they were enough to attract the attention of the State Division of Taxation and the Internal Revenue Service. The contractor was indicted for filing fraudulent income-tax returns, sentenced to ten years in jail, paroled after two years and three months, and was last seen completing his additional 2,200 hours of community service by unclogging drains in an Atlantic City senior citizens' housing tower.

Darrell Pratt guided Monroe past the reception desk. In her glass office, "Dangerous" Delores LiPatti waved her red nails. Pratt kept going, toward a glistening black matte door trimmed in polished brass with red block letters that said MEN.

Monroe began, "But I don't have to go—"

"Everybody's got to go sometime," Pratt said. "No time like the present."

Monroe put his right hand on the polished brass plate and pushed. The door opened smoothly into a small carpeted sitting room of gleaming crimson stone walls, framed in black, trimmed in polished brass, with two matching chairs in brass and red and black leather, illuminated, as if in a showroom, by spotlights sunken in the brass-ribbed ceiling above. Between them a quarter-scale bronze of Atlas held the world on his shoulders. Half the world had been sliced off and filled with sand and cigarette butts.

Opposite Atlas was a shoe-shine station, with seating for six. A brass Art Deco coat rack completed the room.

Monroe went through the sitting room and stepped into a hideous, angular grotto of black marble, polished sandstone, and brass-tinged mirrors and plumbing fixtures. Standing in front of one of the polished brass urinals in a gray, nondescript suit was Marty Gant.

Gant yanked down the urinal handle and water gushed with an explosive burst of power. He caught Monroe's reflection in the brass and yanked the handle again, a wry smile curling under his nose.

"Used to do this for an education," Gant said. "Always had to be somebody doing the flushing when business was being discussed."

Gant looked at his watch. "Glad to see you're on time. If you got to do anything, do it now. Then assume the positions."

Gant directed Monroe to the upper tier of the shoe-shine station. Monroe made the climb awkwardly as Gant and Pratt sat in the shoe-shine chairs on the lower level.

"Now we wait." Gant took a cigar out of his suit and unwrapped it.

"This is a designated smokeless building," Monroe said.

"If there's a place in this building where a man can smoke a cigar with impunity, we're sitting in it. Reminding me of the regulations is a lapse of tact on your part, Lou, considering that this maneuver is being staged for your benefit."

"I don't want anything for my benefit," Monroe said. "I want my job back."

"Relax, Lou, and the world relaxes with you," Gant put the cigar in his mouth and bit off the end.

After the longest ten minutes of Monroe's life, the outer door swept open, emitting a carefully orchestrated pattern of squeaks. In came the sweating, heavily jowled, horn-rimmed face of Atlantic City Councilman-at-Large Harry Todesco.

Monroe flinched at the sight of the man.

"Councilman," Gant said warily, coming to his feet. Pratt remained seated.

Todesco squinted behind his square-lensed, trifocal horn-rims. He made a spitting noise and then went toward the urinals.

Gant waited to hear the water flush. They listened to it subside. Then they heard the almost musical trickle of water running at the sink, followed by the high whine of the electric hand dryer.

The Toad came back and paused, as if he'd just noticed them.

"I want all of you tippy-toeing out of here." He looked directly at Monroe. "Who said you could use this place?"

Gant said, "We felt a call of nature. Considering that we all happen to be here, though, I wanted to bring up the matter of my reinstatement. I'm no longer interested in keeping my retirement status, and as there *is* an opening . . ."

The Toad began to pace. "You want a deal, we make a deal. Later."

"And Sergeant Pratt would like to be the next public-information officer. There is a vacancy for that position, also. Though we're aware that the mayor and the chief have to concur, your ability to influence—"

"My influence? I have no influence," Todesco said, wiping his brow. "It's the men and women of your department who have the influence. I'm happy when they agree with me. You can make me so, so happy if you'd just take yourselves out of here."

"And then there's Detective Monroe. He could use a prorated pension and full disability," Gant said.

"No," Todesco said irritably. "There's a budget crisis on. We've been through that."

"I'd think that the mayor would be beholden to Detective Monroe," Gant went on, "and that even if Detective Monroe's situation is static, that gratitude might extend to Sergeant Pratt and myself."

Monroe began to get angry.

"You're getting nothing out of me," Todesco said. "Nobody plays me like this. If I were Monroe up there, I'd feel pissed off that I was being used."

"I am, Councilman," Monroe said.

"Divide and conquer, hey, Councilman?" Pratt said. "Next you're going to remind me I'm a minority and that you always look out for minorities."

Gant said, "Perhaps if I were to fill the vacancy in Internal Affairs—"

Todesco snapped, "You want to stay in my good graces, get out of my sight, now."

Then they heard the outside door squeak open again and a tall, dapper, impeccably groomed man in a dark, expensive suit breezed in, saw the Toad, and said, "Harry, I'm so sorry I'm late but the limo—"

Then he saw Gant, Pratt, and Monroe, his eyes finally settling on Gant's cigar.

"Mr. Cayleen," Gant said evenly. "I don't think we've met." He gestured back toward Monroe. "This man is married to one of your employees, Mrs. Ellen Monroe. Louis, here, is one of our finer detectives."

Cayleen paused. "Ellen? Oh, yes, Ellie. Hell of a gal. Works out all the time in our health spa. Great legs. World-class Kentucky Derby–racehorse legs."

Carl Cayleen didn't look like the man Monroe had seen in the Miracle Mile brochure pictures. He looked better.

That made Monroe mad. "You come for one of Mr. Todesco's turkeys?"

Monroe was referring to what had occurred on a previous Thanksgiving week, when a freezer truck containing 500 turkeys failed to arrive at 0900 hours in the police parking lot. The police were supposed to distribute the turkeys to the city's poor.

About three hours later the Traffic Safety Division received an anonymous tip. It was a woman's voice, and a check of the incoming phone numbers showed that she was calling from Todesco Luxury Motors, a car dealership out on Route 30 that belonged to Atlantic City Councilman-at-Large Harry Todesco. The dealership was giving away free turkeys to anyone who test-drove a new model car.

More than fifty uniformed men and women descended on Todesco's car lot, cutting off all access to the highway and the swamps behind the dealership, where the freezer truck was parked. The truck was from the same Vineland poultry distributor from which the casinos ordered their Thanksgiving allotment. The packing manifest read 500 hen-type turkeys, frozen, giblets, and pop-up timer included, *deliver Atlantic City, location TBD.*

The driver said TBD meant to-be-determined. He said at 7:50 he was told to deliver the turkeys to the dealership by his dispatcher. He estimated that about 100 turkeys had been given away so far.

A peppy junior salesman corrected him and said, "One hundred and twenty-seven, to be exact."

Street Crimes Detective Jack "Fu Man" Chou stuck his Glock 9-millimeter automatic in the salesman's ear and suggested that the salesman tell him where the turkeys were.

The salesman nervously revealed that everyone who test-drove a car had to sign out in a book. He guided Detective Chou to the book and then began to cry on the showroom floor.

A sales manager at Todesco's lot said that the turkey promotion had been under discussion for a while and that nobody was sure if it was going to come off until the truck had arrived that morning.

The poultry distributor's dispatcher said that on Monday night he had received a call from "someone in city hall" directing him to deliver a load of turkeys to the dealership. He later said "it was just someone. I couldn't be sure who it was. But he sounded like the guy we'd been dealing with all along."

A check of city hall phone records indicated two phone calls to the poultry distributorship made at around the time described. The calls came from a commonly used extension in the Atlantic City Zoning Commission office.

In addition to chairing the Public Safety Commission, Councilman Todesco also sat on the Atlantic City Zoning Commission.

Eighty-six of the turkeys were recovered before Thanksgiving. Four hundred and fifty-nine were delivered to the city's poor. The spokesman for the police department described the incident as "regrettable." Councilman Todesco informed the Atlantic City *Star* that he would not sue the department for harassment "because it's known that I am a long and tireless critic of police excess in this town. The parties responsible for pulling this stunt learned their lesson that next time, there won't be a next time."

The junior salesman was fired. Fu Man Chou was suspended without pay for thirty days, then transferred to the narcotics unit, where he busted one of Harry Todesco's campaign workers for possession of crack cocaine. Chou was suspended after a surprise witness accused one of the officers on Chou's team of planting evidence on the defendant. Chou was then transferred to the arson squad, and suspended a third time after a confidential informant identified him on a line-up as the individual who had been crawling around the driveway of the spacious, suburban Margate house of a full-time podiatrist and alleged part-time arsonist. Though there was no loss of life, the house was completely engulfed in a fire when the podiatrist's BMW mysteriously exploded.

Two months ago Chou had been reassigned to the Traffic Safety Division, where he was supposed to supervise crews of officers securing construction sites on public streets and city property.

No incidents of outrageous, dangerous, balls-to-the-wall police work involving him had been reported since, though rumors circulated that Chou was having his cake and eating it: that a series of wildly improbable Nevada Avenue drug busts performed by unarmed, off-duty officers and, in one situation, a citizen walking her dog, had been orchestrated by the Fu Man, who used the off-duty officers' and the dogwalker's names on the arrest reports.

For that, and other reasons, the Fu Man had the respect, admiration, and downright love of nearly every officer in the department, except two: Louis Monroe, who stubbornly believed that police procedures should be followed to the letter of the law; and Traffic Safety Officer Elizabeth Todesco, who, until she walked out on him, had formerly been known as Mrs. Jack Chou.

"I didn't appreciate that crack," Todesco said to Monroe.

"Hey." Cayleen strode across the room, slipped his hand behind Todesco's shoulders, and shoved him toward the door. "Let's just forget this all happened. Okay, folks?"

The door squeaked shut. Gant relit his cigar and said, "You've made an impression. You also may have made an enemy."

Monroe said, "Is this why you dragged me here? So you can use me to get an edge?"

Gant admired the trail of smoke spiraling up from his cigar. "I wanted him to see you with us. That you're in city hall might have given him the impression that you were not keeping as silent as he might have wished. And I also wanted him to know that Ellie is a mighty important component of Cayleen's executive staff. If he wants to get that casino into his Miracle Mile project, he'll have to take care of people who are involved in that casino. Who, by association with you, Lou, are Darrell and myself. Of course, the Toad won't be able to do this directly. But I suspect we'll see some results shortly."

"Look," Monroe said. "In a few months, I'll have my strength back. I'll take all kinds of tests. I'll prove that I'm not incompetent."

"Contrary to popular belief," Gant said, "proof is not as significant as the ability to inspire the powers that be to act upon it. Jack Chou is the only individual in the department who has got himself out from under a blanket."

"By marrying into the clan," Pratt grunted.

"That is not an option," Monroe said.

Gant blew smoke. "You have other options. You can buy a boat. Go fishing. Think of it, you can be a nice guy all the time."

Monroe got up, slid off the shoestand, and was about to push the door open when Dangerous Delores rushed in, her bright magenta suit dazzling under the recessed spotlights, her two-inch-long red nails fluttering like the blades of a paper shredder.

"Listen, guys, I gotta go to lunch so I want to tell you everything's set and not to worry."

Gant was gaping at her in a way Monroe had never seen: Gant, the savvy, deviously manipulating survivor from the city's wide-open, precasino days, had been blindsided. He had not expected her to come into the Foambutt men's room, not here, not ever.

Pratt, Monroe saw, was downright fearful, like Moses caught before the burning bush.

"Darrell, you'll be the department's public-information officer. Try to make sure we end up looking okay, okay?"

Pratt was almost going to bow down on his knee, but he stopped himself and said, "Yes, momma, I mean, ma'am."

She turned to Gant. "Marty, I want you where I can keep my eye on you. You're heading Internal Affairs. You'll have to wait on the promotion to inspector, but it'll come down. All we're asking is patience. Everything will come out okay."

She stopped, her eyes on Marty Gant. Gant blushed. "Why *Marty,* you're *staring* at me."

Gant swallowed. "I apologize, Delores. I didn't expect—"

"A *girl* in the little boys' room?" She said, running her nails along his cheek.

"Delores, forgive me, I just didn't expect you to, uh,

36

make things happen so quickly. Did this have anything to do with the Toad—I mean—Councilman Todesco?"

LiPatti fluttered her fingernails. "I'm just one of the gals who brings the coffee. *Is that clear?*"

"Yes, Dolores. Crystal clear."

Monroe spoke up. "Mrs. LiPatti?"

She gazed up at him. "Louis Monroe! You look awful in that uniform."

"Can I have my job back?"

"I can give you full retirement, the works. You just have to sign a consent form that you will not hold the department liable for any further complications due to your injuries."

"But I don't want to retire. I want reinstatement."

She stopped. "You ever hear of a gift horse?"

"If I don't want it," Monroe said, "it's no gift."

Gant cut in, "Delores, I apologize for the boy. He doesn't understand—"

"He doesn't have to, Marty." To Monroe she said, "You're quite correct. If you don't want something, you shouldn't get it."

She wrung her fingers and then swished toward the door, her body swaying precariously over her high heels.

"But my reinstatement—"

She paused at the door, looked back at them, as if the lavatory and everyone who had ever been in it was part of a vast infantile scheme. Her last words were, "I don't take requests."

Chapter Three

♦ ♦ ♦ ♦ ♦

Spitting Image

A few days later Monroe opened the door of his car. He smelled traces of his wife's perfume in the seats. He rolled down the window with his right hand.

It took too much cranking for the car to turn over. He would have to look at that engine, he told himself as he stalled five times before seeing his first traffic light. It took him a while to accelerate, brake, and shift with only his right foot, but he got the hang of it.

He parked in Atlantic City General Hospital's garage for his morning physical therapy session. They weighed him, measured him, bent his leg, worked his arm, made him flop around in a pool of warm water. One of his therapists, a blond, pale-skinned woman with the pinched, solemn expression he'd seen on medieval portraits, told him that he should "kick back and enjoy what you have."

He tried to kick. His knee had swollen horribly and wouldn't bend. "I'm supposed to enjoy that?" he said.

"At least don't fight it."

But he fought it and it hurt even more and the pain stayed with him as he drove toward the black cube of city hall. He found Sergeant Darrell Pratt, the new public-information officer, in a tiny, third-floor cubbyhole near the chief's office.

" 'Least you're not in your uniform," Pratt said.

Monroe wore a pair of baggy sweatpants. "I drove my car for the first time today."

"You want a medal? I got a whole box of Distinguished Service Medals here."

"You know what I want."

"You want it so bad, how come you haven't gone to a lawyer? Sue the department. Won't get you far, but it might get you in."

"I don't like lawyers." Monroe said.

Pratt folded callused, thick-knuckled hands over his expanding gut. "Touch your head with your left hand," he said.

Monroe winced. His elbow moved out, like a chicken wing.

"Let's think about what kind of jobs we got for a man that can't move his left hand, can't run, can't fire a gun—"

"I can stand and aim. When I get my gun back I'll practice. Darrell," he began with difficulty, "there must be something I can do."

"You see this yet?" Pratt picked up the current issue of *Rolling Chair* magazine. On the cover was a casino control commissioner holding an oversized sledgehammer—the kind that clowns use to hit each other on the head—in one hand and a rose in the other. She was one of the "Ten Gals with Clout" profiled inside.

"They wrote up your wife inside."

Monroe felt his ears burn red as he opened to the article. The article had a heart-stoppingly gorgeous photo of her, with a few paragraphs that made no mention of Mrs. Ellen Meade Monroe's previous employment history, other than to say that she had worked with the industry "in a marketing capacity."

"You bother turning the page?"

Monroe hadn't. The flattering portrait of his wife as a busy, dynamic executive had made him want to read nothing else in the magazine. The woman pictured smiling proudly across a deep blue craps table did not resemble the woman he'd married.

"I didn't put this into her file yet," Pratt said, and turned to the last profile in the series. It was of Beth Todesco, photographed in her patrolman's uniform, standing proudly before municipal wrecker *Whiskey Alpha Five*, with a beige Rolls-Royce Corniche dangling from the truck's boom.

Her face was dark, angular, framed by a short, thick mop of glossy black hair, her wide mouth compressed into a thin line that was supposed to indicate the arrogance of a person with power but really showed contempt, as if to say she had better things to do than pose for stupid pictures.

The article quoted her as "a person who is drawn to people in trouble. Beth Todesco, the daughter of Councilman-at-Large Harry Todesco, says she harbors no illusions about men, especially those whose cars she's towed. 'Men will do anything to get off the hook. Once I got 'em, I never let them go. The law is the law. You break it, you bought it.' "

He put the article down. "She found my car on Nevada Avenue."

Pratt said, "She's a good one. My predecessor got the magazine to pick her. Women are part of our minority push. She works nights out of the municipal tow lot."

"Why did she split with the Fu Man?" Monroe said.

"Why does anybody split these days?" Pratt said. "Jack Chou was just too much for her. One of these days, I'm going to put Chou on the front page of the *Star*. Let everybody know what kind of a hero he is."

"He does reckless, sloppy work."

"But he's a hero in my book, and everybody else in this department."

"Except Beth Todesco and me."

"*You* are not in this department. Piece of paper in your file says you're on your own."

"We can get rid of the paper if I pass a psych test," Monroe said. "I checked it out. As an administrative sergeant, you have the budget for an assistant. Reinstate me. I'll come in, then transfer out into Vice or some other department."

Pratt glanced at the piles of magazines and media clippings on his desk. "Right now, I need a slave. Somebody to make photocopies, handle media contacts, make the coffee at press conferences—"

"If I have to do that, I could do that," Monroe said.

"But I don't need you."

Monroe closed his eyes, heard the ocean.

"Lou, you're not coming on until the Toad wants you on. Just go home and let Ellie do you and you'll be fine."

Monroe blushed.

"Lou, you getting some off Ellie?"

"I don't want to talk about it."

"So that's why you're making all this noise about a job," Pratt snickered. "I bet you haven't done it since you gone into the hospital.

"One thing I *can* do is get you fixed up with a bad one. Not one of those good girls like your wife. I mean a bad one that does it *all.* The Toad's got a few working for him in his office. Former street girls, some of them. They *say* they can type, you know?"

"Darrell . . ."

"I know you ain't cheated on Ellie, but, lemme tell you about cheating. Took me quite a while to do it. The first time you do it, you learn you can do it again."

Monroe looked away. Pratt was making him sick.

"By the way," Pratt went on. "I wouldn't mind getting comped into that show her casino's got coming up for New Year's. Should I go through you, or should I talk to Ellie?"

Monroe pulled himself to his feet. "Talk to her," Monroe said. "Talk to her all you want."

♦

41

As he squirmed back into his car for the ride back, Monroe watched the people shuffling in and out of the state unemployment office, a low, depressing building at Bachrach Boulevard and Baltic Avenue.

He imagined that some of these people may have suffered unnecessarily. Some may not have deserved to lose their jobs. Some may just be going through the motions, collecting money because it was there, figuring they'd worry about the future when they had to.

Why couldn't he just kick back and enjoy what he had? Then he could hear the ocean again, and the laughter. He started the car and drove aimlessly for a while, searching for the free feeling he'd found in his dreams. He didn't find it.

He found himself on Pacific Avenue, south of the Alcazar, and saw the small sign for Nevada Avenue. He made the turn.

Monroe was still amazed that Nevada Avenue could be the city's new drug mall.

Until now. He avoided the line of vehicles whose drivers were waiting to make their purchases and slowly drove past them, gazing at the forlorn, abandoned, wood-frame two-story bungalows and row houses. Monroe thought he caught the flicker of a crack pipe being lit on the first floor of a house whose top story had fallen in. Another one had suffered a fire on its first floor and had been left to collapse. Other houses appeared, their foundations rotted by floods, slouching as if a light wind would push them over. The few shops on Nevada had been boarded up, with the exception of a grocery store near the Boardwalk. A shiny black Porsche 928 was parked in front of it.

There were other gleaming status-mobiles, whose presence announced that, despite the shabbiness of the street, money was here. Around them stood young kids in black leather jackets and overcoats long enough to hide guns.

Other than these kids, the street had that cruel, shuttered, the-party's-over look that was so common in uptown Atlantic City. Monroe spotted some underage prostitutes in tight, dark winter spandex sitting on broken beach chairs. Some kids in oversized, hooded Detroit Tigers winter warm-up suits, sweatpants and malignant black shoes, fancy warm-up ensembles and oversided leather hats, scanned the traffic coming down for the drive-in customers. These kids, called mules, approached the drivers and took their orders. Behind them, inside the first floors, lurked the dealers, who would bag the orders and give them to the mules to bring back to the cars.

Though Colombians, Jamaicans, a contingent from the Philadelphia junior Black mafia, and, most recently, an exceedingly vicious gang of Vietnamese had operators working Atlantic City, the city's drug business was ruled by Pieto Soladias, a puny Panamanian still in his early twenties who came to the city as a street dealer and had murdered his way to the top of an enterprise that moved more than one million dollars worth of drugs each week. He liked to strut about in brightly colored outfits, though lately he had followed the fashion to rugged outdoor gear, and secured his power with heavily armed street gunners, most of whom were not old enough to vote.

The Homicide Division liked to tie every unsolved juvenile homicide, especially those among the city's poor, to the Soladias organization. Many confidential informants told of how Soladias liked to mutilate and dismember his victims, dumping them on the streets where the victims had lived, as a "statement" of his power. But no one would supply any evidence linking him to a crime.

Only once had Pieto Soladias been taken into custody. That was when he had blatantly ordered the firebombing of a building that Sergeant Vinnie Almagro and rookie vice squad detective Louis Monroe had been using to surveil the corner. Monroe had run down the male prostitute who had set the fire, and Soladias had come in willingly to answer questions, with his lawyer, Chester "Cheezy" Lindberg, standing by. Lindberg mentioned that his client, a self-employed housepainter whose careful investments had, over the years, "more than adequately contributed to Atlantic City's rebirth," would not hesitate to file a discrimination suit against the Atlantic City Police Department if he believed that he was made the target of abusive procedures because of his ethnic heritage.

Municipal Court Judge Francis Unerich ruled that the fact that police had observed Soladias talking to a punk who went into a house and emerged with a bottle of gasoline, and that they had seen Soladias pointing the punk toward the building and the police who were on the roof, was not sufficient evidence to charge him for arson and first-degree murder.

It was for these and other acts of justice that Judge Francis Unerich was known within the police department as the Honorable FU.

As Monroe drove slowly down the ruin of Nevada Avenue he didn't notice a spindly kid in a black leather jacket until he swaggered in front of Monroe's car to cross the street. Monroe took his right foot off the gas and put it on the brake. The car stopped short, touching the kid's jacket. The kid spun back, pulled a small, stubby, gunmetal gray machine pistol out of his jacket, and aimed it at Monroe.

Then he kicked in the car's left front headlight, spat on the car, yelled at Monroe to go fuck himself, and continued across the street.

Monroe wanted to stop the car, get out and take the gun out of the kid's hands, cuff him, search him, arrest him for carrying a concealed weapon, illegal possession of a firearm, and anything else that would stick.

But he didn't. He froze up, put his head down, made a right turn on Jefferson Place, another right onto California Avenue where he stopped beside a fire hydrant and waited until he stopped trembling.

He had never been so afraid.

◆

He spent most of the next day at home, happy only when he was playing with Sere. He could forget himself, forget everything that bothered him and frightened him, when he was with her. Sometimes all he had to do was let her grab his finger and it was as if the pain in his left side was gone.

"Hey," he said when Mrs. Pasecki pulled her away from him to change her diaper. "Let me try to do that."

"Learn on your own time," Mrs. Pasecki snapped. "You'll be having so much to do in the next few years you'll wish it was just some poopie causing the ruckus."

"How am I going to learn if you don't let me?"

"It's not me. A person is particular about who she lets do the changing. If you want to step in, you'll have to earn it."

"So how am I going to do that?"

"By getting out of the way and giving the poor girl some privacy. Take a bath, why don't you?"

He took a long bath. Then he went out to buy a new headlight assembly for his car. As he drove, fat, grayish white flecks of snow fell from the darkening sky.

Monroe used to enjoy the rare times that it snowed because snow transformed the warm-weather fantasy of Atlantic City and its neighboring shore towns into something that belonged under a Christmas tree. The hard-edged, spaceship-modern summer homes that crowded the beach blocks took on softer lines. Snow filled in the cracked sidewalks and potholed streets. The ruined blocks in Atlantic City's Inlet, the rows of abandoned, burned shells, became picturesque in the wintry drifts, as if a miraculously clean, white sand had blown in from the beach to cover them and eventually erase them from view.

The problem with snow in Atlantic City was that it almost never stayed long enough to work its visual charm. What looked good at first became, like so many things Monroe encountered in Atlantic City, ugly and deadly.

45

Snow melted on roadways, and then froze as wind and darkness transformed the mixture of water and roadway slime into flat, glaring sheets of ice offering no traction. The next morning every major roadway connecting Atlantic City to the mainland would have at least one serious automobile accident, blocking traffic for hours.

At the intersection Monroe turned onto Route 30 and drove east, toward the mainland, riding over gray, frozen marshes marred by billboards and the weatherbeaten remains of clam bars, hot-dog stands, gas stations, motels, and Ultimate Pizza Restaurants that had gone out of business and, like Venice, were slowly sinking back into the murk.

On his right, rising from the darkness, bathed in lights as bright as those trained on the casinos, was Todesco Luxury Motors. A Mercedes mounted on a pedestal rose above the rows of gleaming automobiles. Overhead, an enormous American flag dropped into the gloom.

He turned off Route 30 onto Delilah Road, then made a left onto Shore Road, slowing as he entered the ridiculous twenty-five-mile-per-hour Pleasantville speed trap.

Past Pleasantville, he looked to his left and saw the distant towers of the casino hotels in Atlantic City. He felt the car slip and slide on the ice, felt himself tensing, his hands gripping the cold plastic wheel tightly, too tightly.

He gently slowed the car at the entrance to the police academy parking lot, felt the rear wheels begin to slip ahead, but not fast enough to be a threat. Monroe turned right, saw lights blazing inside the rambling brick Georgian Revival edifice that had been, over the last century, a hospital, an insane asylum, an old-age home, a Catholic girls' high school, and, finally, Atlantic County Offices Bldg. #2.

Monroe walked carefully, pulling his storm coat around him. He stepped cautiously down into the basement entrance where the Atlantic County Police Academy had taken over the former school gym. He shoved open the door, heard its groaning hinges echo throughout the building. He passed a row of lockers, picked one, looked down the corridor, and saw a light on in the gym. He put his storm coat, wallet, socks, and shoes in the locker. He straightened his sweatpants and sweatshirt and took off his sling and let his arm hang. Then he slammed the locker shut.

His feet nearly froze on the lineoleum tile floor. He stepped gingerly to the Catholic girls' school gym, saw, through the glass door, Sergeant Vinnie Almagro sitting in a chair at the edge of the dingy, ripped-up tumbling mats. He was dressed in a white martial arts *gi,* his black belt knotted around his waist. He was reading an outdoor camping magazine.

"Uh, hi," Monroe said.

Almagro didn't look at him. He put down the magazine, stood, checked the clock on the wall, put his feet on the edge of the mat.

Monroe hesitated. Then he put his feet on the opposite edge, feeling fear invade him, paralyzing what little movement he had. He hoped Almagro would see how injured he was and just do some warm-ups and give him a pep talk and send him home.

Almagro merely bowed.

"Shouldn't we wait for anybody else?" Monroe asked.

Almagro took three huge, fast steps and drove a punch toward Monroe's face. Monroe pushed away the punch, slipped, and fell forward on the mat. He saw the mat coming to his face. He stuck out his arm and managed to pull himself into a forward roll, but his left leg smacked the mat. He winced and turned, saw Almagro's bare, callused foot poised over his neck.

"Okay, you got me," Monroe said.

"I didn't get you," Almagro replied. "You resisted badly

but escaped. Why are you trying to escape?"

Monroe stood awkwardly. Almagro punched him more slowly this time. Monroe hooked Almagro's wrist with his right hand, raised Almagro's arm, and was about to throw him forward when he felt Almagro's arm coming down, a hand clamping on his, Almagro's shoulder blades hitting his chest, and then he was flying overhead, slamming down on the mat on his ass.

The landing was not happy.

"Again, grasshopper," Almagro said. He was a fan of the blind martial-arts guru in the TV show *Kung Fu* and liked to imitate him when teaching. "Why are you trying to escape?"

"I wasn't trying to escape," Monroe said. "I tried to get you that time."

"You landed improperly. Your mind was on other things."

"I landed improperly because my body's screwed up." Then Almagro was coming toward him, one foot raised high, about to come down on his left knee in a stomping kick. Monroe snagged the foot with his right, shoved it aside, rolled out, felt Almagro touch his back ever so lightly with his fist.

"You got me again."

"Why are you trying to avoid me?"

"I'm not avoiding you."

The foot came down an inch from his head. Monroe grabbed the foot with his right hand, kicked with his right leg, touched Almagro under his ribs. "Better."

Monroe stood, saw another punch coming at him, grabbed the punch, and tossed it—and Almagro—over his shoulder. Almagro fell almost without a sound and rolled to his feet.

"Better still."

Almagro left the mat, picked up a battered, chipped baseball bat behind his chair. He put his feet on the edge of the mat, bowed, opened his mouth, screamed, and swung the bat at Monroe's face.

You can't block a baseball bat. Any attempt to parry a baseball bat with mere flesh and bone will shred the flesh and break your bones. And, given the denseness of the grain, you can't pull any fancy breaking technique because baseball bats are designed to take the impact of baseballs coming in somewhere between fifty-five and ninety miles per hour, and not to break.

And there was no way Almagro could control the baseball bat sufficiently to prevent it from doing serious damage to Monroe.

Almagro's expression, the steely rage screaming from his mouth, the red hatred in his eyes, the sweeping blur of the bat as it swerved toward Monroe's forehead, said, in plain language, that Monroe was about to be hurt, bad.

When you're threatened with a hard, big, deadly weapon, you should immediately avoid it. But Almagro was coming too fast.

There was nothing to do but head right for the man, spin into him just a little bit faster than his swing. You can't do much to defend yourself from a baseball bat, but you can grab the arms that hold it, spin into the body that's swinging it, and by just shoving the body a little harder, a little faster in the direction the baseball bat wants to go, you capture control of the body, the arms, and the bat. Almagro's force becomes your force and then, with a little hip twist, you send it, with the bat, flying.

Almagro went forward, tumbling over, coming down on his back with one arm coming down to break his fall, the other clinging loosely to the bat.

"There," Almagro said. "Now we can begin."

They did a few minutes of stretches, spins, and twists. Then Monroe collapsed on the mat and said, "I can't do this."

Almagro swung the bat and Monroe didn't move. The

bat stopped a half-inch from Monroe's collarbone and he was back under the pier, the ocean crawling up his body, the blows landing, the men laughing.

Then he was aware that he was on the mat, on his side. He touched the mat's worn, dingy canvas skin.

"You made it easy for me," Almagro said. "I didn't even have to touch you and you went down."

"It was like I went somewhere," Monroe said. He saw that Almagro had gone back to his magazine.

Monroe pulled himself up until he could sit, his right leg curled under him, his left sticking straight out to the side.

"Sir, will I ever get it back?"

Almagro turned a page. Then he said, "What have you lost?"

Almagro closed the magazine and put on his glasses. His pale, sagging, drooping face seemed to harden behind them, as if the glasses were a mask that might protect him. He looked at his watch. "I'm sorry, but I have an appointment. Perhaps we'll do this again sometime."

◆

When he got home he realized he'd need two hands to take out the old assembly, put in the new one, and align the light.

At least you have a car, he told himself. He wanted to thank Beth Todesco for spotting it.

"Sure," he told himself. "Why not?"

It was dark, Ellie had gone to work, and Mrs. Pasecki was putting Sere to bed when he called the municipal tow lot and asked to have Officer Todesco paged.

"Sure I remember you. Datsun two-eighty Z, robin's-egg blue, Nevada Avenue beach block."

"I just want to thank you again."

"And tell me you saw my stupid picture in that dumb-ass magazine and you're hot as hell to meet a celebrity."

"I don't want to disappoint you. . . ."

"Listen, they say that when you get your picture in the magazine, it's supposed to be a turn-on for a certain type of guy."

"I'm not that type," Monroe said.

"You saying that because it was your wife in the article and you're so used to it, being married to somebody that gets all the attention?"

"No. I mean, as far as I know, this was the first time she was—"

"And she's not celebrating with you? Popping open the champagne? Painting the town red?"

"Not really. She's at work."

"She works nights. I work nights."

"I used to work nights."

"And now you're all alone?"

"Not really . . ."

"I used to be married to a guy wanted attention all the time."

"What happened?"

"I'll tell you one of these days."

"Why do I have to wait?"

"Suspense, intrigue, I don't know. I like the sound of your voice. Maybe I'd want to hear it again someday."

"But I'm . . ." Monroe had always been painfully shy with women. "Nothing."

"Nothing what?"

"Nothing like you'd . . . I mean, I'm *married*."

"So we'll go dutch on lunch."

"Sure. No. I should pay. I owe you that. One day, if you're free. . . ."

"Long as I hook cars I'm free as a bird. How about right now?"

"I'm . . ."

Mrs. Pasecki said, "Is that Ellie? I'll bet she's got something cooking at that casino."

Monroe put his hand on the mouthpiece. "Could you...?"

"Stay late? Whatever. Where the hell I'm going to go, such a cute one like this within walking distance?"

"I'm getting on my coat," Monroe said to the phone.

Chapter Four

♦ ♦ ♦ ♦ ♦

All Men Are Jack

Seen from the passenger seat of *Whiskey Alpha Five*, Traffic Safety Officer Elizabeth Todesco's city tow truck, the darkened Inlet looked just as dark and dangerous as it had been before the slums started coming down. Streetlights cast a baleful glare on graffiti-scarred housing projects, boarded-up tenements, and broken, potholed streets covered in slick, slippery glare ice. The lights didn't illuminate the Inlet streets as much as they defined the territory: anything they didn't touch became no-man's-land.

Rising above the gloom, the floodlit, billion-dollar casino hotel towers glistened against the dark, cloudless horizon like an incomplete set of capped teeth.

As Todesco drove her wrecker through the darkened Inlet, with the Georgia Satellites doing "Battleship Chains" on the tape player drowning out the sharp mutterings on the police radio, Monroe stared at the tower of the Alcazar shining brightly along the Boardwalk. It was so easy to pretend that, even on streets whose lights hadn't been shot out by drug mules trying out their machine pistols, there was no city around him, no once and future Queen of Resorts: just a row of casino hotels beckoning, like the working girls along Pacific Avenue, for the opportunity to be a "force for positive change."

She drove him to a twenty-four-hour delicatessen that glowed brightly in a strip of abandoned shops and shuttered storefronts on the north end of Atlantic Avenue.

Schneckle's Delicatessen to the Stars was deep enough in the Inlet to miss the daytime lunch trade from city hall, the county office buildings, and the casino hotels along the northern stretch of the Boardwalk. But it was close enough to the senior citizens' housing towers and the few slums that were still inhabited by their original owners to have survived before the casinos. And it showed every indication that it would continue to survive in the big, bright, and empty post-casino city.

Monroe saw the steam-clouded front window of Schneckle's Deli glowing warmly on the freezing night. Above it was a weathered, painted sign lit by a single, baleful bulb.

Todesco rolled down her window and, a block away, Monroe smelled chicken soup, pickling spices, and maximum-strength coffee. She parked on the street. Monroe winced as he swung his left leg over and down to the sidewalk. She shouldered open the glass door at the front. Monroe scurried in behind her as the door closed.

What had been an aroma now became a dense fog of grease suspended in steam. Todesco, in her police-issue storm coat, sauntered past the narrow counter with the deli case, waved at the mustached geezer in faded white shirt and shriveled black bow tie yawning behind a cash register, and took a banquette behind the dessert case where dessicated cheesecakes spun slowly behind the glass.

Monroe slid in opposite her, and watched as she shrugged out of her coat, tossed back her black mop of hair, put her portable police radio on the table, and threw a uniformed leg up on the banquette. It was a long leg, Monroe noticed, longer than his wife's.

She caught him noticing and he fumbled with his coat.

The dining room had a few people in it. Some bums were sleeping on the tables. A shabbily dressed couple in their forties stared vacantly past each other, chewing their food like cows. At another table Monroe was sure a drug transaction was taking place between a casino floorman with perfect hair and a kid in a long black leather jacket.

A puffy woman with a pincushion face and an enormous bosom, whose name tag said BABE, asked, "You wan' the coffee, hon?"

"Two as usual, Babes," Todesco said, "and leave the pot."

It was the strongest coffee Monroe had ever tasted. It seared his mouth, scoured his teeth, and burned harder than liquor. The aches in his body receded to a dull throb. He became ravenous and opened the menu and ordered the first thing he saw: the roast-beef special platter.

Todesco asked for her usual. Monroe took off his gloves and wrapped his hands around the coffee cup, touching his wedding ring to the scratched, dishwasher-eroded surface of the porcelain.

"So," he began, "I guess you've been having a quiet night."

"Who you talking to?" She yawned. "We had a three-car pileup at Route Thirty and Brigantine Boulevard, a mile from that trailer you were sitting in. This van was hit broadside by two kids in a Jeep, knocked them both into a head-on with a station wagon. Had to use the jaws of life."

"The kids—"

"Bunch of Jesus freaks, actually. No drugs involved. They were talking about Blessed Virgins when they hit a patch of glare ice, couldn't slow down, and whammo. Everybody lived, but that roadway was *gleaming* from ice and broken glass. It was weird, with all the lights on it, like we were in some kind of fairyland. That glare ice is incredible. Slick as hell, and you can't see it until you're on top of it and even then it's too late. I've pulled vehicles out of people's front living rooms and the drivers had been only doing thirty-five miles until they hit the ice and went sailing right out there.

"And there was a stop-and-search on Arkansas, going

toward the expressway. Somebody gets stopped and we find drugs, I have to tow the car. Get a lot of tows that way. Soladias's turned this place into the drug capital of south Jersey."

"Is anyone in the department working on him?"

"Every week there's a small-scale operation that gets a couple of mules or a corner boy. Keeps the stats up."

"We should get him," Monroe said.

"We should shoot him," Beth Todesco said. "But that's murder, and cops aren't supposed to do that. You can, though. Say it was in self-defense."

Monroe shuddered.

"You cold or something?"

"No, I . . ."

"Listen, Jack, as long as you're paying, I'll talk your ear off but it's you I want to hear from."

"My name isn't Jack," Monroe said sheepishly.

"All men are Jack to me when they piss me off. You got a problem with that?"

"No, I—"

"I have this thing for men with obvious problems." She nailed him with her milky green eyes.

Monroe waited for the blush to come, but it didn't. He took in her long, triangular face, with its wide mouth, sharp, almost hollow cheekbones, prominent brown eyebrows. He pegged her age at the middle thirties. She could be his age. She was the kind of ballsy female who would never have lowered her eyes to see the five-foot-two-inch Monroe staring up to her.

But she was looking at him now. "So, are you going to be suave and ask me how I got into this business?"

"I don't ask people about how they got into their business."

She stretched her legs and her knee brushed his thigh. "Ten times a night, I tow a car and the owner is a male and he catches up to me, the first thing he wants to know, after he figures out that he parked illegally, is how I got into the business. You know the line I tell him?"

Monroe said, "You ask him if it's his first time with a hooker."

"You read about me in the magazine."

"I liked what I read," Monroe said.

"The media always gets it wrong."

He smiled and she smiled and he glanced up at a set of vaguely medieval imitation wrought-iron chandeliers. Every third bulb was yellow.

"So," Todesco said, "your marriage getting any worse?"

Babe slapped the roast-beef special in front of him. It was two fat slices of white bread with gray, leathery hunks of roast beef piled on top, drenched in a gooey sea of brown gravy that seemed to have erupted from a mashed-potato volcano at the far end of the plate.

He'd have to saw it up with a knife and there was no way he could do that one-handed.

He looked at Todesco's usual: a pepper, egg, and cheese sub sandwich. Next to that was a large plastic glass of orange juice and a side order of french fries slathered in melted yellow cheese.

She picked up the sub sandwich, opened her mouth wide, and chomped down, a trickle of grease running down her chin. She put down the sandwich and dabbed her mouth.

Monroe didn't touch his knife or fork. "I don't recall saying anything about my mariage."

"I read about your famous wife." She tore another chunk out of her sub. "You don't have to say a thing about your marriage. I have a sense about some things. Like I can pick up on you checking me out."

Monroe pushed up his left arm, put a fork in it, closed his fist around it and pinned down a slice of meat, and started to saw with his right. He actually tore off a chunk.

"Wow," he said.

She put down her sub. "I have wrinkles around my eyes,

buck teeth, a crooked chin, one nostril's bigger than the other, I wear my hair long so you can't see my ears, and I'm fat."

"I don't see any of that."

"I know," she said. "I'm grateful."

Monroe face suddenly felt hot. He put the roast leather in his mouth, chomped down hard, began to chew.

"It's hard as hell to be grateful when you're married," she went on. "You take it for granted that the person who was so wonderful when you met him is going to be wonderful ten weeks, ten months down the line. Things happen. Weird things. You find out stuff you never expected."

Monroe thought of his wife. "People change."

"Tell me about it, Jack."

Did she really want him to tell her? Did anybody? Was it possible that seeing Sere come into the world had changed him so much? Before she had been born, he didn't care about the death penalty. Now, having seen the effort that goes into creating life, and having held in his arms the helpless splendor of an infant, he could not bring himself even to think of death.

And then it was as if the lights went out. He was back under the pier, the ocean rising around him, hearing the sound of the surf and men laughing as they beat him. Five shots were fired from his gun and he asked himself if he had killed anyone. He couldn't remember. He couldn't be sure.

She had her hand on his. "Earth to Louis, Earth to Louis. Whatever it is, it's not important. Earth to Lou, you're clear for reentry."

He felt the warmth of her rough, slightly greasy palm. He tried to remember the last time Ellie had touched him like that.

Then he pulled back his hand and put another chunk of leather in his mouth. "You pick up on a lot of things," he said.

♦

She didn't tell him anything about her relationship with Jack Chou, other than to hint that the man was not what he seemed. When Monroe pressed her, she changed the subject.

Monroe paid and they went back to the wrecker.

"You got time?" she asked as she started the engine.

"Some."

She drove up Maine Avenue, to the edge of a seawall that extended past the docks around flattened point that used to be Captain Starn's Pier, up to Gardner's Basin.

Several cars were parked in what was Atlantic City's traditional lovers' lane. The cars seemed dark and abandoned, until Monroe saw, in the glare from the casino hotel across the channel, that the cars' windows were covered by an opaque film of condensation. One car was even rocking slightly.

She asked him, "You ever take a girl here?"

"No," Monroe said, taking in the broken, gray sheets of ice that reached into the inky black waters of the creek and would close it if the clammers didn't break the ice each morning with their boats. "This place was always too far," he said.

"What the hell did you do when you wanted to get laid?"

Monroe grinned. "I went under the Boardwalk once. We didn't really get that far. The sand . . . it got all over."

Monroe saw her smile. "No sand in the backseat of a car," she said. "Don't you say it!"

She startled him. "Say what?"

" 'Do you come here often?' "

"I wasn't going to say that."

"But you were thinking it."

"I was not thinking it," Monroe lied.

"This is where the rumrunners used to come in, trying to

beat the Coast Guard," she said. "Before that, the priva-teers might hole up here, waiting for a fat British frigate to sail by."

"I didn't know you were into history," Monroe said.

"Family history. My family's been doing stuff they weren't supposed to for going on three hundred years. Smuggling, rum-running, blockade-running, privateering. My grandfather got himself into the automobile business after Repeal. That big lot of his out on Route Thirty started with a bunch of trucks he had to sell. The trucks used to run the hootch into Philadelphia and Jersey City. He got rid of them and used the lot as a front for a stolen-car ring out of Atlantic City. Had the poor folks run 'em in."

"And your father? He stay in the family business?"

"My father carried on the family tradition in his own ways. I could sink him, what I've seen go on there, but I don't believe in turning people in. Not my own flesh and blood. I split with him when my mother died, and we haven't had any contact for eight or nine years."

"In a town this small you've never run into him?"

"You can avoid somebody, if you put your mind to it. It's not that I haven't heard things about him, like that he's laundering cash on the used-car lot and maybe chopping stolen cars in the shop, but, if he's still doing that, it's small-time. The big money in Atlantic City's always been in real estate scams. I'm sure he'll be getting a big piece out of this Miracle Mile, if he gets someone stupid enough to put down the seed money."

Monroe marveled at her toughness. "How come you turned out different?"

"I wanted to. I grew up around him. My mother didn't care—she was a Depression baby and she liked money. She didn't want to think about what my father did any more than you don't want to see how the cow died that put that meat on your plate. I did. I worked around the lot, learned about cars. I always wanted to feel I was built of stuff that wouldn't fall apart. I joined the department to be as unlike my father as possible."

Monroe didn't want to tell her about his father, and how his father's dishonesty had affected him the same way. But there were other reasons he became a cop. There was that night when he was hanging around on the Boardwalk and looked down an alley and saw what appeared to be a drunken bum getting mugged. But as quick as you can blink, the bum turned the tables, started beating the tar out of the muggers, while plainclothes cops jumped out of the darkness with police dogs.

It was a decoy operation, with a police sergeant dressed as a bum as bait. The bait took two would-be muggers off the street for a while, though the sergeant had taken a few hits in order to do it.

Monroe told Beth Todesco about it. The cop who took the hits was Sergeant Vinnie Almagro, a member of the vice squad who also worked as a part-time unarmed combat instructor at the police academy. Monroe thought that what Almagro was doing was the most heroic thing, setting himself up like that, laying it on the line. The muggers could have had guns and they could have used them and Almagro could have been hurt bad, even killed. "I saw that and I said, here's somebody who's making a difference."

When Monroe came on as a rookie and began to train with Almagro, he discovered that one of the reasons Almagro got hurt doing decoy operations was that he *wanted* to, that there was a part of him that felt guilty because his daughter had been mugged a long time ago, and he hadn't been there to stop it.

But Monroe never lost his respect for the man. He never stopped training with Almagro. When Almagro broke his elbow and was transferred out of Vice to became a full-time instructor and weapons qualifier at the academy, Monroe showed up as many as three times a week to the open unarmed clinics Almagro would have in the academy's gym.

"Then I got married and I got hurt and I haven't trained . . . I can't remember. But it's always been amazing to me: you get close to people, you find out they have flaws, things that piss you off, and you want to run from these people, or lock them up. And then there are others, you see the flaws plain as day, but they don't become important."

They were quiet for a while and she put her hand on his head, turned him toward her, and Monroe managed to pull back just before he caught a taste of fried onions and melted provolone.

She let go and they watched as the occupants of the other cars gradually noticed that a city tow truck had pulled up. First one engine, then another roared to life. Headlights winked on, and the cars backed out and headed away.

She put her hand next to his leg and said, "We're alone."

He said, "It's getting late." The roast-beef special was fighting his stomach, and his stomach wasn't the only part of him that was giving way. He told himself that he was supposed to be a happily married man who had never cheated on his wife and never wanted to, and that this was one of life's little tests.

Todesco put her arm on the back of the seat, her hand dangling near his ear. The hand came down to his collar, touched his neck. Her glove was off and her fingers were warm against his skin.

He looked at the clock on the dash. He felt her breath on his neck. Is this what it feels like to be on a date with someone who is pushing you to do something and you don't want to be pushed? Monroe wondered.

He reached forward and turned on the other radio, the police scanner.

"I knew you'd do that," Todesco said.

The rasping, choppy sound of the dispatcher's voice, and the officers responding, was like opening the door and letting in the cold.

"I'm sorry," Monroe said.

"You're thinking that you want to be someplace else."

From the chatter on the radio, someone had run a road-block down at Congress and Island Avenues. "Beth, I just wanted to—"

"I'm picking up on it," she said, sounding oddly serious.

"Please, just take me back."

"That's not what I'm picking up from you."

The dispatcher called for a clear channel, giving radio communications to the street crimes apprehension team for pursuit of suspect in a black Jaguar with New Jersey plates, 10YR63.

Todesco paused. "My father used to drive black Jags. For a minute, that sounded like his tag."

She turned down the radio.

"So let's just go back."

She looked away from him, far to the left, at a traffic light swaying in the wind over Maryland Avenue. Maryland Avenue ran between the northernmost sections of the Inlet, the Boardwalk casinos, the commercial fishing docks, and the marina casinos to the west. A jitney tried to stop at the light and ended up skidding and sliding halfway into the intersection.

He would have looked at something else, or asked her to drive back to the lot for a third time, if the jitney hadn't stayed where it was.

Todesco said, "His brakes must've locked up. He stays in that intersection and it's slam city. We're going to have to pull him out of there."

She put the truck in gear, snapped on the flashers, and floored the gas. Monroe felt his seat belt pulling at the damaged muscles on his right side as the truck leaped forward, the wheels spinning on the gray glare ice that covered much of the street. The truck lurched to the left, slipping into a skid. Todesco spun the wheel, and they were on Maryland Avenue, heading west, toward the jitney. Then she glanced into the rearview mirror and said, "Hold on," and swerved to the side of the road, almost running into a low-income housing project.

Monroe saw a black Jaguar shoot past them at what must have been ninety miles an hour. The car tried to steer past the jitney, hit the ice, slamming through a chain-link fence and into the low sheds of the commercial fishing dock.

Todesco backed the wrecker into the street while the jitney driver freed his brakes and moved off as she hit that broad stretch of glare ice and slipped to the right.

This time Monroe saw, to his right, about twenty-five feet of bent chain-link fence that separated the street from the docks. The fence had been pushed in toward the docks, and the ice and the open water beyond it, finally breaking at the gate, which had been torn open by the black Jaguar with its right taillight ripped out. The Jaguar had kept going, smashing into the side of a shed, bouncing off the shed, and crashing through a wall of metal clam bushels that had slowed down the car just enough to make it stop, its front wheels hanging out over the edge of the dock toward the ice-sheathed Absecon Inlet.

Elizabeth Todesco picked up the transceiver and called the accident in to the dispatcher.

"I'm going in," she said, dropping the truck down to second and slowly pushing away the remnants of the gate. "He's hanging right off the dock. The wind changes and he's in the creek."

"Roger, Todesco. You sure know how to find 'em," the dispatcher said. "Blue situation at Maryland and Huron Avenues. Emergency blue units respond."

"You don't think that's your father—" Monroe began.

"In a blue situation, you don't think," she said quickly. "No time."

Monroe heard the other emergency vehicles call in as the metal gate twisted and broke around them. Once through, Todesco rolled down her window, spun the truck around with her head out the window, and backed toward the car until the flickering yellow lights on the cherry bar over the cab were reflected off the XJ-12 numbers, in chrome, next to the rusting license plate.

"The XJ-twelve has twelve cylinders in it." Todesco said. "It's one of the heaviest cars ever made. If it was any lighter, that guy'd be a frozen Popsicle by now."

She switched on the rear floodlights. Monroe had his seat belt off and the door open before she could tell him to get out. He heard someone bark over the radio about a plate number, but then he was out, slipping and sliding across the smooth, glossy gray ice that coated the pitted asphalt pavement around the docks. Over the low grumble of the idling truck, he heard the high whine of the Jaguar's engine racing.

The car seemed to be frozen in its final leap into the water, hanging with its front end in the air, over a ten-foot drop to the water, which was covered with jagged plates of ice. Monroe knew that this part of the Absecon Inlet was dredged every year to accommodate the deeper drafts of the commercial boats. Even with the water at low tide, it was deep enough here to swallow the car completely.

The car's engine was still turning the front wheels. The windshield was intact and without shatter marks. This meant that the driver's-side airbag must have worked. The spinning of the car's front wheels indicated that the driver still had his foot on the accelerator.

Todesco left the truck, crawled to the edge of the dock, and shone the light under the car. "No noticeable fuel leaks, but it might be too soon to tell. He's going to have to turn the engine off."

She stood and shone the light through the windshield. Monroe saw a man hunched over the wheel, a line of blood dripping from his nose. His eyes were open. Todesco wiggled the light and he blinked, turned his head toward them.

It was Pieto Soladias.

Chapter Five

♦ ♦ ♦ ♦ ♦

Slip-Sliding Away

Monroe saw the fear on Soladias's face increase, and then he couldn't see anything as Todesco lowered her flashlight and went back to the truck.

An awful splitting sound emerged from below and Monroe felt the wooden planks along the dock twist and dip downward as the car slid forward a few inches.

Monroe scampered off the dock. Inside the truck, a spatter of noise came over the radio, then the wild growl of Detective Jack Chou.

"Chou, repeat, black Jag ten YR sixty-three, he's *mine*. Nobody gets near him until I get there."

The dispatcher said, "Officer Todesco, respond."

"I hear you, Jack," Todesco shouted into her radio. "You're dead meat, you come near me, you roger that, Dispatch?"

Monroe took in her crimson face, her hair blown back in the wind like some magnificent mop-headed mascot on the prow of a ship, and he wondered how Chou could have let her go.

Beth Todesco pulled a portable megaphone out of the truck and went to the car.

Soladias's eyes went wide, his mouth opened, and he appeared to be fighting to get the door open. He was probably screaming but Monroe couldn't hear him over the roaring engine.

She raised the megaphone and yelled at the car, "Take your foot off the accelerator!"

She repeated the command a few times. A few more of the planks beneath the car split and the car jumped forward again before Soladias realized what she was saying. Then the engine died.

"Turn the car off," she said, but Soladias was too busy trying to open the door, and failing.

"Sit tight. Turn the car off. We're going to get you out of there," she said.

Soladias finally turned off the car and shrieked as the car sagged deeper, slipping forward. Monroe saw that the only thing preventing it from falling into the water was a crumpled metal clam bushel jammed between the left rear wheel and the base of the broken concrete tie-up piling.

"You," Todesco said to Monroe. "Sit down on the back of the car over the left wheel."

"I'm not sitting," Monroe said. "I want to help."

"With your weight it'll stay there until I can get the hook on and pull it back."

Monroe looked at the car and shook his head. He called back to Todesco, who was beside the truck, powering up the tow-bar hydraulics. "My weight could push it forward and we'd both be in the water," he said.

"Then I'll pull both of you out," she yelled at him over the hydraulics' squeal. "Now sit!"

"You just want me to sit on it?"

"Over the left wheel," she called from the side of the truck, dropping down the tow bar.

Monroe was wearing gloves. He put his right gloved hand on the side of the car, noting the streaks and dents of freshly injured metal. He backed his buttocks against the bumper, braced himself with his left arm, winced at the pain in his shoulder, and hopped backward. He hit the car, pushing it slightly toward the water, and slipped off, landing flat on his ass and then sliding back against the left wheel as he heard the groaning sound of old wood bending too far, but holding.

The hydraulics stopped squealing and for a second Monroe heard a request from Detective Chou on the truck's radio for Officer Todesco to confirm the Jaguar's license plate number.

Todesco flinched and told Monroe to sit *on* the car. "Don't push it in." She knelt beside him to hook the tow bar under the Jaguar's back end.

"I'm trying," Monroe said, struggling to stand on the tilted surface. He managed to ignore the freezing, stinging cold creeping through his cotton-polyester blue jeans as he planted himself, more firmly now, over the left taillight, settling down, ever so gently, as the dock squeaked and groaned below him.

"There," Todesco said, standing up. "You just stay put and don't move *at all*. Stay on the car. I'm going to pull it back. Normally I'd pull it up first, but that might shift too much weight to the front end and that might put you over. So I'm going to pull it *back*. Do whatever you can to stay on the car, okay?"

She went back to the truck and Monroe heard a say-again on the plate number from Detective Chou.

Todesco turned up the radio, slammed the door, stuck her head out of the window, and popped the truck into first.

Monroe heard the engine drop down an octave, and then Beth Todesco on the radio.

"Responding to Jack the fat Fu Man fuck. I'm involved in a blue situation here, which means all unauthorized vehicles back the hell away. Your sardine's still in the can. New Jersey plate one-zero-Yuma-Romeo-six-three."

Chou roared back, "Suspect in vehicle is mine. I want him alive."

Todesco put the truck in first. It groaned ahead. Then

Monroe noticed that he was still on the car, and that the car hadn't moved at all. In the backwash of the wrecker's rear floods, he could see Todesco as she stared at him and the car, her face hanging out of the window.

She was worried.

He turned around and saw Soladias screaming at him in the car. Monroe tried to make out what he was saying. Something about not going anywhere.

Monroe nodded. It was true, they weren't moving. Todesco was popping the truck in and out of first gear, and nobody was going anywhere.

He looked back at the wrecker, and at the truck's four fat rear tires spinning behind salt-spattered black vinyl mud-guards. They were snow tires, but without chains or studs. A recent amendment to the municipal vehicles code banned tires with chains or metal studs—even in snow—so as to preserve city streets.

Without studs there was no way those wheels would grip the ice; they were spinning on the slick surface. The former Mrs. Chou was popping the truck in and out of first with the expectation that the spinning wheels would create friction and the friction would melt the ice and sooner or later the wheels would hit the asphalt and away they'd go.

Sooner or later.

Monroe turned around to give Soladias the okay sign when he felt the car shudder and heard more wood splitting under him. In the second before the car dropped Monroe locked eyes with him.

Then the dock collapsed and Monroe reached for something as he felt himself tumble back and managed to snag, with three of the fingers on his bad left hand, the rusted edge of the license plate, while the back of the car seemed to come up and smack him in his face.

The pain in his left shoulder was excruciating and he almost forgot about anything but that, until he looked up and saw through a ragged hole where the wooden decking had been, the boom on Elizabeth Todesco's wrecker. The car had pulled the wrecker backward, and the only thing that was stopping the truck from coming down was the broken concrete tie-up piling that had somehow wedged itself between the truck's right rear tires. He heard an odd squeaking sound as the left rear tires slowly inched toward the edge.

With his right hand he pushed himself up and away from the trunk of the Jaguar, and saw, straight through the rear window, a black hole that the front end of the car had made through the ice.

He heard a banging beneath him. Soladias was trying to kick open a window but he lacked the fortitude. The part of Monroe's mind that was oblivious to the shredding pain in his shoulder and the corrosion-sharpened edges of the license plate digging into his fingers was thinking, from his years of unarmed combat training, that most people don't know how to kick properly. They think you have to muscle through things like wood and bricks and human torsos, and, in some situations, muscle helps.

But if you want to be effective with kicks, Sergeant Almagro had told Monroe, you must first develop the calm, confident, concentrated, peaceful attitude that does not recognize that which you are kicking as an obstacle.

"You do not kick to your target," Almagro had said. "You kick *through* your target."

The part of Monroe's mind that was calm, confident, concentrated, and peaceful gazed down at the guy in the car and realized that Soladias would never kick out the window.

Monroe looked up and saw the wrecker's rear tires almost over the edge. Todesco spun the wheels and they grabbed some concrete, showering ice and dirt down upon him, but they didn't budge.

Maybe it was the pain that made Monroe so calm. It was strange. He had stopped taking the painkillers except during the mornings and after his physical therapy sessions, and he told himself he had no right to be this peaceful. He was about to fall into water that would kill him within a minute. He should be screaming his guts out with Soladias. It should be a buddy thing, a male thing, in which macho dudes facing mortality reenact the birth howl.

Soladias must have smacked his nose on the last plunge. The dark red blood dripping on his mouth gave him the appearance of having a mustache that, because of Soladias's peculiar relationship to gravity, was turning up on one cheek.

Turned up. Turn. Monroe held up his right hand and made a turning motion with his wrist. Soladias went hysterical and began to kick again. Monroe waited patiently (while the part of his brain that was feeling all the pain in his shoulder and his fingers informed him that he had no right to wait patiently) until Soladias looked up again. He repeated the motion.

As if to prove that organized criminals have intelligence, Soladias turned the ignition key and those magnificent twelve cylinders roared to life.

Monroe made a lowering motion with his hand. The car had power windows. Soladias lowered the driver's-side window and stuck his head out and screamed words that Monroe didn't quite hear. "Help!" was one of them.

Monroe was aware of Beth Todesco screaming something from above. He had to wait patiently for Soladias to quiet down. Then he told him to open the door.

"Wha' you say?" he asked, his oddly squeaky voice hoarse, his eyes closed to slits.

Monroe said, his voice as tranquil as the narrator of a TV commercial for sleeping pills, "Open the door."

Soladias sprayed a streak of blood-laced profanity. Then he said, "You think I'm so fucking stupid I didn' do that before?"

"Did you?"

Soladias screamed more obscenities and Monroe felt darkness crawling over him. The pain had become so intense that his arm was numb. He had complete confidence that he would die holding on to the car.

Soladias's cries died to a whimper.

Monroe said, "Open the door."

"Fucking won't open, man." His eyes were wet and Monroe caught the scent of loosened bowels. "No way I can get myself out through the window."

"Unlock the door," Monroe said.

Soladias paused, as if to indicate that, though organized criminals possess intelligence, they tend to ignore the obvious. He said, "Oh," and the car door swung open.

Monroe felt no emotion. "Now come out and reach for my hand."

The car slipped and Soladias went hysterical, whimpering about not wanting to die. Then he crawled out, clinging to the door, extending his hand, his brain recalling a lecture he'd heard when he was taking a humanities class at Stockton State College about the image of God giving life to Adam on the top of the Sistine Chapel. The positions of the fingers were important. God had a big beard and his arm and finger thrust out, all fired up to give Adam life, and Adam was sitting back, his hand out as if it was a hot day at the beach and he was expecting another piña colada.

The fingers are important.

"Reach for my wrist. Hold my wrist," Monroe said as he felt Soladias's fingers brush his. "I'm wearing a glove. You don't want the glove to slip off."

Soladias spat out something incomprehensible, then exploded into sobs as he clamped his hand around Monroe's right wrist and dropped like dead weight.

The pain that Monroe thought he didn't have to feel returned. He almost lost it there. Then he remembered to tell Soladias to let go.

Soladias became alert. "Is this a trick?"

Monroe coughed from the engine exhaust blowing in his face. "No. It's just what . . . you have to do. You're out of the car now. Find something else to hold on to. I need my hand."

Soladias became childlike, almost docile, as he wedged one foot onto the dashboard, another onto the door handle, put his free hand on the car's roof, where Monroe's foot hung down. Monroe felt the tension around his wrist relax. The pain in his shoulder disappeared until he realized what he would have to do next.

He flung his good arm around and grabbed the edge of the car's trunk. Then he hunched himself forward, inch by inch, slipping, falling back, but finally at the point where he could stick his face past the license plate and examine the tow bar strapped to the Jaguar's back end.

Elizabeth Todesco was yelling at him about pins at the edge. He saw them—the tow bar was fixed to the frame by twin steel-reinforced rubber straps that were held together by a heavy latch. In the middle of each latch was a grimy metal pin. A quick release?

Monroe fumbled with the pin on his right side and the car plummeted down, rotating out toward the water, with Soladias telling him that he was going to kill him and his mother. Monroe felt Soladias's hands around his old, beat-up walking shoe. He felt his shoe come off and the cold wrap around his toes as hands grabbed his ankle.

The other pin was not going to stay in for long. Monroe said, "Hold on to me, tight," locked his right hand around the tow bar, and yelped as he opened the fingers of his left hand and tried to pull them on the tow bar.

He waited for the car to drop out from under him. Nothing happened.

From above he heard Beth Todesco's voice beginning to curdle with panic. She told him she'd tried to wedge the truck's front wheels but nothing was holding. He'd have to pull the other pin.

To pull that pin Monroe would have to reach with his left arm and hold it with his left hand. When he remembered that his left hand was his bad hand a red ring of panic seethed around him and he yelled, "I can't!"

"You sumbitch you gotta or I kill you dead," Soladias said. "Kill you. Kill you dead. Cut your fucking head off and hang it from the truck. Kill you sumbitch mutherfucking . . ."

He heard something squeal overhead. Pieces of debris hit the car's hood. Monroe hooked his right arm around the tow bar and pushed his dead left arm toward the pin.

Don't reach to the target, grasshopper, Almagro said in his mind. *Reach through.*

But there was nothing past the pin, nothing for him to focus on, just a blur of pain and the rising fear that the water would claim him and take him away from this.

He told his fingers to open. They didn't move. He willed his fingers to open. They wouldn't budge. He pushed his shoulder toward the pin. A finger snagged it, slipped off. He closed the finger, closed another. He twisted, he pulled.

The car dropped from under him like a living thing suddenly let go. He heard what sounded like ripping cardboard as the ice broke and shredded, taking the car and pieces of the dock. He heard the car's engine rumble, sputter, and die. He felt the tow bar dig deeply into his right armpit. He felt his right leg straining at the hip socket. He wondered if there was a pin in his hip that he could pull that would send the leg, and the man holding on to it, down with the car.

It was then, on the triumphant squeak of functioning hydraulics, that he rose toward heaven as a patrol car skidded in, stopping short of ramming Todesco's truck. The door was open before the car stopped moving and the bulky form of Officer "Bigfish" Tony Filmont tumbled out and came up with both hands clamped around his Glock automatic.

He said, "Hands in the air and freeze!"

Monroe was hanging on the tow bar and Soladias was

hanging on him and both were hanging over the creek. Todesco had to go back into the wrecker and drive forward before they would be on solid ground.

"Move your damned car!" Todesco yelled at Filmont.

"What car?" said Officer Jerry "Jerry Lad" Ladzinski, who stepped carefully out of the patrol car and now had his gun on Todesco.

"The goddamn one you came in on!" Todesco yelled. "You move it or I'll move it."

Bigfish Filmont said, "Don't move," to Monroe and Soladias, went back to the patrol car, and backed it up as a yellow Buick, the right front end smashed in like a wadded-up piece of aluminum foil, bounded in. The Buick made a hard left, spinning around and then backing up until the Buick's rear end blocked the truck.

Monroe couldn't see Todesco in the cab. He thought he might have heard her yelling something. He looked down at the broken ice and inky black water swirling around the trunk of the Jaguar and willed himself to hold on. He felt the truck move forward with a slow, powerful inevitability, watched its front touch the butt of the Buick and shove it forward as a wide, squat man in a fur-collared storm coat jumped out and started yelling at Todesco.

"What the fuck they doing? They gonna get us out of here or what?" Soladias said, his breath foul in Monroe's face, his body hanging heavily on Monroe.

Monroe wanted to tell him to shut up but every bit of energy he had was going to the numbed muscles holding on to the tow bar.

The man went back to his car, moved it out, and the truck started forward again and the slight swaying of the tow line almost pulled Monroe's shoulder out. He looked down, watched the ruined dock slide under his feet, felt his shoeless foot brush ice and snow.

"I'm going to let go," he told Soladias, who began to panic again.

"Nobody let go until I—"

Monroe folded forward on his bad leg. It wasn't supposed to bend as much as it did, at least, not outside of the physical therapy classes, and Monroe felt muscles and tendons stretching, ripping, pulling as the dirty ice rushed up to his face. Without thinking, he slapped his hands—*both* hands—down in front, to break his fall. His hands and his arms vibrated from the shock, but he hit the ice without injuring himself.

Soladias fell off him and hit the ice on his side. Monroe rolled away from him and looked up to see Soladias rising just in time to take a right hook near his eye from Bigfish Filmont. The hook put Soladias on the ice, hard, next to Monroe. Bigfish had his boot up and was about to stomp Soladias's hands when Monroe yelled, *"No!"*

The last time Monroe had encountered Bigfish and Jerry Lad, he had watched them remove a group of junkies from an abandoned boathouse by spraying aerosol deodorant in their eyes. Bigfish and Jerry Lad had a reputation for unusually sadistic brutality and excessive use of force. Monroe had no doubt that Bigfish was going to "take his piece" from Soladias. Monroe didn't have time to ask himself what he was going to do about it.

As the foot was coming down Monroe smacked it to the side. The foot went wild and Bigfish came down on Monroe, knocking the wind out of him.

From the hesitant way Bigfish clambered over Monroe and toward Soladias, Monroe guessed that Bigfish wasn't sure what had brought him down. Monroe saw Bigfish draw his gun and held it as if he was about to pistol-whip Soladias across the face.

Monroe got to his knees and came down hard on the arm holding the gun, pinning it, and the gun, to the ice.

Then Monroe felt the muzzle of a gun in his ear. "Freeze, fucker," Jerry Lad said.

Monroe would have frozen if Jerry Lad hadn't pushed

the gun into his ear and twisted it, in an effort to nick his ear with the pistol's sight.

He stuck out his left arm and whipped it back quickly, surprised that the arm wasn't as stiff as he had expected, banging his balled fist into Jerry Lad's forearm with enough force to penetrate through Jerry Lad's jacket and police blouse, all the way to the pressure point at the elbow joint, giving Jerry Lad a funny-bone jolt. Monroe opened his hand and grabbed the elbow with his left hand, grabbed a piece of Jerry Lad's jacket with his right, twisted around, and with his hip, pulled Jerry Lad down and forward, hoping, in that half second that he saw Jerry Lad flying above him, that Jerry Lad had taken enough unarmed combat courses to know that when someone is throwing you forward, you bend your arm, tuck in your head, and roll off your shoulder.

Jerry Lad hadn't taken enough courses. He landed face-first on Bigfish's back.

Bigfish yelled first. Jerry Lad yelled louder. Monroe rolled out and was in a crouch when he saw Jerry Lad's gun on the ice. Soladias also saw the gun. Monroe gave Soladias a look that said, *Don't even think about it.* Soladias stopped as if he'd run into a concrete wall.

Monroe reached over, picked up the gun, held it. Bigfish had turned on him and was about to lunge for him when he saw Jerry Lad's revolver in Monroe's hand.

Everybody stopped and stared at each other and Monroe, astonished at what he had just done. Here he was, a guy with so many strained, sprained, broken, and slowly mending parts, and the unarmed combat stuff *worked.* In fact, it worked better than it had before he'd been injured because he hadn't had time to think about what he could or couldn't do.

"What the fuck is this!" the voice of Detective Jack Fu Man Chou roared at Bigfish and Jerry Lad.

Monroe stared up at a wide, lumbering, storm coat–

encased slab of meat, its blunt, potato-shaped face bulging under a lumpy, shapeless knitted cap on his head and eyes as wild as the blinking jackpot lights on a slot machine.

"He, uhh, dropped his gun," Monroe said, standing awkwardly with his woolen sock on the ice.

Bigfish and Jerry Lad were glaring at Monroe as Chou moved between them toward Soladias. Soladias cowered behind Monroe. Chou reached past Monroe for him, and Todesco yelled over the sounds of approaching sirens, "Don't you lay a goddamn hand on him!"

Chou halted, but Monroe saw him tremble, a quaking volcano on the edge of eruption. He reached again for Soladias and Todesco said, "Lay off him, Jack. He's *mine*." She radioed a check on the license plate.

"*Who's* yours?" Chou growled.

She came from behind the truck with a crowbar in her hands as the emergency vehicles skidded onto the dock. "I was first on the scene and I got him on reckless driving. I might have him for operation of a stolen vehicle if this car belongs to who I think it does."

"*You* don't got shit." Chou turned to Bigfish. "You pat the scumbag down?"

Bigfish said, "Yes and"—he reached into his jacket—"I discovered fifteen vials of crack cocaine in his possession." He held up a plastic bag secured by rubber bands and then tossed it at Chou, who snatched it out of the air.

"Possession means *we* got him," Chou said. He reached for Soladias a third time.

"What the fuck, you think I'm stupid?" Soladias sputtered. "I never carry nothing on me, man."

"You're carrying if I say you're carrying," Chou said.

Monroe shook his head. "You're not planting it on him."

"Who the *fuck* asked you?" Chou growled.

"Only thing you got is the car, man, and it not even my car," Soladias continued. "It's some politician's car and he don' need it no more."

The dispatcher said the car was registered as a fleet vehicle owned by Todesco Luxury Motors.

"It's my father's car. This asshole stole my father's car."

"I couldn't get to my car because this fat fuck wouldn't let me!" Soladias yelled.

"You shut up!" Chou pointed at him. He put both hands on his waist, stared down at Monroe, and said, "Who the fuck are you, taking over my operation?"

Monroe introduced himself and said, "It's Officer Todesco's operation."

"You're the guy got the blanket," Chou said. "You can't hold a guy like this on anything less than possession."

"He can be put in a tank for reckless operation of a motor vehicle," Monroe said as the emergency crew shone flashlights on them. "But you'll have to prove he's intoxicated."

"I'm nothing like that, man," Soladias said. "I don't touch that booze shit."

"He's whatever I say he is!" Chou screamed, stomping his feet on the ground.

"Hey, it's the Fu Man!" The emergency crew's flashlights found him and his face changed. The rage dripped out of him, replaced by the broad smile Monroe had last seen him wear at the Ancient Mariner Bar & Grille.

"Hey guys," Chou called, his anger mellowing, becoming smooth, almost like a stand-up comedian with a good crowd. "We caught a live one here. Caught him coming out of that fag bar on New York Avenue. You should've seen it. His bodyguards slipped on the ice but this son of a bitch steals a car, drives it into my Buick, goes on this joyride you wouldn't believe, and we had to fish him out of the drink."

"Who's *we*, Jack?" Beth Todesco said.

He faced her. "I'm not fucking around. He's the bad guy and we get the bad guys—"

She looked him in the eye. "Not if we have to become as bad as they are to do it!"

79

Monroe asked himself if he'd said that. Then he saw Chou put on his smile again. "Hey. We're all on the same side, right? Let's take him in and you charge him with what you want, and Bigfish and the Lad'll charge him with what they want and—"

"No, Jack," Beth Todesco said firmly. "I'm charging him."

Chou looked at Monroe, and then back at his ex-wife.

"What the hell you two have that gives you the balls to gang up on me?"

Todesco looked at Monroe and said, "We're in love."

Chou's jaw dropped.

Twenty-four hours later, Louis Monroe would be reinstated as a detective in the Atlantic City Police Department.

Chapter Six

♦ ♦ ♦ ♦ ♦

Armed and Dangerous

Cheezy Lindberg, Soladias's lawyer, claimed police entrapment. He came to the department with a statement from Harry the Toad that Todesco Luxury Motors made fleet vehicles available to numerous persons, that the vehicle was fully insured for all damage, and that Todesco Motors had no intention of pressing charges.

Soladias was ordered to pay a $500 fine for reckless driving. He paid cash. Other charges against him were thrown out.

At two A.M., Ellie had not returned. There was a message on the answering machine from the woman who had wanted to see Ellie.

"I saw you in the magazine and I couldn't believe it. How you can go so far and . . . nobody questions you. I mean, getting into government isn't *that* difficult—you take the test and you work on a campaign, but . . . What I have to talk to you about is, if I file harassment charges against my boss, how can I stop them from finding out what I was? My friend said if they find out I used to turn tricks out of the casino lounges, they'll think I'm street trash and it'll never get to court and that bastard will keep doing it to other women and . . . How do you get them to not care about what you were? How do you get them to understand you for what you are?"

She didn't leave a phone number, but promised to call back.

Monroe left the message on the machine, hoping that Ellie would hear it; hoping that she might have an answer for the woman and for him.

When Sere woke him at six A.M., Ellie stirred beside him. He wondered if she would ask him where he had been last night.

But she was with him now. He felt her rise from the bed, put on a blue and green hooded terrycloth boxing robe with ALCAZAR CASINO HOTEL lettering on the back, and go down the hall, into the living room of their one-bedroom apartment, where her daughter lay squalling in her crib.

Monroe tried to go back to sleep. He heard Sere's cries end. Outside the engines of a fishing boat rumbled as it headed out of Clam Creek Inlet into Absecon Channel, its prow making popping sounds as it broke the ice that had crawled out in the night. When Ellie returned forty minutes later, Monroe said, "There's a message on the machine for you. The woman who came—"

She erased it without listening.

Even with that edgy, panicky look on her face, she was, in the dim morning light, so beautiful to him. He asked her to stay with him tonight.

She propped herself up on the pillows, as she did whenever they argued and he was in bed. "You just say, 'hop' and I jump, right?"

"It's not that. I'd like to spend some time, you know, together."

"We've had this argument before."

"We've had this *discussion* before."

"Call it what you like. My job is what I do. It's what I am. I don't *think* about what I used to do for a living."

"Ellie, I wasn't talking about sex."

"I *am*, and if you don't like it, you can leave." She went to the bathroom and gently closed the door.

♦

Ellie was still in the bathroom when the phone rang. Monroe had drifted off to sleep. He didn't answer and heard Marty Gant say on the answering machine, "You got yourself into something that I might be able to make pay off for the both of us. I can't be specific about the payoff at this point. It depends on a lot of things you're probably just guessing at. If you want to stop guessing, you should see me, today, before lunch. I'm seeing Dennis Newton, captain of Traffic Safety, around then, and your name is definitely going to come up for—something. You get out of your physical therapy session at, what, eleven hundred hours? I'll expect you after that, preferably. And I dearly hope Mrs. Chou was confused in referring to you as . . . these rumors can be dangerous. I'll try to stomp it from my end but there's no guarantee that it won't make trouble for you."

The phone rang again.

"This is for Monroe," Soladias hissed. "We don't have much time to say anything about what you did, so I call you and we make time, or you come to my club, you know, the Demimonde on New York Avenue, and we work something out, okay? You come to my club, we talk about doing something, make everybody happy."

Monroe erased the messages. Ellie came out and he thought that it wouldn't take long for her to hear about what had happened last night. Ellie had many contacts in the police department, and Beth Todesco's comment about them being in love. . . .

The phone rang and Monroe said, "I'll get it!"

But Ellie had it in her hand. "Carl," she said, and he saw her smile come on, a special lilt in her voice, a way of talking and agreeing and laughing as she discussed casino business with Carl.

She promised to come in early and bring the baby this time. "Anything you say. Buh-bye."

She hung up and Monroe said, "Carl."

"Carl is Carl." She stretched.

"That says a lot."

"He's tall, has perfect hair that he fusses over all the time. He's silly about clothes—can't ever match his tie with his pocket square. He can flirt like crazy but he's really very shy—a hopeless romantic ever since his wife died. This man won't flinch when a customer drops five million, but he'll shed tears if he sees a hungry dog. When he gets depressed he goes out and buys himself lots and lots of expensive toys. He's also the CEO and my boss."

"He calls you at seven in the morning?"

"If it's important."

"This was important?"

"Extremely. A few hours ago he got a call. Councilman Todesco found a backer for the Miracle Mile. Somebody with land and enough seed money to put it through. He said the backer had been holding out, but last night he had a change of heart."

Monroe saw the headline: MILLIONAIRE DRUG DEALER BACKS HALF-BILLION-DOLLAR REAL ESTATE SCAM. Then he told himself he was only guessing. "He say who this backer was?"

"It's under wraps. But he's very excited. Now if we can only get the guy that owns that land we need to build a second hotel tower, we could link up to the Miracle Mile, and then it would be just perfect. Carl says we'll just have to pray for that. God, Lou, I think it's going to happen! It's really going to happen!"

"He calls you at seven in the morning to tell you that?"

"What's wrong with sharing good news with somebody you like to talk to?"

"What's wrong is we're married," Monroe said, meaning that Carl Cayleen should have known that and called at a decent hour.

But it didn't come out that way. Ellie grabbed the covers and turned away from him in the bed. "Don't remind me."

◆

He wanted to spend the rest of his morning playing with Sere but Ellie swooped in on the girl, giving him silent, cold looks. This made his physical therapy session even more attractive. He decided to head out early, take the car for a drive.

But the car wouldn't start. He pumped the gas, gunned the engine, cursed, prayed, did all the things that worked before. Nothing.

Ellie would drive him but he didn't want to ask her for anything. He didn't want to go back into the house to call a cab.

That left the jitney. He put his face to the thick, raw December wind, and limped two blocks east to Mediterranean Avenue. Each minute he waited drained more of the life out of him. When the jitney arrived, the driver stared straight ahead as Monroe winced and groaned and pulled himself into the van-sized bus.

The jitney jolted and bumped its way past low- and middle-income housing construction sites. Monroe sat among casino workers on the tightly packed fiberglass benches. It was nearing ten A.M., when the casino domestic and restaurant staff reported for work. The majority of the 65,000 people who worked in the Atlantic City casinos and related businesses lived outside of the city, in tightly stacked condos and tract houses on the nearby island of Brigantine, in wider, larger residences in Ventnor, Margate, and Longport to the south, or in the vast stretches of what had been pristine wetlands and pine barrens, which were now denuded of trees, creeks, and some 38,000 species of wildlife dependent on the region, and transformed into tidy, sodded, subdivided, suburban plots, ringed in concrete and asphalt, conveniently situated near shopping centers, malls, and schools.

The few who worked for the casinos and stayed in the

city did so because they could not afford to leave. The worst-off lived in the Inlet. They did the manual, menial jobs far removed from the giddy highs and lows experienced by the millions of gamblers who flooded the casinos, and, like the tides, left a few hours later.

The jitney stopped on one of the rebuilt blocks of the south Inlet. A guy stepped on in wearing a black cashmere coat, black knitted cap, sunglasses, a stained white scarf, rumpled black wool pants, and spotless hiking boots.

He resembled one of Pieto's people but Monroe couldn't be sure. He felt the same fear as when he saw the punk on Nevada Avenue kick out his light. He wanted to put his head low and hide, but there was no place to hide.

The guy lurched as the jitney started up. He mumbled something to the driver, and then shouted, "Fuck you!" as he threw his fare money on the floor. He grabbed for, but missed, a handhold, falling on a wide, mean woman in a waitress uniform. She shoved him away and he had hauled back to strike her when the bus lurched again, throwing him down on the empty gray fiberglass seat beside Louis Monroe.

He thrust his head back, slouching in the seat, and spread his legs wide. Monroe sniffed at a faint wisp of cologne that could no longer disguise the acid breath and sour body odor exuded by people who had been up all night drinking, smoking, eating, and pill-popping, and were now falling to earth like the jettisoned aircraft toilet-tank waste that freezes into dark, vile globs that everybody hopes will vaporize as they plunge through the clouds before they slam into your house and only then begin to melt on your living room rug.

At a traffic light the driver bent over to pick up the guy's fare money. "You owe a quarter on the fare," he called back.

"Suck it," the guy said, his head bouncing like one of

those spring-loaded porcelain dogs sold in the Garden State Parkway gift shops.

Unlike the city bus drivers, who work for the state transportation company, Atlantic City jitney drivers were self-employed owner-operators whose loosely confederated association was one of the few proofs that, when left alone, enlightened free enterprise could solve some social problems, at least those involving transportation. The Atlantic City jitneys were more dependable than Saint Bernard dogs. They ran at all hours of the day or night, in the best and worst weather. When a lunar high tide and a northwest wind pushes the ocean past the beach and into the city's streets, you'll always see a jitney parting the waters, moving grandly past stranded cars and waterlogged municipal buses.

The jitneys' interiors were always clean and sometimes even personalized by their individual drivers. Among the more famous examples were the *Elvismobile*, in which the hip-shaking music and illustrations of the King predominated; the *Frank-We-Love-You*, a similar vehicle driven by a Sinatra worshiper; the Jesus Saver, whose densely clustered crucifixes and icons rivaled any stationary chapel; and the *Bozo Bus*, a moving memorial to the hippie days of the 1960s crowded with Peter Max prints and reproductions of Jefferson Airplane and Grateful Dead album covers.

The jitney in which Monroe rode was not personalized. No music played. Every rattling jolt and shudder as the jitney hurtled over Atlantic City's pitted and potholed roads emphasized the numbing misery of the morning.

The guy sitting with his legs spread on Monroe's left turned his head and spat. A gob landed on Monroe's left leg, making a dark gray blot on the his winter-weight sweatpants.

In any other city, spitting in a public bus would be seen as a regrettable display of careless manners. Passengers would turn their heads, and the driver, whose union contract forbade him from doing anything other than driving the bus and opening and closing the doors, would pity the guy back at the bus barn whose union contract forbade him from doing anything other than wiping public flotsam off the vehicle.

But because the Atlantic City jitneys were owned by their drivers, the passenger who let fly a hocker on the spotless black, no-skid rubber-stripped floor was doing more than demonstrating his contempt. The act was the kind of insult that provoked retribution.

From his position near the back of the jitney, Monroe could see the driver remove his left hand from the steering wheel and reach for a crowbar, that, judging from the way the driver gripped it, had the same function as a baseball bat in a saloon—something you have around because you think it would force obnoxious assholes to back down.

The guy saw the driver's hand on the bar. He put another glob of spit on the floor, this time in the aisle, and shouted to the driver, "You wanna use that stick, go ahead. I'll shove it up your motherfucking ass."

Monroe felt the tension within the jitney rise, as the dozen or so passengers who would have been content to mull over their private woes suddenly woke up to what could be a nasty situation. Only Monroe was aware of how dangerous it was: after the guy spat, he sat up and a portion of his jacket fell open and Monroe saw, riding low over the guy's stomach inside a tooled and inlaid leather holster, the dull, blunt steel and two-inch barrel of a Cobray M-11/9.

An American-made refinement of the infamous Ingram MAC-10, the Cobray was sold as a semiautomatic, single-shot pistol that could be easily transformed into a fully automatic machine gun capable of spraying thirty-two nine-millimeter rounds per second. More than the Uzi, AK-47, Bren-10, Tec-9, MAC-10, and MAC-11 assault weapons, the Cobray had become the status weapon among inner-city drug dealers for most of the last decade. It was enormously more lethal than Monroe's Smith & Wesson .38 special revolver, which Marty Gant had confiscated.

The fact that the state of New Jersey had banned the sale and ownership of assault weapons hadn't reduced the number of weapons in the hands of street criminals. Street scum didn't buy their weapons and ammunition over the counter. The law of the street held that money and intimidation could obtain anything, and that law, rather than those passed in Trenton and Washington, D.C., prevailed.

It wasn't that the cops could do nothing: narcotics was the biggest growth industry in law enforcement. Politicians promising to get tough on crime loved to throw money at the numerous federal, state, and local drug cops because the drug cops delivered impressive arrest statistics. More significantly, the drug cops had a license to steal. Property seized as part of the bust. Boats, cars, houses—anything whose purchase could be tied, however tenuously, to the "ill-gotten gains" deriving from the sale of controlled and dangerous substances—could be confiscated by the arresting body and either kept or resold at auctions, with the funds disappearing into the bureaucratic maze.

All of this was, of course, completely ineffective. The supply of illegal drugs coming into the country continued to rise because the demand was high in a society that placed such an emphasis on feeling good. It was easier to feel good with a drug, and, if you were part of the urban underclass, surrounded by reminders that you were unwanted, unloved, and locked out of a society that wished you hadn't been born, it made more sense to get in on the ground floor of the drug business and start dealing on the street. This was in spite of the fact that you might get maimed, killed, or arrested and put in jails so crammed with street dealers that time in prison became a finishing school for career criminals.

But nowhere else in the world was it possible to make

your first million without learning how to read. If you stayed in a run-down, inner-city public school long enough to learn to read, you knew that for the last three centuries America had been the land of opportunity for millions of immigrants who turned to crime because they were denied the straight and narrow path. And immigrants weren't the only ones breaking the law and getting away with it. Open a newspaper and you'd read about a bank president, corporate head, some guy with a college degree who had stolen millions, sometimes billions, of dollars, and—if he got caught and was found guilty—got a lighter sentence in a country-club jail than the kid who holds up an all-night gas station for twenty bucks.

The jitney hit a pothole, and the guy pushed Monroe, hard, in the ribs. "Don't touch me, pussface," he breathed.

Monroe was trembling with fear. He asked himself why. He hadn't been afraid last night, when he had stood up to Jack Chou, Bigfish, and the Lad. He hadn't had time to think then. He hadn't been in the situation long enough to doubt himself. Someone had needed defending, and he had just jumped in and done it.

The guy shouted at the driver. "Hey, suck-ass. You can't drive this thing, you pull over and get the fuck out."

Monroe said, "Uh, hi."

The guy sat up, rubbed his sunglasses. "You say what?"

Monroe tried his best Boardwalk smile. "Let's take it easy, okay?"

The guy opened his mouth and Monroe saw stained, rotten teeth, and below the shriveled gumline, little scars and open sores that might have been made by needles. Some junkies like to shoot into their mouths, because the needles don't leave marks on their skin and, as a junkie had told Monroe once, "when you get happy, you start to bleed, and there's nothing like the taste of your own blood."

"Only thing I'm gonna take is your fuckin' head off, you skanky piece of dago shit."

Monroe's mother was Italian and so he was aware that he should feel insulted. He was also aware that he'd better not let this idiot know that he had no idea what the hell he was doing.

"I'll let you try," Monroe said.

The guy rubbed his sunglasses again. "What's this 'try' shit?"

"The next stop," Monroe said, loud enough for the driver to hear. "At the next stop."

The guy's mouth curdled into a smile. "You wanna do me?"

Monroe nodded, smiling. The guy put his gloved fist under Monroe's chin, tilting Monroe's head. "I'm gonna rip your face off, motherfucker. Feed it back to you." He extended a finger and was about to jab it into Monroe's throat when the driver pulled over, pushed the lever that opened the door, and announced the street corner.

"This is it," Monroe said.

"Sure be it!" the guy said, slapping his hands on his knees as he stood. He swaggered toward the door, then turned to look at Monroe.

"You with me, pussy?"

Monroe pushed against the chair, wobbled to his feet. He brushed against a casino coffee-shop waitress, shrank back.

"Sorry," Monroe said.

"I make you sorry," the guy sniggered, one foot on the jitney, another on the pavement. "I make you so sorry you gonna beg me to cut you. Cut you deep then I piss in your mouth."

Monroe took one step, then another, until he was beside the driver. He stared down at his nemesis, who was grinning, his gums bleeding in anticipation.

Monroe still had no idea of what to do. He was sure that anything he did to fight this guy would get him hurt, if not killed, fast.

The guy stood with his arms wide. "Come 'n' get me, dago shit."

One of the guy's arms brushed against the jitney's folded open door, which was connected to a polished chrome lever within the driver's reach. The lever was on Monroe's left side.

Monroe smiled. "Uh, bye," he said. He put his left hand on the lever and pushed. The door closed and swept the guy backward, nudging him away from the jitney and making him land flat on his back, his head bouncing on the concrete sidewalk, like a fighter going down for the count.

Monroe saw through the panel that when the guy fell, the impact had knocked off his sunglasses, and that the swaggering, machine-gun-toting menace was actually a tall, gangly-limbed young boy, no more than fifteen years old.

The boy began to get up as the driver gunned the jitney's engine and pulled away from the curb. He was soon on his feet, yelling and running into the street toward the jitney, and Monroe wondered if he would bring up the Cobray and perforate the jitney with the kind of weapons fire designed to mow down an advancing army.

But the kid just waved his fists and bellowed a challenge made inaudible by the jitney's engine.

Monroe turned back and looked at the driver, who said, "His quarter is on the floor someplace. You find it, it's yours."

Chapter Seven

♦ ♦ ♦ ♦ ♦

Newton's Laws

Monroe was in agony as he limped past the junkies on his way out of Atlantic City General Hospital. He wanted to go home and play with his daughter. He wanted to stop guessing about a city councilman using a drug dealer to supply seed money for a redevelopment project.

If it was true, it was another deal with the devil, the kind that Atlantic City had specialized in for well over a century, and the Jersey Shore centuries before that. The arguments were different, the people advancing them were always very educated and reasonable, but everything boiled down to, *If you can't beat 'em, exploit 'em.* Why should government deprive the public of what the public was willing to cross great distances and pay significant amounts of money to obtain? Let the people pay for what they want. Let government take a share of the proceeds, throw a few pennies to charities and public works, and sin becomes salvation.

For well over 300 years the Jersey Shore had had a history of permitting, condoning, or benignly ignoring privateers, smugglers, highway robbers, backroom gambling casinos, bootleggers, prostitutes, and enslavers of Native Americans, African Americans, and migrant laborers. History created tradition, and, as long as the cash flowed to the people with power, no one questioned the consequences that such actions had.

When Monroe was single and was in moods like this, he would go running on the Boardwalk. As he swung his left leg, he told himself that running was out. For a while.

Thinking about the Boardwalk brought back the ocean and the laughter and the sound of his gun discharging. He had to stop and let the scene clear before he could recognize the hospital's drive-up entrance where, before he risked driving, Ellie would wait for him in his car.

The thought of her picking him up made him feel guilty. She had had a terrible life as a prostitute. Now she had gone legit, and was enjoying it, and he really should do something to get along with her better. Be considerate. Say something nice about how she looked.

He imagined tall, dapper Carl Cayleen eating one of those ridiculously opulent dinners that Monroe hated in the casino's "gourmet" restaurants with her. Monroe hated those meals because their purpose was to make gamblers forget how much money they'd lost. As the head of a casino, Cayleen would enjoy talking about how much money his "customers" lost. He would appreciate having time to smell the roses. He would tell Ellie how nice she looked, and she would look great, in those expensive clothes she'd buy at a discount in the casino boutiques. The casino industry had an insatiable demand for good-looking women— one more reason for those old, rich, high-rolling guys to come on down and lose their money.

There were worse ways to earn a living, Monroe said to himself as he saw the homeless addicts hanging around the hospital's entrance.

But there were better ways, too.

He told himself that if Ellie didn't arrive to pick him up, he could deal with it. He didn't need her to listen to him talk about how much it hurt to have his arm bent backward, his neck rotated, his leg lifted and pulled, or how the fat old guy with the broken hip was always trying to make the nurses touch his crotch, or how warm and sticky the water was in that swimming pool that everyone in the group had to go in.

He thought of calling Beth Todesco. She worked nights. She'd be sleeping now. He remembered the way the fight had gone out of Jack Chou when she had said that she and Monroe were in love. Chou had just given up then. He'd let them all go back to the station, hadn't said a thing when Soladias walked, hadn't been able to look Monroe in the eye.

Sooner or later, Monroe was going to have to tell Fu Man Chou that what his ex-wife had said was a lie. He'd have to tell a *lot* of people. Like his wife.

He hesitated in front of the sliding glass doors that led out to a concrete driveway where a line of taxis waited. Around him milled the junkies, in their soiled coats, mismatched shoes, and matted hair, waiting to pick up sanitary hypodermic needles that were being distributed free as part of an experimental program that was designed to limit the spread of AIDS among crack and heroin addicts. The idea was that if addicts could get free, sterilized needles, each would use his own needle and the spread of AIDS would be confined to those who already had it.

He thought he saw a few ruined faces that he recognized: prostitutes he'd busted while on active duty with the vice squad, homeless men and women he'd met during the years he worked the Boardwalk as a patrolman. They didn't recognize him and he made no effort to renew the acquaintance.

He could tell, though, that the free-needle program wasn't working. Most junkies don't care about their health. They viewed their bodies as vehicles that brought them to inexpressibly wonderful, drug-induced highs. When junkies were high, the filth they lived in, the diseases they had, the neighborhood punks who beat and tortured them, the drug dealers who threatened to kill them if they couldn't pay what they owed didn't matter.

When the high faded, they wallowed in depression and hateful despair, some of them hoping that AIDS, or something "better," would help them die so they wouldn't have to feel so bad.

Monroe found it ironic that the statistics for the average life expectancy of a drug addict stumbling about the streets and back alleys of the city were roughly similar to the figures charting the financial "health" of a high-rolling gambler living it up in a top-floor casino suite. Once a casual user of illicit narcotics crosses the line to heavy-use dependecy (defined as more than three large doses a day), he, or she, has between a year and a year and a half of life left.

In the same way, once a casual gambler starts rolling high, visiting a casino twice a month and wagering in excess of $25,000 to $50,000 on each visit, he will go broke within sixteen months.

So it did not surprise Monroe that those who came to the hospital for free needles sold those needles or traded them for drugs. Addicts will do anything to get what turns them on. Compulsive gamblers were the same way: they lived their lives between bets, and the losses they suffered only made their need to gamble more acute.

What continually surprised him was how many addicts there were. For every needle-pocked corpse that was found dead in the back of some Inlet crack house, a dozen came from nowhere to take his place.

The same thing happened with busted-out gamblers, only they didn't have to die. They might have squandered their kids' college money, lost their families, embezzled or stolen to fuel their habits, but to this addict society offered hope, which was called bankruptcy. If a player was rich enough, he could pay a lawyer to sue the casinos. The lawyer claimed that the player was a compulsive gambler, and as a compulsive, he was insane at the time he was gambling and therefore not responsible for his actions. Enough of these suits were settled out of court to make compulsive gambling suits an industry among lawyers who could trust their clients to hide enough money to pay their fees.

There were better ways to make a living than dealing with compulsive gamblers, Monroe told himself as he saw a few junkies ogling something that was just past the hospital lobby's glass entrance doors. Monroe limped past them, and saw his wife sitting in a navy blue Mercedes sedan with tan leather seats and a whip antenna that screamed "car phone."

Monroe looked through the broad, glossy windshield and saw her dolled up in variations of blue: a dark blue serge chesterfield coat with a summery azure business-woman's suit beneath. Behind her, he saw Sere strapped into her car seat.

Ellie got out of the car, came around and held the passenger's-side door open for him.

Monroe couldn't move.

"Get in," she said, beaming at him.

"I can't."

"Louis, relax. It's just a car."

"It bothers me," he said, getting in.

She closed the door, went back to the driver's seat, closed her door. "If you're feeling bothered, then . . . then I think it's time that you *did* see a psychiatrist. You could have that post-traumatic stress syndrome that the Vietnam vets have. I used to see it in girls I counseled that had been worked over really, really bad. It's like they can't shake whatever it is that happened to them. They can't get past it."

Monroe eased himself onto the lusciously soft leather seat. "There's nothing to get past," he said. "What happened, happened."

He pulled the door closed with his right arm. She pushed the door and went around to the driver's side, her high heels making clopping sounds on the concrete ramp. She got in and one of the junkies sprawled facedown across the windshield and said, "Washerwindow?"

Ellie scowled. She honked the horn. The junkie opened his mouth and drooled on the window.

Ellie shuddered. "Why is he doing this to me?"

"He's not doing this to you," Monroe said. "He's doing it to the car."

"You'd think that, with a car like this, he'd show some respect."

"He's an addict. He'll do anything for money so he can get a fix," Monroe said.

She honked the horn again and muttered, "Make him go away."

"He'll go away once he figures out he isn't going to get any money out of you."

The junkie began to lick the windshield with his tongue.

"This is getting gross. Louis, look around and make sure Sere isn't seeing this."

He twisted his neck, loosened from the torturous physical therapy session, and saw Sere sleeping in the car seat.

"She sees no evil," Monroe said.

"What's that supposed to mean?" Ellie snapped.

Monroe shrugged and he was astonished. "Hey, I just shrugged my shoulders. Both of them."

"I will not have that creep ruining this car," Ellie said. She honked the horn, put the car in gear, and let the car inch forward. The junkie grinned and held on tight as Ellie feathered the brake pedal, making the car jerk and stop, jerk and stop.

"I'm going to shake him off," she said.

"If he falls off the car and hurts himself, he can sue you," Monroe said.

She stopped the car. "This is a case of self-defense."

"His tongue doesn't appear to be threatening your life."

"He could have AIDS or something."

"He probably does. But whatever he has, you can't get it through a windshield."

"But he's being *disgusting*. People have a right not to be disgusted."

"Not in Atlantic City," Monroe said.

Her breath hissed. "Maybe if he falls off the car and *dies . . .*"

Monroe had never heard his wife talk this way, about anyone.

"If you run him over accidentally, you've committed manslaughter. If you do it intentionally, it's murder."

"Right. And who cares enough about a piece of crud like him to arrest me?"

"Me," Monroe sighed, aware that, this time, he had said the wrong thing. With his right hand, he pulled a dollar bill from his pocket, pressed the button that rolled down the window, and waved it to the junkie, who snapped up the bill and hopped off the windshield.

"I can't believe you did that," she said as the car glided off the ramp onto Pacific Avenue. "You're just encouraging him. Now they're all going to see it and when I come to pick you up again they'll be waiting for me."

Monroe said nothing. Ellie used to give money to every panhandler on the Boardwalk before he married her. She had once told him, "These people have had so much taken from them, and I have so much to give."

He decided not to remind her of that as she drove down Pacific Avenue, past the turn that would take them home.

"We're going to the casino," Ellie said brightly. "I have to run down some details with Carl about our player parties. You'll play with Sere in the executive employee day-care center and then you'll join me for a staff lunch meeting. That reminds me, *Rolling Chair* magazine's hosting a happy-hour reception coming up at the Olde Salt for the girls with clout. I want you with me for that. Councilman Todesco is going to be there with his daughter. They haven't spoken in years. That's going to be something."

He felt warm air blowing on his face, arms, neck, chest, legs, and feet. He closed his eyes. "Ellie, I can't deal with this right now."

"Oh, come on," she said. "Carl said he wanted to meet my family. That includes you."

"Please, Ellie. Not right now."

"If my boss wants to see my husband and my husband has nothing better to do but mope around all day feeling sorry for himself, why can't he just do it? Why do you have anything against casinos? You don't even gamble. It's a business, Lou. A place where people dress a certain way and try to make as much money as they can. What's so scary about that?"

"Nothing," Monroe said, thinking of the new drug mall of Nevada Avenue, another place where people dress a certain way and try to make as much money as they can. "I just don't like the way you make the money."

"We've *been* through that, okay? Just grin and bear it, for a while. Until we get settled on the mainland. You'll like being able to look out your window and not see casinos and slums."

"When we got married, you said you wanted to live where I wanted to live. You said you loved Atlantic City, and that you wanted to work to make it better."

"I *am* working to make it better and so is everybody in the casino industry. Something's got to be done, Lou. At least we've got Councilman Todesco on our side."

"Nice guy," Monroe said. "Corrupt, but nice."

"If you mean that he takes care of the people that take care of him, I don't call that corrupt. I call that helping out. Councilman Todesco understands that unless we get the Miracle Mile built, this city is *not* coming back anytime soon."

"It would come back if we made it a place that appeals to people who *don't* gamble," Monroe said. "If we encouraged people to stay here, raise families . . ."

"Atlantic City is not a place to raise a family. I will not have my daughter—" She stopped short for a traffic light.

Monroe said, "*Our* daughter."

"The only way I'm going to let you establish a relationship with her is if you quit the department. As long as I'm the one with the job, I—"

Monroe opened the door.

She glared at him. "Just what are you doing?"

It took him a while to get out of the car. He tried to ignore the horns honking behind them.

He steadied himself with his hand on the door. He looked into her angry, beautiful eyes. He wanted her to say something that would force him to get back into the car.

"The next time you see me you're not going to be the only one with a job," Monroe said.

How could Ellie believe him? How could she do anything more than lean over, shut the door, and drive off toward the tall tower of the Alcazar Casino Hotel that loomed over the Boardwalk just a few blocks ahead?

◆

He imagined himself a marionette with tangled strings as he limped up New York Avenue to the dull black cube of city hall. The vaguely slovenly assortment of pedestrians, most of them heading in the opposite direction, toward the Boardwalk and the casinos, slipped past him, their faces gray with faraway thoughts.

He crossed the broad, four-lane expanse of Atlantic Avenue, grateful, for the first time, for the ridiculously long traffic lights that tied up traffic on that street. He asked himself how he could expect to get anything out of that building.

He crossed the asphalt parking lot that surrounded city hall like a brackish moat and saw two TV news vans. The familiar city-hall-lobby tang of ammonia and stale cigarette smoke was replaced by the morning scents of fading aftershave and the aroma of portable coffee urns riding on a table at the far end of the lobby, where reporters milled about, exchanging low, muttering gossip with city hall wage slaves and, here and there, a police officer in dress blues.

Monroe saw Pratt laughing it up with Kevin Urlenmeyer, a reporter with the Atlantic City *Star* who was universally despised by the department for his ability to misspell officers' names. That he distorted and confused facts wasn't a problem; the media *always* got it wrong. But misspelling simple names, like Monroe, was unforgivable.

To see Pratt acting as if he were having the greatest time of his life made Monroe ill. He looked up and saw a few technicians clamping microphones to a lectern in front of the Christmas tree on the lobby's information booth. Monroe guessed that the mayor was going to make a speech that had something to do with the police. He saw many department officers and civilians coming into the lobby.

He went to the fifth floor where Efrum Traile, the former head of Internal Affairs, had his barren, drab office behind the lavish Foambutt suites. Monroe passed Dangerous Delores's glassed-in lair.

She winked at him.

He found Marty Gant in Traile's office, with Captain Dennis "Sir Isaac" Newton, commander of the Traffic Safety Division.

Both Gant and Sir Isaac were in their dress blues, their blouses fitting tightly across their paunches. Sir Isaac sat in a plush, padded chair that had been taken from the Foambutt reception room.

"Detective Monroe," Gant said, pointing to one of the cruel, uncushioned wooden chairs that Efrum Traile used to torment his visitors. Monroe sat and Gant put his dress black patent-leather shoes on his desk, close enough to Monroe's face so that he could examine the erosion patterns of the soles.

"You've run into Captain Newton from time to time," Gant began.

Monroe hadn't, but he nodded. Sir Isaac had a painstakingly trimmed mustache, brass wire-frame spectacles, and a purple port-wine stain across his nose.

"Want to ask you something, Lou," Gant said. "What's the job of the Internal Affairs unit?"

"To police the police, sir."

"That's right. Now, without looking at your wristwatch or calendar," Gant said, "tell Captain Newton what today's date is."

Monroe thought about it. "I'm sorry, sir. I don't know."

"What about the day of the week?"

Monroe shook his head.

"Want to guess? It isn't Saturday or Sunday, is it?"

"I'd rather not, sir."

Gant took his shoes off his desk, pulled out a piece of paper, and began to doodle on it. "Because you're still experiencing dislocation with time. It's not just that you don't notice it anymore. Folks who been through serious physical and psychological calamity typically have difficulty remembering the month, day of the week, time of day."

Monroe forced himself to remember the month and he couldn't. Then he remembered the Christmas lights in the city hall lobby.

"It's December," he said.

"All well and good. I'm just pointing out that whatever conclusions we reach in this informal get-together, we're going to wait a while before we put you on a witness stand. Now I want you to jog your mind a little bit and come up with something you'd like to tell the commander of our Traffic Safety Division."

"Something I'd like?" Monroe was confused.

"A violation you've seen. Procedural error. A vast and horrible crime that has been going on in our midst."

"There's a stolen-car scam going and I think we can bust it," Monroe said.

Sir Isaac picked his nose for a minute. Then he said, "I have a law for that."

"You what?"

"Newton's Third Law of Interpersonnel Relations: 'Any officer who indulges in behavior sufficiently dangerous and obnoxious to piss off the entire department will either find himself stomped out of existence or earn the favor of someone within that organization.' "

Gant grinned.

Monroe said, "What's that supposed to mean?"

"Laws have no meaning, but they can explain things," Sir Isaac said. "You still busting cops?"

Monroe became uncomfortable. "That's like asking somebody if he's still beating his wife," Monroe said.

Sir Isaac's eyes widened, observing the sling holding Monroe's left arm. "Looks like you're not doing much of that, either. You want to hear Newton's First Law of Domestic Tranquillity?"

"Tell him, Newt," Gant said.

" 'Whatever it is, it's your fault.' "

Gant laughed. Monroe didn't. "That's supposed to explain something?" Monroe said.

"If you're married, that explains *everything*."

Gant looked up from his doodling. "Tell us about this car scam, Lou."

Monroe told Sir Isaac about casino valet-parking attendants running cars out of the lots and abandoning them on Nevada Avenue so that busted-out gamblers could collect insurance money.

"When I was a patrolman on the Boardwalk beat," Monroe said, "I found out about a narcotics dealer and Captain Gant put me in the vice squad so I could run it down."

"You're suggesting," Gant said, "that Captain Newton issue a personnel transfer request so that you can be reinstated into Traffic Safety?"

"Isn't that what you have me here for?" Monroe asked.

Sir Isaac put on a serious, concerned expression. Then he

giggled and pulled on his nose. He said, "No."

"No? You want me to do more legwork?"

"Newton's Law of Affirmative Negativity: 'Yes means nothing. No means no.' "

Monroe wanted to strangle him. "I've just made you aware of a probable case of felony theft and insurance fraud and you're telling me you don't want me to do anything about it."

Sir Isaac appeared sad. "I didn't say that. I just said no."

"But this is going on. You wouldn't be here talking with me if you didn't know—"

"I'm talking to you because I want to be late to Sergeant Pratt's silly swearing-in ceremony in the lobby," Sir Isaac said. "If I'm late it will appear as if I was doing something significant."

Gant made little triangles on the paper. "We've had swearing-ins four times a year, every year," he said. "It's tough for us old-timers to live with Sergeant Pratt using them to promote himself."

"So the two of you are just killing time?" Monroe said.

Sir Isaac picked wax out of his ear and examined it on the end of his finger. "The public has an impression that we are in the business of righting wrongs. Fortunately, we are not the public."

Monroe sat up. "I sure as hell am."

Sir Isaac continued, "Even though they say they're not responsible, those casino garages are private property, and there is an implicit contract between the purveyor of the space and the owner of the vehicle that the purveyor of the space will use all possible care to maintain the safekeeping of said vehicle. If cars are wandering out of these garages, the owners of the vehicles can sue. The casinos have a fuck-you fund they dip into to settle petty lawsuits out of court."

"But it's still against the law and we should be doing something about it," Monroe said. "If you put me on, I could get a warrant to go over the surveillance tapes they get from the cameras mounted in the garages. I could catch them in the act."

Sir Isaac folded his arms. "Newton's Law of Surveillance: 'Anything that reveals, conceals.' The feds, who keep track of these things, say that between ten and fifteen percent of all stolen-car claims are fraudulent. I think it's closer to twenty-five, but the feds don't talk to me and what do I know? I know what happens when I sit at this desk after a major holiday weekend—it's like the cars just walked out of those casinos. Now, you'd think that it's just a question of numbers—more people drive in on those weekends, so the number of cars stolen would increase to reflect that. But you talk to the owners reporting the theft. You bullshit around a little, like I'm doing with you. You ask them, as if it's just part of the conversation, how they did at the tables."

"They'll tell you that they lost," Monroe said.

"And they'll tell you that it's not so bad—the casino is sending them home on the train or the bus or, if they're big players, in a limo. How lucky can you get, eh? I bullshit around a little more with them. Some of them tell me that not only have they lost their car, but they had their hotel room broken into, or got robbed in the hotel lobbies, right where there was no surveillance camera, or when the cameras were down, and it's always some fat diamond ring that's missing, that they're insured for. That's when I wink and give them Newton's Law of Insurance. 'If you want to win, you have to lose.'"

"So you've got proof that what I've been telling you is true."

Sir Isaac looked at Gant. Gant said, "Tell him."

"What I have," Sir Isaac said, "are two encouragements. You wouldn't know about encouragements because you're not management. An encouragement is not an order. It is not a memo. It is not official policy. It is not unofficial. It's not written down and I can't say where it came from, but, this department, and this division of this department, has been encouraged to relax observation and enforcement of questionable practices occurring within the casinos. The casinos need every loser they can get, and, because our state, county, and municipal governments have become addicted to the tax revenue that comes from a gambling economy running at full throttle, it's suddenly become our job to make sure the casinos get as many losers as possible. If that means looking the other way while they bilk the insurance companies, then we might be encouraged to do so. If that means staying off Nevada Avenue because Pieto Soladias paid the street money to get the mayor elected—"

Monroe stopped himself from jumping out of his chair. "So there was a link," he said. "I don't have to guess." He heard the words in his mouth slow and blur as *glass* faded into the churning roar of the ocean. He felt a baseball bat on his head, felt it crack his skull and smash his eye socket and rip the skin off his face. He felt the bat return and shatter his collarbone.

Then he did something and the shots fired and . . .

"Newton's Law of Laws—"

"I don't want to hear about any more laws," Monroe said.

"That's it, exactly," Sir Issac said.

"What?"

"The Law of Laws is that the ultimate function of laws is to interfere, limit, and render ineffective law enforcement's ability to solve the unsolvable problems of human nature which it is our duty to solve. In other words, the more laws we enforce, the less significance we have. Being insignificant is no picnic, believe me. It isn't for nothing that men like Jack Chou go crazy."

Monroe stood. "That's why you want me here. You want to put me up on the witness stand about him trying to plant evidence on Soladias so you can suspend him and make Harry the Toad happy. The Toad is part of it, right? The Toad is the link with Soladias. The Toad is getting him to come up with the seed money for the Miracle Mile, right?"

Gant continued to doodle. Sir Isaac looked at Monroe and said, "Jack Chou is one of my detectives and I don't care how sloppy or reckless his police work is. Jack Chou puts out the message to scum like Soladias that no matter what kind of deals he cuts, no matter how rich he is or how much land he owns or how deep he gets into local politics, he's still meat."

He turned to Gant. "I'm here to tell Captain-Soon-to-Be-Inspector Gant that we need personnel like Jack Chou. We need cops who can go the distance, if anything to make up for the ass-kissers and floor-suckers who don't and wish they could. The man is an inspiration we cannot do without. I'm here to tell Captain Gant that I am proud of Jack Chou and that I will do everything in my power to frustrate, obfuscate, interfere, hinder, thwart, impede, and otherwise prevent any action from Internal Affairs against him."

Gant put down his pen. He smiled at Monroe. "In addition to his many responsibilities within the department, Sir Isaac is the vice president of our union, the Police Fraternal Association." He picked up the pen again and added, "An elected position."

"As an elected official of the PFA," Sir Isaac continued, "it is my obligation to make sure our men and women are treated fairly."

"I'm in the union," Monroe said. "Where were you when Harry the Toad put me under a blanket?"

Sir Isaac picked his nose again. "To be honest, I was pleased that justice was done. You bust cops. It's bad enough the kind of shit we have to take from the media, the lawyers, the politicians, and the scumbags on the streets, without one of our own making things worse."

Monroe took a step toward Sir Isaac. "Even if the guy I arrested was dealing drugs from his patrol car?"

Gant said, "Sit down, Lou."

Monroe took another step toward Sir Isaac. "And you have all this respect for Jack Chou. What's going to happen when he fucks up? When a civilian gets hurt or killed or he does some damage that can't be swept under the rug?"

"He gets the bad guys," Sir Isaac said. "He could have had Soladias if you hadn't backed up Todesco."

"He doesn't get anything," Monroe said. "He takes the law into his own hands."

"Sit *down*, Lou," Gant said.

Monroe waited a few seconds before he complied.

"In point of fact," Gant said, "Jack Chou doesn't take the law into his own hands. He ignores it completely."

"He also ignores encouragements," Sir Isaac agreed. "I get some heat because of him, but I hold my hands up. What can I do when one of my men simply doesn't give a shit? Suspend him? Fu Man Chou has been up for three suspensions in two months, but nothing happens because nobody *wants* anything to happen and it's very tough to prove he did anything because he finds some flunky— Bigfish Filmont, Jerry Lad, or the like—and lets them sign off on the charges. It doesn't matter that the cases are thrown out of court, or that a marginally competent lawyer can grind Bigfish and Jerry Lad into shark bait on the witness stand. What matters is that members of this department can point to Fu Man Chou and know that somebody out there is doing something valid."

He adjusted the cap on his head and stood.

"I don't want to work for you," Monroe said.

Sir Isaac grinned. "You'll excuse me, but the media beckons and I must pretend to be significant." He slipped out of the office, leaving the door open behind him.

Chapter Eight

♦ ♦ ♦ ♦ ♦

Walk the Walk

With his pen, Gant turned the triangles on his paper into squares. "Let's have the air clear a while," Gant said. Then, reluctantly, he rose, came around the desk, closed the door, and put his hands on Monroe's shoulders. He held them there affectionately for a few seconds, then went back behind his desk.

"Believe it or not," Gant said, "I didn't screw that one up for you."

"What he said was for my benefit?"

Gant began to doodle again. "Lets you know what kind of game you're in for if you get yourself a desk job. Folks think it's all paper and rubber stamps."

"Internal Affairs is not paper and rubber stamps," Monroe said.

"It can be. My predecessor made it appear that way. He knew where the roaches hid when the lights came on, but he didn't put down the poison to take 'em out."

"You're going to put down the poison?"

Gant put down his pen, folded his arms, leaned back in his chair, and replaced his shoes on the table, the soles facing toward Sir Isaac's empty seat.

"Lou, you've kept quiet about our relationship. Harry the Toad finds out about that—"

"He could what? What could he make you do that you wouldn't do anyway?"

Gant sighed. "He could hurt your wife. Folks find out

she has a different father than she said, they'll ask about her mother."

"What's wrong with that?"

"There are only four folks aware of our relationship," Gant said. "The one that held the gun on me while you were getting beaten up is in jail. Then there's Ellie. Ellie's mother is missing in action."

It came back to him again, vividly now, the memory exact, the pain as sharp as if the blows had just been inflicted, the silhouette of a woman rising against the hazy fluorescence of the ocean.

And with it, the sound of his gun firing five times.

His throat went dry. He couldn't stop himself. He had to ask, "Did I kill her?"

Gant said, "No."

"Did I kill anyone?"

"I don't have to—"

"You do," Monroe said. "Because you were aware of a deal between Soladias and the mayor, and now I'm aware of it, and I'm aware that if you hadn't kept your mouth shut, what happened to me under that pier would never have happened."

"And the mayor wouldn't have been elected and the momentum that was pushing the city forward would've been lost—"

"Did I kill anyone?"

"If the body had been recovered," Gant said, "and you'd been tried before a jury for the murder of Reuben Claymore, you'd have been acquitted. If you'd been tried before a judge, the judge would probably have charged you with manslaughter but suspended the sentence because it was in self-defense. You were being tortured, for God's sake. If you hadn't fought back, if you'd just given up, I can't say for sure what those bastards would've done to the rest of us."

"Why didn't you tell this to me when I asked you the first time?"

Gant began to doodle. "I can't answer that."

"Because you don't have to?"

"Because . . . oh, Jesus. Believe me, Lou, when I say that . . . I didn't tell you because I didn't want you hurting anymore. I might have to go around pretending you're just another cop in here, a pain-in-the-ass cop at that, but, dammit, Lou, you've married my girl."

He had killed. He had done the worst possible thing. He waited for the ocean to rise around him, the blows to come down, and the laughter to drag him under.

But the floor remained solid, the floor below his feet.

He became aware of the scratching of Gant's pen. He asked, "Who made the deal with Soladias?"

Gant seemed to shrink behind the desk. "What deal?"

"You're going to deny it?"

"It's not so much a deal as it is an understanding."

"Who set it up?"

Gant was silent.

"Was it you?"

"No. I have too much contempt for him and his kind."

"What about Harry the Toad?"

"He was involved. I think that that's obvious at this point."

"You have knowledge of a conspiracy within local government and organized crime, and you haven't done anything about it?"

"I am uncertain if I want to do anything about it."

Monroe sat silently and fumed. "When did this understanding begin?"

"Depends on how you look at it. Four years ago, when our mayor got elected the first time, certain distinguished members of the clergy and other civic bodies let it be known that Sunburn Bernie would need to distribute more than the usual amount of street money if he wanted in. Sunburn Bernie didn't have the cash. Soladias did, and the money got put on the street and . . . I'm not saying you have

112

to buy votes in this town but it's always nice when you get what you pay for.

"Curious thing about Soladias was that he had been shut out of the drug trade back then. He was head of a gang that was mostly stealing cars out of the Inlet. But things began happening for him."

"Because we let them? Because, in exchange for the money, we went light on him?"

"There's no proof of that, but I can't see how it could happen any other way. I guess it was a matter of dealing with the devil you knew. If you go over the narcotics unit arrest statistics for the last four years, you won't find many suspects from Soladias's gang, and those that are there were mostly low-level kids. I can imagine him using the department to trim staff."

"But you have no proof?"

Gant shook his head.

"Sometime around the end of the summer, after Soladias tried to burn down that row house you and Almagro were using as a surveillance post, the city had got a green light for a state/casino-financed low-income housing project at that site and he just up and went to Nevada Avenue. Word has it he invested rather heavily in local property, but, once again, that's hard to prove."

"You can't buy property in Atlantic City with small bills," Monroe said.

"You can if you have somebody like Cheezy Lindberg set up dummy corporations and money-laundering operations through local businesses. They say he's quite good at that thing."

"But you have no proof."

"That Cheezy's good? The only proof I have is that I have no proof otherwise."

"Can't we get this guy?"

"Legally? Not at the moment." Gant made little circles on the page. "And Soladias is actually holding his end up.

Depending on who you listen to, he's believed to have murdered, or have caused to be murdered, upwards of a dozen rival drug dealers in this city and possibly more in other parts of the state. He hasn't committed any aggressive activity against tourists, locals, or members of our police department."

"Nice guy," Monroe said.

"I wouldn't be so sarcastic if I were you."

"How come he hasn't gone after Jack Chou?"

"I have no answer for that, though he just might, after what Chou pulled last night. But the story I've heard is that he's had a change of heart, that he saw his own death staring at him and he wants to get out of the drug business and go legit."

"So he's backing the Miracle Mile?"

"Possibly. If he truly wants to go legit, Harry the Toad is the logical person to seek out. Todesco's family made the transition without any of them going near a jail, much less a courtroom."

"Why can't we build a case against Soladias that's so solid that we can convict him and confiscate every penny and piece of land he owns under the ill-gotten-gains statute?"

Gant leaned back from his doodle, gazed at Monroe with the quiet compassion a rich man has for a village idiot. "You didn't listen to what Sir Isaac said about the Law of Laws. The ill-gotten-gains statute, which gives law enforcement the power to confiscate property and finances that are believed to have derived from illegal activity, has only made it more difficult to put a big drug dealer away.

"Before the statute, if a drug dealer only had a fine or a jail term to worry about, he might turn some of his buddies in, or negotiate a plea bargain. But if he stands to lose everything he owns, it's in his interest to hire the absolute best legal talent there is, and drag as many people into the fight as he can.

"Let's say we get a rock-solid case on Soladias. The first thing that happens is his defense lawyer starts running interference, asking for this, protesting that. Pretty soon it's just like Miami, where it can take five years before a major narcotics case comes to trial. Meanwhile, the Miracle Mile goes belly-up when we need it the most."

"But if our case is tight, we'll convict him," Monroe said. "He'll go to jail. The land will be sold, the cops who busted him and the prosecutors who convicted him will feel as if they've done their jobs. And there'll be one less drug dealer on the streets."

Gant shook his head. "One less drug dealer? Soladias is doing a better job of keeping down the number of drug dealers in this town than we ever will. There comes a time, Lou, when you have to work with what you've got."

Monroe stood. "Are you finished with me, sir?"

Gant shook his head one final time. "No. You're going to stop picking on your wife just because she's a success and you're a goddamn failure. She's got a shot at making a name for herself now, and you're not going to hold her back. And you're not going to make trouble for yourself by hanging out with Mrs. Chou."

"She calls herself Todesco," Monroe said.

"They never got divorced. It still says Chou on her paycheck."

Monroe went to the door.

"Lou, I want to keep you safe so you can be a husband to my girl. When Sere gets older, you'll understand why I feel the way I do. You won't believe the shit you'll get yourself into, just because you want things to be okay for her. Be grateful you're not in my shoes."

"I don't think they'd fit, sir."

Gant muttered something foul as Monroe slammed the door.

♦

As he rode the elevator down to the lobby, Monroe remembered the long nights when he had had to find someone or look something up or get a piece of paper stamped, authorized, filed, photocopied, or indexed and he would mount the stairs or take the glacially slow city hall elevators to other departments hidden within the building, where he would recognize people on similar missions.

There had been no wink, no glance, no indication of camaraderie among Monroe and his fellow bureaucratic wanderers. If they had anything in common, it was the certainty that if their search ever came to an end, the effort would not have been worth the pursuit, and they would be left with the feeling that their lives had been reduced, robbed of the spirit that is more valuable than the mere time spent tracing and retracing steps.

Monroe felt that way now. Somewhere in this town was a kid with a Cobray machine pistol hanging at his side. That kid should be locked up for packing a gun like that. It was likely that the kid had an arrest record behind him. If Monroe could identify him in the Kiss-Off (Known-Suspect/Offender) files, he could write and file an incident report and . . .

What would happen?

Monroe forced himself not to think of that question as he pushed himself to his feet and moved slowly down the corridor. You have to have faith, he told himself. The system might be frustrating, but you have to have faith that it still can work. You have to believe that, every once in a while, when the moon was in the right position, the tide was high, and the stars shone down from a cold, clear winter sky, justice would be done.

Each police unit, squad, and division had its own set of Kiss-Off files that were almost never crossreferenced. Monroe figured he'd start with the files with which he was most familiar, the huge set in the vice squad office, and then move on to files in the juvenile, narcotics, and street crimes units. The search might take him all day, and even then he might not come up with a photograph that matched the kid's face.

But, with his wife and *his* child at the casino, he couldn't think of anything better to do.

Unlike most police department units, the vice squad's office was located outside the department, just off the ground-floor city hall lobby behind the Senior Citizens Outreach Center. As he neared the lobby, he heard Pratt's voice, amplified now, filling the granite cavern that was now blocked by the backs of men and women, some in the dark blue police dress uniforms, their hair lit by the wash from TV-camera lights.

"I'm not looking at a bunch of recruits here," Pratt said. "I'm looking at some real heroes."

Monroe moved into the crowd until he could see Pratt clearly. He certainly seemed larger under the lights.

"Check 'em out, everybody. This is the front line, here. This is all we've got between us and the kind of human trash that takes our property, endangers our children, rapes, murders, and exploits the system to get back on the street and do it again. These men and women aren't the first line of defense, they're the only line. Every one of them is a hero in my book. As public-information officer of this great police department in this great city, it's my job to make the world know of your heroism."

Pratt stared unblinkingly into the floodlights. "With these brave men and women, I will be able to tell the world that a hero isn't just somebody who keeps the streets safe. A hero is a source of love, strength, and human dignity."

"Yeah," a low voice muttered, "and you can put shit in coffee when you run out of cream."

Monroe could see the flicker of annoyance in Pratt's face. "Now some of you remember me when I worked the vice squad, and, let me tell you, my life was threatened on a daily basis. I did not understand, until I was shot and lay, semiconscious, on an emergency-room operating table, that I might lose everything for a community. Let me tell you once and for all, a hero survives. Ladies and gentlemen, I survived."

"You shoulda died," a low voice muttered.

Before anyone could react, Pratt raised his hands like a country preacher and the applause came, on cue.

"I'm looking for heroes, now. I'm looking for police officers who will tell the story of our great department, not in words, but in deeds.

"It is our pledge as officers," Pratt continued, "to uphold ourselves with deceny and honor, to respect and defend the rights of all citizens of the United States, regardless of race, sex, color, or creed, to serve—"

"Anybody who picks up the check," Jack Chou growled. Monroe looked to his right and saw a broad, wide paunch bulging beneath a purple, black, and red flannel shirt.

"But it is our duty, as human beings, to improve our community and ourselves," Pratt continued. "We officers are not defenders of our community, we *are* the community in which we serve."

"Just don't get out of your patrol car," Chou muttered, "or the community will shove itself up your ass."

Monroe couldn't help but grin. What Pratt said about service and dignity was true, but it was the kind of party-line truth that, when handed to new patrolmen, tended to get them humiliated, injured, and even killed on streets in which pistol-packing pimps and heavily armed drug dealers, many of whom were born on those streets, *did not* want them in their community.

Monroe saw a shadow of anger cross Pratt's face. He heard a few officers chanting, "Fu Man, Fu Man, Fu Man!"

Kevin Urlenmeyer wrinkled his nose as if he smelled a dead fish. Monroe saw no reaction among the civilians, probably parents of the cadets, who stood rigidly in their dress blues, the bills of their caps gleaming in the lights.

"For the men and women assembled here, every tour of duty will not be a walk in the park." He acknowledged the laughter.

"Depends on what you step in," Chou said.

"Rather," Pratt continued grandly, "it will be a walk in honor, a walk in justice, a walk in peace, a walk in freedom, a walk"—he paused for the maximum effect—"in heroism. Ladies and gentlemen, let's walk that walk!"

While the department's former street beast promoted himself, Monroe imagined how fast those cadets might *run* if they saw a kid flashing a Cobray machine pistol. He went down the corridor leading past the Senior Citizens Outreach Center to the heavy, steel-reinforced door of the vice squad office.

The door was locked. Monroe's left hand instinctively pulled down on the sling. He used to keep his keys in his left pocket, and one of those keys had been to the vice squad office.

He had had to surrender the key when he was declared incompetent.

He put his hand on the doorknob and twisted it again, just to make sure that it really was locked. Then he stepped back, so angry and frustrated that he wanted to kick down the door.

He looked at the steel door-frame. He looked at the scuff marks, dents, scratches, the dark smears and stains on the door. He remembered how Sergeant Almagro, the deal maker, had explained the correct procedure for kicking in a door.

"You check out the hinges," Almagro had said. "If you see hinges, you're going to have a problem, because the door opens out. Fortunately, most front doors open in. When it opens in, the weakest part is the lock. You check out the lock. If there's one lock, you check out how it's mounted. If it's just sunk into the wood, you're set. You take out the lock by coming in with your foot on the side. You want to be on the side because you never know if the scumbag is going to be behind the door with a portable rocket launcher aimed at your stomach. You come in from the side, but not so far to the side so your foot doesn't slide, and hit under the lock."

Almagro had stepped back, raised his leg, delivered a fast, brutal side kick and, "Wham! No more door."

You need two legs to do a side kick. One of them has to be strong enough to stand on. Monroe lifted his right leg and felt the left wobble, buckle, and strain under the increased weight.

He stood back and asked himself if he still had a brain. Here he was, a police detective, trying to break into his own office.

No, he corrected himself. The office wasn't his because he didn't have the key, and he wasn't a police detective because he was disabled, injured, a cripple: too useless and ineffectual to carry a badge or a gun.

Then he saw, to his left, an open door at the end of the corridor. It was the narcotics unit's office. He peered in, saw a smaller, shabbier version of what the vice squad had: a windowless crypt filled with battered, grimy, green steel desks, each with a telephone. One desk had a computer with a cracked casing and a monitor that seemed encrusted in spit. The chairs were standard police-issue: steel frames with ripped fake leather upholstery. The floor was a filthy gray-and-red-patterned tile.

A row of narrow gray lockers lined one wall. Against another was a bulletin board with sheets and mug shots. On the third wall was some city hall plumbing that gurgled, clicked, and pinged. A shelf made of stolen plastic milk crates had been crammed into a bend in the pipes. On the shelf were three huge yellow loose-leaf binders, with KSO on their spines.

Monroe went toward the Kiss-Off files. He put his hand on the first one.

"First you freeze, *now*."

Jack Chou. He was in his early forties, his face lumpy and fat but not soft. He reminded Monroe of a nasty version of Ho Ti, the fat, laughing Taoist saint whose image, usually with his arms in the air and his enormous belly bulging over his pants, is frequently mistaken for the Buddha.

"Now you put the other hand up where I can see it—move anything else and I'll kill you. And I *will* kill you."

"You're not going to kill me," Monroe said. "My arm's in a sling."

"Then take a slow, steady step back."

"I can't. My left leg—"

"A fucking whiner. Is there any goddamn thing you *can* do?"

"I came here to find out," Monroe said. He turned and saw Chou's Glock aimed at his forehead.

"You banged my wife and you came here to tell me all about it."

"I didn't bang your wife."

"What was she wearing? She's got a couple of outfits, when she wants a man to do her. She wear the red spandex bra, or the black bodyshirt?"

"I didn't do her and she was wearing her uniform and there's absolutely nothing between us. Whatever reason she had for saying that—"

"You're lying," Chou said, the gun trembling in his hand. "I can pick up on that."

"I told you. There was nothing—"

"Listen, prick. I *like* violence. I get all warm and squishy inside when I think of busting your fucking face in, kicking in your knees, and, if you fall facedown, stepping on your neck and stomping your head into the floor."

Monroe took a step to face the broad paunch, descending like slag off a mountainside, narrow, worn, and faded blue jeans, a crew cut and round face with bad skin marked by narrow, feral eyes, huge black eyebrows, and blunt, bent nose.

Monroe said, "Try."

Monroe looked at Detective Chou's Glock, the thick, meaty hands holding it, the hideous purple, red, and black plaid flannel shirt, the eyes bearing on him and the face, with its cratered, pocked, and dented skin that reminded him of the vice squad office door.

"Not before you tell me how she got in your pa—"

By then Monroe had lifted his right leg, and had felt the left wobble, buckle, strain, and *hold* as he sent a side kick into Chou's groin.

Later Monroe would reflect that kicking someone in the groin is not an intelligent counterattack, because pain can make people contract and if a guy has his finger on a trigger of a handgun, the pain can make him squeeze off a round.

But, he would tell himself, anyone who is stupid enough to put his faith in a gun deserves what he gets.

Which, in Chou's case, was a sudden implosion as the paunch came down, his legs collapsed, the arm holding the gun bent, and Chou went forward and down, his head banging the edge of an armless metal chair, his body rolling over, landing on his right side, legs drawn in, a great, fat log of a man across Monroe's path.

He was still. Monroe saw Chou's left hand go down to his right boot, to the handle sticking up, taped against the leg. Monroe waited until the hand was wrapped around the handle and then he grabbed another armless metal chair and, with his right leg, pushed the chair on top of Chou's side, pinning Chou's left arm in place.

Monroe leaned forward, put his weight on the chair until he saw the dark black Mace canister in Chou's right hand. The canister was less than a foot from Monroe's face.

Monroe was trapped by his own weight. He couldn't move back fast enough before Chou could release the burning blast of chemical, or pepper, or whatever might be in the canister, into his face.

Chou said, "Gotcha."

Monroe waited a half second and the blast didn't come. He pushed himself backward and smacked his spine on the edge of the desk, tumbled over, and went down on the floor.

Chou was crouching, his arm extended, a long, hooked hunting knife inches from Monroe's throat. "That's two for me," Chou said. "I win, you gotta tell me."

"I don't have to tell you anything," Monroe said, his eyes on the knife.

Chou pounced and Monroe twisted rapidly, excruciatingly away. He rolled across the floor and heard a deep, metallic *thunk* as Chou crashed into the desk, tipping it over, sending a telephone, calendar blotter, and purple, green, and red ALCAZAR LUCK-E STAR coffee mug crashing to the floor.

Chou pushed himself up, turned around, and saw that Monroe had his gun in his hand.

"Uh, hi," Monroe said.

Chou rubbed a dark red welt on his forehead. His eyes were on the gun. "I, ah, must've dropped that," he said.

Monroe noticed that the safety was on. He checked the chamber and popped the clip.

Then he heard the chief of police leading the voices outside:

"I do solemnly swear to support the Constitution of the United States and the Constitution of the State of New Jersey; to respect and defend the rights of all citizens of the United States, regardless of race, sex, color, or creed; to serve with courage, courtesy, and compassion; to uphold myself with decency and honor, and faithfully discharge, to the best of my ability, the duties of police officer in the Atlantic City Police Department."

Monroe went to the Kiss-Off files and wrestled down a huge volume.

"You think this is a library?" Chou growled.

Monroe told him what happened on the jitney. "I want to see if he's in here."

He stopped and saw a picture of Pieto Soladias when he was younger, his eyes wild and defiant, as if the mug shot were a fashion shoot. Soladias's first arrest was for grand theft auto by Sergeant Dennis Newton of the Traffic Safety Division, but the charges were dropped.

"You'll find them all in here. But then what?" Chou growled. "The Cobray is a classic status weapon. Soladias's big enforcers get them the way executives get company cars."

"Those guns are illegal."

"So let's take some off their hands. You can't beat these suckers, but you can sure exploit 'em."

Monroe stopped. "How?"

"Wouldn't you like to find out."

Monroe hesitated. Monroe thought of his wife and child at the casino. He was dejected and disgusted, and he had a feeling he was about to get himself into trouble.

"Sure," he said. "Why not?

♦

Chou pulled his coat out of a locker in the Traffic Safety Division office and was out the department's back door going so fast that he could have been running. He started the engine and opened the door of a faded yellow Buick with a smashed front end that had brown, dried-out chunks of marsh grass sticking to the metal. The car had never been washed, waxed, polished, much less emptied of wadded-up sandwich bags, take-out trays, cardboard coffee cups, stained plastic lids, and rancid cream containers.

"But listen to this," Chou said as he twisted the ignition key and the car awoke with a throaty growl. "Hear that? This baby has been loved."

Monroe, sitting beside him in the front seat, was out of breath from trying to keep up with him.

"That the fastest you can move?" Chou demanded, turning around his short, bullet head as he backed the car out and aimed it north, toward the ruined Inlet section.

"For now," Monroe said. "I used to run the Boardwalk. One time, I ran the whole length of the island and back."

"Then no more limping around like a goddamn cripple. . . ."

"I'm not a—"

"Then don't act like one!" Chou yelled.

Chou floored the gas pedal. As the car shot forward he looked down between his legs, found a cup of something, wiped his mouth on his sleeve, drank the contents of the cup, and threw it in the backseat and then hit the brakes in time to stop at a red light.

Monroe had his hand out, flat on the dashboard. "Uh, about last night and your wife. There's nothing between us."

Chou floored the gas and the car left the road. "You think I'm stupid I don't know that?"

"Then why did you take it the way you did?"

"Because it's part of the show. I put on a show. I gotta act like she can hurt me. But I don't feel nothing for her anymore."

"How come you broke up?"

"What, I got to tell you my life story?" He swung the car down Utah Avenue. "First we get some food. I don't work on anything less than a full tank. Maybe we'll find somebody who can write the arrest report."

"I can write an arrest report," Monroe said. "I mean, I could, if I was reinstated to active duty."

"You'll get reinstated."

"How?"

"Become a hero, like me."

Chapter Nine

♦ ♦ ♦ ♦ ♦

Fu Man

The Ancient Mariner Bar & Grille took up the ground floor of an old, mildew-green boardinghouse where Utah Avenue dead-ended at the Boardwalk. Like all bars within the Atlantic City limits, it served booze twenty-four hours a day. Unlike any other bar in Atlantic City, its primary patrons were cops.

Exactly how the Mariner became the cop bar is a mystery buried in lies, legends, and stories that, if they weren't true, should be.

The best of these stories had to do with the low wooden ceiling that hung over the Mariner's circular bar. Even in Atlantic City's heyday, no visitor wanted to spend the night in a boardinghouse room over a noisy saloon.

It was not an act of generosity for the Mariner to permit on-duty police to sack out, without charge, in those rooms, though both officers and the Mariner's management (which owned the boardinghouse) liked to pretend that it was. In order to approach a somnolent state, an officer had to drink heavily of the beers and low-proof beverages, thereby paying more than the room would have netted, assuming the Mariner's management could have rented it out.

If the officer was needed for anything so annoying as an emergency, a call was made to the Mariner's bartender, who would discreetly deny having seen the officer in question, hang up, then take a stout broom handle and bang on the ceiling in the approximate location of the officer's bed. The

127

officer could tumble out of bed and down a staircase leading to the Mariner's infamous back room, which, during more exciting times, housed an assortment of gambling devices. All backroom casinos had emergency exits so patrons could leave slightly ahead of a raid, so the officer could depart the Mariner without the folks around the bar seeing him go.

The Mariner was one of the few bars in Atlantic City to survive the coming of the casinos, which bankrupted more than half the taverns and restaurants in the city by doling out free drinks and meals to gamblers. The places that flourished set themselves up as adamant denials of the newfangled glitz and glamour: they were dark where the casinos were bright; slow where the casinos were fast; accommodating to the losers, misfits, empty dreamers, power jockeys, and nutcases in the old town, where the casinos only wanted gamblers with money to burn.

In his days as a rookie, and then on the vice squad, Louis Monroe had hung out at the Mariner, hoping to mix with the changing array of bleary-eyed officers, some in, some out of uniform. Though he had the loner's suspicion of cliques, he had the lonely man's desire to belong, to fit in, to be one of the guys.

But even before he busted Patrolman Reuben Claymore for possession of methamphetamine with intent to distribute, and subsequently earned the hatred of the department, he never felt quite comfortable in the Mariner. On nights when he went with Darrell Pratt, he sensed that he was a guest on somebody else's territory.

Now, as Chou threw his yellow Buick into the badly paved lot opposite the Mariner, Monroe tensed, not wanting to get stares, glares, and cold shoulders from the cops inside.

He thought of going up on the Boardwalk and getting a pizza slice when Chou, perhaps reading his mind, said, "You're coming with me."

Warm, humid air rolled out when Chou elbowed aside the Mariner's door. The familiar reek of spilled beer, frying oil, and briny, steamed seafood penetrated Monroe's coat, sweatpants, soaking through his skin, into his stiff muscles and sore bones.

Heads turned and voices rose, welcoming the big-bellied detective sergeant with cries of "Fu Man, man!" and "Jack attack!" Chou parted the Mariner's thick air like a wide, overpowered speedboat tearing up the placid waters of the back bays, stopping to slap backs, punch ribs, mutter jokes and obscenities with other officers, old and young, who brightened as he passed.

And when their eyes turned to the short, limping guy in Chou's shadow, they expressed neither surprise or disgust. To be with the Fu Man was to have your past erased, if only temporarily, and be accepted, acknowledged, embraced, if only in spirit, as one of the guys.

"Good guys," Monroe said to himself and was surprised when, over the roaring voices and murky oldies tunes spilling out of the jukebox, Chou turned to him and said, "They wouldn't've pissed in my shadow two years ago. You kick some butt and all of a sudden, everybody knows your name."

Monroe desperately wanted to agree with him.

It took time to go around the Mariner's oval bar. Chou had a good word for everyone, and finally they took a pair of seats where he could survey the crowd.

The Mariner's bartender, who moved so fast during the lunch rush that he rarely stayed in one place long enough for anyone to figure out who he was, *stopped* in front of Chou and *waited* while Chou grimaced at the menu and said, "The usual. But make it *hot* this time. Tell 'em to kill me."

The bartender filled a tall soda glass with ice cubes, poured a steaming pot of coffee, and set it in front of Chou. He was about to buzz off when Chou said, "And the kid's having . . . what are you having?"

Monroe awkwardly climbed onto the stool beside Chou. He asked for a tunafish sandwich on whole-wheat toast and a diet Coke.

"Cat food," Chou growled. "You eat that, it does nothing for you." Chou patted his gut. "I earned this. You're looking at body armor."

Chou gulped the coffee, smacked the cup on the bar, rattling the cubes. He blew coffee breath into Monroe's face. "You married, kid?"

Monroe sipped his diet Coke. He felt the ring on his finger. "Yes."

"You ever wonder why? You ever sit there and ask yourself how you got into this?"

"Oh . . . sometimes."

"Beth likes guys that have broken parts inside them. She walked out on me when I put those parts back together. Sometimes I say to myself I wouldn't be doing any of this shit if I wasn't getting regular nookie and the occasional sidedish of love and affection, but . . ."

Monroe saw him relax for just a second, and in that second, he realized that Jack Chou missed his wife deeply.

"It's a trade-off. If I was getting regular fucking, I wouldn't be so fucking famous."

♦

It was seeing Chou's hidden need that helped Monroe open to him. He found himself talking easily to the man, telling Chou about growing up off Route 30 in Galloway Township. Chou told him about the old neighborhood.

"Two or three times a year, Nevada Avenue used to flood. And, growing up there, you'd get this feeling that, no matter what happened, you could take it. As bad as things could get, one day the tide would go out, and it was over.

"It used to be a place you'd know everybody, where everybody would hang out and say, 'Hello Mrs. Morello, having a nice day? Mr. Savitsky, want to have egg roll at

Chou's Chinese?' That grocery store next to what's now Soladias's office used to be my uncle's restaurant. We lived upstairs. My parents were illegal immigrants and they were afraid of being seen and too superstitious to go to the hospital. I almost died. So they decided they were going to be citizens, and they memorized all the presidents, and they saved everything they earned from working in my uncle's restaurant, and when they became Americans, they did the American thing. They bought a house, settled down. I was working on cars in this gas station used to be up by California and Atlantic. Became a cop because, I figured, hey, all you do is walk around on the Boardwalk, right? My folks had this liquor store up on Pacific they figured they could make some money from, and the kid that murdered them with a sawed-off twelve-gauge shotgun for twenty-seven dollars in the cash register was a fucking junkie they were asked to hire as part of a Good Neighbor Juvenile Minority Rehabilitation Program."

"They get the kid?" Monroe asked.

"Sure they did. But there was some procedural complication about the way the evidence was obtained, so he got seven years, and they let him out in two and a half, and around the time they let him out . . . I was the token Chinee cop, you know, the nice, respectable guy, married to another respectable cop, and we're both playing by the rules. I was getting promoted, not because of anything I did, but so the department could show it had minorities moving up the chain of command. And it is a chain, let me tell you.

"One day, it was the summer, I'm in a patrol car around the Inlet and the junkie that killed my parents is sitting on top of this car that was stripped, you know, obviously stolen out of someplace, and I start asking him questions about the car, but he recognizes me from the trial and he starts in, you know, ranking me, calling me a piece of shit, saying what he's going to do to me.

"And there's this other kid, on a corner across the street,

131

and he's taking it in, and he's saying I should kill the junkie kid and that if I don't do it, he'll do it for me. And the junkie is shouting back, daring him to do it, so I just drive off, like I'm supposed to. Next day I come back and I see all these seagulls poking and pointing around the stripped car, and I look in there and it's the junkie that killed my parents, but he's been chopped up and his head is on the seat and the seagulls are picking at it and I look up and there's the kid across the street, says I owe him one. I try to chase him but he's gone.

"So I call it in and, naturally, I'm the first person everybody suspects. And this pisses me off, because if anybody knew me, they'd know that I was incapable of that. But nobody wants to know you until everybody wants to know you, and it gets to me. I mean, it really gets to me. And . . ."

Monroe waited. "And what?"

Chou took a breath that seemed to span years. "And then Harry the Toad took those turkeys and all the stuff that was broken in me came together like *that*. I just said, 'So what?' and decided to go for the bad guys, and fuck the procedures and fuck the evidence and fuck everything in my way. I put some street justice on Harry the Toad, and Beth walked right out."

"You like that?" Monroe asked.

"Absolutely. Nothing matters but going for it, and, when you go for it with everything you have, it's like, you don't need to really *arrest* the bad guys. You kind of want to throw the fish back so you can catch it again."

"So you really weren't planning on getting Soladias last night?"

"Only thing I was planning on was fucking around and giving the boys something to talk about at breakfast time."

"But look at the cost," Monroe said. "You wasted man-hours and equipment. You could have accomplished something."

"I accomplished plenty."

"I mean something really significant," Monroe said. "Something that would make this town better."

Chou laughed. "You're full of shit, you know that? But you can't help it. You weren't born here. I was. When you're born here, the message you get is, the town is going to be the town, no matter what. People are always going to have fun here, and people are always going to exploit other people, so you might as well do both, which is to have fun exploiting the bad guys."

"That's not the job," Monroe said. "The job is to get rid of the bad guys."

"You think like that, anytime you're going to do anything, you'll freeze up, you'll get depressed, you'll get on people's bad sides for no decent reason, you'll get into moods when you're sunk up to your neck in the worst possible shit and you just want it to be over—you'll be like me before I fixed my parts. You want to survive, you gotta loosen up, blow it out, *play to the crowd.* They want to see a show. They want to see you walk that walk. So let 'em. It's so much easier. There's no problem with right or wrong, good or bad, this procedure versus that one. You can let it happen. Go with the flow."

Monroe shook his head. "You're lucky somebody else hasn't gotten hurt, or even killed."

"I don't believe in luck, but if I did, I'd be the luckiest man alive," Chou said. "The way I see it is, my job is to have the most fun possible fucking around, so the front-line kids that really have to do the work will look at me and feel inspired. Sir Isaac's got some kind of law about me. But I don't care about laws."

"What *do* you care about?"

"Me. Sooner or later you figure it out that the only person you're up against out there is yourself. When you stop fighting yourself, everybody wins."

♦

133

Chou zoomed past some casinos on Pacific Avenue and made a hard left down Nevada Avenue.

"You know about the deal Soladias cut with the department?" Monroe said.

"I heard about it. It won't save him from the Fu Man. Nothing saves the bad guy from the Fu Man. Now shut up for a minute and let me scope the scene."

Monroe wasn't aware that he'd been talking. He turned his attention outside and saw the mules, the enforcers, and the cars lined up for purchases. A few out-of-state cars were parked at the top of the beach block, one with a window shattered, hood open, and significant parts of its engine missing. At the far end of the street, opposite the grocery store, was a black, glossy malignant-looking Porsche 928GT (New Jersey plate MR-KRAK) and two cream-colored Mercedes sedans (New Jersey car-dealer tag). The Mercedes came from the same dealer that had leased the Alcazar's fleet: Todesco Luxury Motors.

"I love it. There is more firepower concentrated on this street than the entire SWAT arsenal," Chou said.

"Then what are we doing here?" Monroe demanded, seeing someone he thought resembled the kid on the jitney. "We're not going to fuck around—"

"That's *exactly* what we're here to do," Chou said, swerving out of the line of cars, making a hard right on to Jefferson Place and leaving the car in front of a hydrant. "Somebody who's fucking around makes a tough target. You ever try to shoot somebody who has no idea what he's doing?"

For a moment Monroe tried to remember.

"You want, you can stay in the car," Chou said. "Or you can watch me get the bad guys."

"I still have your clip," Monroe pulled out the thirteen-shot clip that fit into Chou's Glock.

Chou gave him the gun. "You might as well keep the rest of it."

"You're going up against all those guys without a gun?"

Chou paused. Monroe saw his hands trembling. Then he said, "Yeah," and opened the door and set off for Nevada Avenue. Monroe followed him, trying not to limp, but Chou moved too fast, disappearing behind some parked vans where Jefferson Place met Nevada Avenue.

When he reached Nevada, Monroe turned right and went up a seagull poop–spattered ramp to the Boardwalk and got a blast of cold, briny wind in his face. He heard the ocean and it was real this time.

He turned to face the street. The Boardwalk rode about nine feet above Nevada Avenue. From that height, as far as Monroe could tell, it seemed to be business as usual in the new drug capital of Atlantic City. Vehicles listlessly wandered down from Pacific Avenue, paused in front of one or more houses. A mule approached, took cash, went back to a house, emerged after a few seconds, and returned to the car, where the goods were handed back.

Then he saw Chou sitting on the steps of a bungalow porch a few houses up Nevada Avenue, across from the glossy black Porsche. Chou seemed to be killing time until several cars came down the street at once, causing a backup that put a customer's dung brown Dodge van between him and the Porsche. As mules scurried to make their transactions, Chou stood and nonchalantly moved into the street until he was close enough to touch the van's passenger door. Then he dropped into a squat and crawled quickly under the van.

Monroe watched him get up on the other side of the van, now close enough to touch the Porsche. Chou remained low, just out of the van driver's sight.

The mule returned with the goods, holding them under his Detroit Tigers jacket. Because the mule was intent on giving the goods to the driver, and the driver was intent on getting them, no one noticed the bulky man crouched beside the van's rear tire. In the time that it took the mule to pull the goods from under his jacket, Chou pounced, grabbing the mule and the hand holding the goods, then came up under the mule and, with his shoulder, heaved the mule up and over the van.

Before he could open his mouth and yell, the mule let go of the goods, a tightly wrapped bundle of tiny plastic envelopes. As the mule fell back on the street, Chou dropped down again, ripped open the bundle, and hurled the envelopes overhead, where they fell like brightly reflective confetti on the street, on the van, and on the surface of the black Porsche.

The driver opened his mouth but the mule's yell had already summoned the enforcers. A gunman stepped between the Porsche and the van, the gun held under his jacket, and Chou jumped up, pumping his right fist into the gunman's throat, his left fist on the arm that was about to bring up the gun. The gunman snapped back from the impact but Chou kept coming, pounding him flat on the street.

The next events happened almost too quickly for Monroe to follow. He heard a brief clatter of automatic weapons fire, saw the Porsche's passenger-side window and a portion of the windshield shatter as the van driver yelled, "Shit!" and spun his vehicle hard to the left, right into a crowd of enforcers who were still fumbling with their weapons. When Monroe looked back at the Porsche, the car's passenger-side window was gone and the passenger door was closing with someone inside. By the time Monroe recognized that it was Chou, the car's engine screamed to life inside and the Porsche rocked back, smashing in the front grille of the first cream-colored Mercedes, then out onto the street, heading straight for Monroe and the Boardwalk.

Through the shattered windshield, Monroe saw Chou wave at him. Monroe heard the shriek of expensive tires on cheap asphalt as Chou hit the brakes, then threw the car into reverse, aiming the Porsche's rear end at the other cars on the street that were buying drugs.

The street itself was suddenly flowing with people: mules, prostitutes, the kind of shabbily draped denizens who disdained education, employment, status, and family values but gleefully risked their lives to pounce on the plastic envelopes scattered across the street. These street denizens crawled like roaches through a few of the enforcers who had their ugly, hideously lethal weapons out but apparently were not sure if it was more important to recover the goods or yell macho threats at an expensive automobile that was careening toward them without exhibiting any intention of stopping.

The denizens chased the envelopes that were being blown about capriciously by the wind, which tended to move them in eddies working outward from the center of the street. Two enforcers tried to keep up with the denizens, conveniently removing themselves from the path of the approaching car. The enforcer Chou had knocked down had long ago come to his senses and fled.

Five gunmen remained in the street, sensing a macho contest. One of them gestured to a crowd that had gathered behind Monroe on the Boardwalk. Another acknowledged a person emerging from the bungalow adjacent to the grocery store: Pieto Soladias in an oversized, beige camping jacket, woolen cap, and black leather hiking boots. At his side was a hulking monster of a man, evidently a bodyguard.

Monroe saw Soladias sweep the scene. His eyes came to rest not on the group of gunmen in the street, but on Monroe.

The men in the street had their weapons drawn and pointed at the Porsche, but they hesitated to fire. They were waiting for a signal from Soladias, but Soladias didn't move.

Alas, the proverb about the perils of hesitation did not occur to anyone. The Porsche slowed as it bore down upon the nearest man, who lost his nerve at the last second and was about to flee when the low, flat, horizontal blade of the Porsche's rear spoiler caught him in his gut. Chou hit the brakes and the man seemed to fly over the Porsche, miraculously holding on to his machine pistol as he bounced off the Porsche's hood and tumbled onto the street beside the driver's-side door. Before the others could react, Chou had the door open. He yanked the machine pistol out of the gunman's hand. Then he slammed the door, spinning the wheels as he moved back into gunmen who, having seen the perils of hesitation, threw themselves away from the car.

Chou didn't stop. The Porsche continued in reverse, racing toward the few customer cars that still hadn't cleared off the street. They cleared, and Chou put the car in forward, heading back toward the enforcers.

Another machine pistol clattered and Soladias dropped, the bodyguard ducked in front of him, and Soladias dived into the bungalow as the Porsche aimed for a gunman who was firing his Cobray into the air, like a movie bad guy who expects to be obeyed.

The Porsche put on speed and the gunman watched the three enforcers standing beside him peel off. He hollered something and went down on one knee, holding the machine pistol in front with both hands, cop-style, aiming it straight at the Porsche. But the Porsche swerved drunkenly and the gunman was apparently nervous about hitting a moving target that would kill him no matter how many rounds he fired. Before he could pull the Cobray's trigger, Chou swerved hard to the left and opened the driver's-side door, catching the gunman in the face, dragging him under the door and almost under the car's wheels.

Chou stopped long enough to grab the man's weapon before throwing the car into a tight reverse curve at a pair of gunners who were coming up behind him. They scattered and, this time, Chou spun around and couldn't quite stop.

The front end of the Porsche slammed into the wounded Mercedes. Chou put the car in reverse, its rear end heading for the Boardwalk.

The Porsche's high-impact polymer bumper hit a pier and Monroe felt the impact come up through his knees into his skull. The Porsche shot straight ahead, made a wide curve, and hit the first Mercedes's already injured front end, pushing the car up and back until it landed on its side like a beached whale.

Chou backed off again, having made an opening, and aimed the car at Pieto Soladias. Soladias ducked behind his bodyguard, who grabbed him and leaped out of the way as the Porsche bounced up on the curb and came down on the sidewalk and continued into the front porch of the bungalow, blasting through its rotting timbers, and then pulled back onto the street just before the façade of the house groaned, leaned forward, and crashed down on the sidewalk, bringing down expensive pieces of furniture from a second-floor office with computers, a television set, and what looked like a bar trimmed in jaguar skin.

Then the windows and the black skin of the Porsche and the ashpalt around it puffed, crumpled, and shattered from the impact of thirty-two rounds of what would later be identified as Winchester 9-millimeter 147-grain Black Talon bullets.

The street was suddenly quiet. "You dead yet, motherfucker?" the voice howled gleefully. "You gonna beg me to do you?"

It was the kid, the kid in the jitney.

The Porsche's engine was still idling, but the car stood still, its tires shot up, its recessed headlights gaping like empty eye sockets. Monroe was off and limping down the ramp, wondering if Chou had survived.

No one moved on the street. Then, a lone figure stepped out of the rubble, his Cobray aimed and ready, his leather jacket blowing behind him like a cape, his head held high, his mouth red, as if he'd just drunk blood.

He let off another spray of bullets and the Porsche's windshield erupted in a spiderweb of fractures.

"Pepe, you fuck!" Soladias yelled at him from behind his bodyguard. "You shoot my fucking car! Nobody shoot my fucking car but me!"

But Pepe was in his glory, swaggering into the street like an archetypal cowboy gunman at high noon, though the sun was low behind him.

His shadow reached the motionless Porsche and Pepe let forth another spray of bullets, blowing away what was left of the Porsche's windshield.

He popped out the Cobray's clip and was reaching into his jacket for another when Monroe raised the gun and shouted, "Police, freeze!"

Pepe looked at Monroe, and the Porsche was already moving forward as Pepe spun toward the voice and had the clip out and in the machine pistol. Then the Porsche was on him, the shattered front of the car hitting him in his legs, snapping them like sticks as he fell forward onto the hood and into the shredded windshield. Chou halted the car, climbed through the windshield, the guns under his arm. He wrestled with Pepe's Cobray.

Then he paused, looked around for a second, caught Monroe's eye, and gave him the strangest grin Monroe had ever seen.

When the gun went off, Chou roared as both men fell off the car and onto the asphalt.

Monroe had to push his way through a crowd before he found Chou rolling back and forth on his back, his hands red as they tried to staunch the blood that was shooting out of his thigh.

"Oh, it hurts. Oh God, oh God, it hurts, it hurts, it hurts, hurts like fucking *hell*!" he yelled, his eyes squeezed tight, the pain contorting his face.

Monroe removed a portable radio from Chou's jacket

and called in a 15 LOD. He put down the radio, grabbed a Cobray, and yelled at the crowd to stand back.

Pieto Soladias, his bodyguard, and four of his enforcers were halfway across the street when they saw Monroe standing, a Cobray in his right hand aimed at them.

Soladias stopped and his gunmen clustered nervously in front of him. No one had a gun out. For an instant, Monroe realized he could kill Soladias, right now. With a weapon like a Cobray, he didn't even have to aim. Pull the trigger and the man's life, and that of anybody near him, would end right here.

Soladias realized it, too, and the confident smirk bled from his face.

"Freeze," Monroe said.

For a second nobody moved. The anguished cries of Pepe, Jack Chou, and an approaching police siren cut through the wind.

Monroe hesitated a second too long. Soladias's smirk returned; he looked even more confident. He put his back to Monroe, lifted his hiking boot, and brought it down on Pepe's face. Pepe screamed again.

"I said *freeze!*" Monroe shouted.

Soladias walked with exaggerated calm back toward the ruined bungalow. His gunmen drew close and Monroe saw the snouts of their weapons projecting through their coats. Any advantage he may have had over Soladias was gone.

Soladias's crew stayed with him. Then everyone piled into an uninjured Mercedes. After what appeared to be some fumbling for the keys, the car hummed to life and slowly took them up the street.

Chapter Ten

♦ ♦ ♦ ♦ ♦

On the Street Where You Live

A single ambulance arrived to take an unconscious Pepe and a delirious Fu Man to Atlantic City General. As the ambulance doors closed around him, Chou muttered something like, "My house, my house is my house."

Monroe watched the ambulance go past the barricades at the end of Nevada Avenue. He saw crime-scene investigators wandering around, taking pictures, collecting shell casings, bagging weapons, congratulating Monroe on seeing Chou in action. Patrolmen drove their cars up and down Nevada Avenue, waving at Monroe, giving him a clenched-fist salute.

The supervising officers kept their distance, making wide circles around Monroe, whose sweatpants and jacket were splashed with Chou's dried blood. It took Captain Dennis Newton of the Traffic Safety Division, who had been called in because Chou was in Traffic Safety, several minutes to ask who was submitting the report.

"Fuck the report," one of the patrol officers said. "Who's going to write the screenplay?"

Sir Isaac was about to recite Newton's Law of Diminishing Reruns when Monroe pulled him away and told him exactly what had happened.

"Very imaginative," muttered Sir Isaac, staring at the blocked-off street as if he were in a movie theater and the picture was late in starting. He chewed on a piece of his

142

foam coffee cup, spat it out, and said, "Except that our Fu Man does not shoot himself."

Newton went to the coffee urn on the back of the Emergency Services van, put more brew into a fresh cup, and stirred in nondairy creamer. The steam from the coffee fogged Newton's glasses as he drank from the cup. "I think I'm being followed," he said finally.

Monroe waited for a Newton Law. It didn't come. "Sir, I witnessed the whole thing," Monroe said.

"I hope you were impressed."

"It was the most courageous thing I've ever seen, but it was also reckless, sloppy, and stupid. People could have gotten killed. And then, it was like I told you, he looked at me, and the gun went down and he shot himself in his leg."

"All the people on the Boardwalk, and he looked at *you*?" Sir Isaac sighed. "Why *you*?"

"I got the feeling he was looking *for* me," Monroe said. "He wanted to make sure I saw him do it."

"We've conducted extensive interviews of other eyewitnesses. No one backs up your claim."

"That's because people see what they want to and they don't want to see a cop who could take those guns away and then shoot himself."

"But you want to see that, don't you? Because you bust cops. You only see the worst in us. I see what I see, but I don't turn my own people in."

"I only busted one cop,"

"I have no doubt that you'll bust some more of us, or try to. You'll work for Gant up in Internal Affairs. He has his eye out for you, like the Toad has his eye out for Jack Chou."

Monroe pulled back. "They hate each other. Chou's been on his case since the turkey thing."

Sir Isaac shook his head slyly. "There you go, seeing

what you want to see. The Toad looks out for Chou like you wouldn't believe."

"But Chou's been hitting him and Soladias."

"Hitting, but not hurting. Newton's Law of Aggressive Affection: 'You always love the one you hurt.' " He gazed back on the street. "When a man gets hurt, we only have two alternatives: throw a blanket on him or make him a hero. Much as I loathe Pratt hogging the cameras, I'm going to get him on this. I want this on the front page of the *Star* tomorrow. Chou's a minority. He's been injured against the big, bad drug dealers. We can't miss."

"You're going to miss if Jack Chou doesn't get help, sir."

"Jack Chou is going to get everything he needs, and more." He straightened his cap. "You'll excuse me, but justice must be served."

♦

The sky had grown dark and the few streetlights along Nevada Avenue that hadn't been shot out winked on as municipal wrecker *Whiskey Alpha Five* positioned itself behind the ruined Porsche.

Beth Todesco would pause every few seconds as she attached the bar to the front end. Monroe watched her put her hand on the car, on the truck, on the ground to steady herself. He saw another hand go to her face.

She noticed him and uttered something low and wordless, putting her hand over her face and turning away.

"Beth—"

"Go away."

"I want to tell you—"

She faced him and her eyes were red, her cheeks marked by tears that the wet wind had turned to raw, scarlet streaks. She seemed to be forcing herself to calm down. "That's his blood on you. Go away."

"I want to tell you that what he did was—"

144

She went to the winch controls on the side of the truck. "I've seen what he did. I've seen *him*."

"You've been at the hospital?"

She uttered a low, wordless cry as she pushed down the winch control.

"Is he okay?" Monroe asked over the roar of the winch.

She waited until the front end of the car had been raised. "They're operating. He could die from the blood he lost. If he lives, they might have to cut off his leg."

"He won't die," Monroe said firmly.

"How do you know? How do you know anything? I wouldn't be surprised if you were the reason he did this. It was just you and him, right? He was showing off, showing you what a big macho guy he is, standing up to Soladias."

Monroe fell silent. "We came here because—"

"Because he *lives* here. He needs an audience for what he does. With you, he could play cowboy."

"Beth, he didn't say anything about living here."

"He would if you'd seen through him. See that house?" she pointed to one of the bungalows, the one where Chou had sat, waiting to pounce on the Porsche. Monroe saw for the first time that it was the only one on the street with a new coat of paint.

"When he walked out on me, he moved back in there. It was his parents' place. They bought it after they had their liquor store."

"Wait. He told me you walked out on him."

"Same difference."

"So he moved back here. Have you—did you ever try to find him here and talk with him?"

"Why should I? He knew where *I* was. If he wanted to talk, he could find me."

Monroe looked at the house because he didn't want to look at Beth Todesco. He was certain that her husband desperately needed her as much as he needed his wife. How could he tell her?

"He lived in that house and he put up with Soladias moving into his neighborhood and destroying it?"

"Of course he did. He's been obsessed with Soladias from the moment he met him, and Soladias knows it. There's no way in hell Soladias's pricks would've left that house alone unless Soladias told them to lay off."

"You're not suggesting that—"

"We broke up when I found out Jack's been the contact with Soladias. Jack got street money to get the mayor elected. Jack got Soladias to move to Nevada Avenue. It's been Jack every step of the way." She bounded into the truck, rubbed her eyes, slammed the door in Monroe's face, and moved slowly up the street.

◆

Monroe watched to see if any of the remaining police on the street went into Chou's bungalow. They didn't. He waited, shivering in the wind, until the last police car left.

He wasn't the only one waiting. As soon as the patrol car turned right at the intersection of Pacific and Atlantic, the mules returned, the enforcers took up their positions. A minute later, the first customer cars began to come down the street.

Monroe imagined that with dried blood on his sweatpants and jacket, he'd get some attention. But in the evening darkness he merely appeared filthy, and he was ignored as he approached the bungalow's screened-in porch. The screen door was not locked. He opened it. The hinges were well oiled and didn't squeak. In the dim light from the streetlights he could see a stack of empty, upended flower pots and a pair of weatherbeaten wooden rocking chairs. The solid wooden door was locked.

On a hunch he moved the doormat aside. He saw nothing but wet, grimy floorboards. He went to the flower pots and found a key between the first and the second pot.

It opened the front door.

Monroe groped for a light switch and turned on a single bulb hanging from a ceiling socket overhead. The heat was low enough to make Monroe's breath come out like steam. Straight ahead was a narrow flight of wooden stairs with a frayed brown runner. To his right was a narrow, shabby sitting room with worn, faded pale yellow and green rugs, dented, mismatched wooden furniture, and yellow-and-green floral-print wallpaper whose edges were beginning to curl.

Behind the sitting room was a small dining table and a door leading to a kitchen with yellow enameled cabinets.

He wasn't sure what led him up the stairs. He turned on another light and saw the bedroom in the rear had a broad, queen-sized bed, with its red, floral-print spread pulled tight.

This room had not been lived in for several years.

Next to the bathroom was a smaller room with a mattress on the floor, a rumpled sleeping bag, a stained pillow, a half-empty coffee maker, and a stack of car magazines.

On the walls were calendars and garish posters of women in bikinis, in negligees, sprawled on the hoods of gleaming, glossy automobiles. The posters were sold in the sleazier Boardwalk shops a few blocks from Nevada Avenue.

Near the head of the mattress was a small wedding photo of Chou and Beth Todesco.

On another wall was a set of shelves with meticulously assembled plastic models of Fords, Chevys, and fancy racing cars. In the closet were a grease-stained mechanic's coverall and boxes of arcane Buick parts.

It was the last room, the one that looked over Nevada Avenue, that took Monroe's breath away. It was orderly, purposeful, and so functional as to be intimidating. A pair of very small TV cameras were positioned in the window, connected to a bank of time-phase videotape recorders similar to the one the casinos used to monitor their public areas and parking garages. There was also a telescope, trained down at the street.

A computer stood dormant on a card table against a wall. Beside it was a box of disks, and a notebook of license plate numbers and dates. Monroe thumbed through the pages and saw his license plate among them, on a date in November when . . . Ellie *could* have parked the car on Nevada Avenue.

He heard a small electronic beep and a tape recorder on another card table began to move. Monroe heard a conversation in Spanish. Monroe heard the names Chou, Newton, and Todesco mentioned. It was grainy enough to sound as if it was coming from a car phone.

One of the voices Monroe recognized as Pieto Soladias's. The recorder shut itself off when Soladias ended the conversation.

Beneath the table was a fax machine. In a tray in front of the machine were several documents that had been sent to Cheezy Lindberg's office. One Monroe could see had something to do with a Crack Properties Corp., headquartered in Panama.

Behind the fax machine were stacks of tapes. All were dated. Some were labeled *Transactions, Large Deals, Panama, C Lindberg, H Todesco, Miracle Mile.*

He found no warrants authorizing the wiretap in the stack of papers beside the tape recorder. He did uncover a large white envelope with the Alcazar's logo on it. Monroe opened it and saw an unsigned agreement of sale for a piece of property at the corner of Montana and Pacific Avenues, just up from the Alcazar.

The owner of the property was listed as Happy Land Wine & Spirit Shop, Inc.

Clipped to the agreement was a note in Ellie Monroe's handwriting. The date matched the one in the notebook beside the computer.

Dear Mr. J, the note said, *Carl really hopes this works out. Neither of us can see why you have to be so hush-hush about this, but Carl wants me to emphasize that we can keep secrets. If there's anything the casino can do for you, give me a call.*

Ellie had signed it, *Mrs. E.*

Monroe heard cars outside on the street. He went to the window and saw that the cameras would be able to capture nearly everything happening on the street. The telescope was trained directly on what had been, before Chou destroyed it, the upper floor of Pieto Soladias's office.

He stood for a while in the window, gazing at the transactions going on below him, hoping that Chou had a warrant for the wiretap. Even if he didn't, the visual evidence alone was enough to bring in the feds, who would have no compunctions about shutting down Nevada Avenue permanently.

He saw a cream-colored Mercedes swoop around the line of customer cars and stop in front of the ruined bungalow. He watched Soladias get out, in a different outfit now. He saw him ranting and fuming, kicking the wreckage. He sent one of his crew into the grocery store.

Monroe told himself that Soladias would have to suspect that Chou was surveilling him from the window. You can't do the kind of business he did on a street without getting to know who lives where. If someone looked at the second-floor front window with a good pair of binoculars, he'd be able to see the television cameras during the day.

Monroe saw the crew member come out with a glass juice jar. Soladias opened the jar and spilled out the juice on the ice-streaked street.

Soladias ordered one of his crew to open the trunk of the Mercedes. Inside the trunk was a red gallon container of gasoline.

Monroe told himself that it may have been possible that

no one looked in the window because Soladias was in so deep with city hall that he didn't care.

Or that, if what Beth Todesco had said was true, Chou had set up the understanding with Soladias, then Chou was working undercover, and those sloppy actions against Harry the Toad and Soladias were part of that cover.

But Sir Isaac had said that the Toad was *protecting* his son-in-law. For a moment, Monroe hoped that the Toad was doing a better job for Jack Chou than Marty Gant was doing for him.

Then he thought about working undercover and concluded that the way Chou was behaving was the wrong kind of cover. You don't risk your life so extravagantly as Chou had a few hours earlier when you're undercover. And you don't shoot yourself in the leg. The goal of an undercover operation is to stay undercover long enough to build a case.

And you can only push people like Soladias so far until they push back. Soladias had almost died when he ran his car off the fishing dock.

No, Monroe corrected himself, the Jaguar didn't belong to Soladias. Though Monroe did not doubt that Soladias had crashed the Jaguar accidently, psychological profiles of drug dealers and others who made their living in a dangerous, illicit fashion emphasized that they enjoyed trashing expensive cars and toys that did not belong to them. They considered it their due.

But touch something that *did* belong to them . . .

Monroe watched one of Soladias's crew fill the juice container with gasoline. Monroe remembered a regulation about transporting cans of gasoline in a car. Was it illegal on the streets, or only on bridges and in tunnels? Now that he was in Traffic Safety, he'd have to find out.

While one of his crew held the jar, Monroe saw Soladias knot a handkerchief and stuff the knot of the handkerchief below the mouth of the jar. Soladias pulled out a lighter, lit the handkerchief, and pointed the crew member at the window Monroe was standing in.

No, Monroe said to himself. It wasn't going to happen *again*. He wasn't going to be in a building, watching Soladias, and have Soladias burn the building down beneath him.

He watched the crew member haul back and hurl the flaming jar directly at him. He ducked, bending his right leg, and heard the jar make a *thunk* on painted wooden shingles above the window. He saw it drop down below the window, heard it bounce and stop, and heard the guy out front say, "Fuck."

Monroe came toward the window, inadvertently knocking the telescope aside. He peeked over the sill, saw that the jar had rolled over the porch roof and got stuck sideways in the drainpipe, where the ocean breeze was blowing out the flame.

He watched the tiny wisp of blue flame flutter and die. One thing about criminals that never makes it into the movie and TV shows is that they aren't that bright. These guys didn't know that the repeated freezing and thawing of wood shingles on an ocean beach block will actually soften them, so that a glass jar wouldn't necessarily shatter, even if hurled from the street.

He heard another *thunk* and saw the red gas can on the porch roof now, all the way down at the far end, with a much bigger rag stuck in it, and a brighter flame that, even though the can was on its side and the flame was being fed by gasoline, was still dying in the wet ocean breeze. Weren't those idiots aware that the traditional Molotov cocktail only worked when the glass jar broke and spilled gasoline over a flammable surface?

Then he heard something he hoped he would never hear again in his life. It was the noisy, staccato shriek of soft shingles, damp drywall, aluminum trim, and double-pane glass exploding on top of him from a rapid-fire machine gun spraying Black Talon rounds. If the can had been tossed any closer to him he'd probably be dead and he wouldn't notice that some of the rounds had punctured the can, and he wouldn't have heard the proud, hot *whump* of low-octane, no-lead engine fuel gasoline discovering its true purpose in life. He said to himself that it was time to get the hell out of there.

He crawled back, got into a crouch, and took off at a run.

It was when his left leg wouldn't move that he remembered that running was something he couldn't do anymore. He went down on the hall carpet, started crawling, which was difficult because his left hand wouldn't support his weight and his right hand still had the front-door key in it.

Something was bothering him, a weird little fact tucked in the back of his brain, about keypads and intruder- and fire-prevention systems. If Chou had stuck all this expensive survelliance equipment in a high-crime neighborhood, why hadn't he put in a burglar alarm?

And why the hell was Soladias burning down a house on the block where he made his bacon? Hadn't he learned once already that displays of violence were bad for business?

He heard another spray of automatic weapons fire penetrate the front of the house. Knowing that those extra-heavy grain rounds could slice through just about anything in this house, including himself, he kept his head down, which was silly, he conceded, because anyone firing that gun was firing it from the street, which meant everything was being aimed up. If anything was going to hit him, it was going to get him in his gut, so he'd better get downstairs as fast as he could.

He had squirmed around to the top of the stairs, pulled himself up so he could hop, one-legged, down the stairs, when the lights flickered and went out, catching him in mid-hop. He went down, missed the step, felt himself falling sideways into dark, stuck out both arms to break his fall, and snagged the banister with his right hand. He tried to grab it but missed because he had the damned front-door key in his hand, and he hit the stairs on his right side, skidding and sliding over the runner.

Monroe could hear voices outside, calmly discussing the fire, and then some cries to *vamanos,* or vamoose, or gedda fuck ouddadaway over the sound of an engine, an automobile engine whose throaty rumble would have been more familiar if he was like Mrs. and Mr. Chou, who had that talent for *knowing* cars, probably better than people.

After all, he said to himself as he braced his right arm against a stair and took the pressure off his leg, sliding down a few steps, binding his left leg under him, bending it sharply at the knee, and feeling that deep, excruciating physically therapeutic agony from muscles and joints that were taking their sweet time healing and would tolerate no encouragement to do otherwise, cars either work or they don't or they work badly. People, on the other hand . . .

He was sitting on the stairs, about two-thirds of the way down, when he heard an engine race and the headlights come on, shining through the porch, casting odd shapes of white light on the walls of the darkened living room.

Though the light didn't hit him, Monroe, who had managed to stand by now, froze like a deer on the highway and, in an instant, understood why animals who have become accustomed to darkness and must navigate such a bizarre and uncomfortable circumstance as a heavily trafficked road will lose all sense of self in the glare from a headlight. It was because the light was so *inappropriate.* It didn't belong. It had nothing to do with anything, and yet it was there, intruding with such finality that it changed the situation, *became* the situation.

Monroe was smart enough to recall that when an animal froze in the path of an oncoming vehicle, that was generally the *last* thing the animal ever did. So he stopped thinking about why those assholes would shine automobile headlights into a burning building and began moving toward the back of the sitting room. He had his hands on the dining room table when he heard the car's engine race, followed by a terrific groaning and snapping sound as Chou's even more smashed-up yellow Buick came roaring through the porch and the front sitting-room window and wall, pulling everything down like a collapsing balloon. The headlights caught Monroe in the act of hitting the kitchen, the bitter odor of spilled gasoline preceding the car, which stopped in the living room, its whirling rear tires trapped on the porch. The headlights shone, a flickering glare from the front seat, the car's front seat, where Monroe didn't have to imagine more Molotov cocktails, because something obligingly detonated, throwing another wash of heat into his face and blowing him backward into the kitchen. There he got up, turned, and staggered into the rear door, prayed that there would be an alley in the back.

The door was locked.

He heard another *whump* behind him and the house was getting *seriously* hot. He banged on the door and threw his body against it, but the door wouldn't budge.

In the glare from the Buick's headlights, which were still shining but had no right to be, Monroe observed a very strong dead-bolt lock sunk deep into a metal door-frame, the kind cops tell every moderately paranoid suburban homeowner to install.

Well, this *wasn't* the suburbs, Monroe told himself as a third *whump* blew half of the dining room table into the kitchen. The kitchen door had no glass in it, and the kitchen window was about the size of phone book. Nothing could crawl into it, and he certainly couldn't crawl out.

It was when the headlights went out that he began to panic. Things have to be pretty damned hot for a car's electrical system to fail, or it could be an old car, or the gas tank under the car was about to blow, and he definitely did not want to be in this house.

He might have been screaming when he realized that he still had the front-door key in his right hand. Some people had different keys for the front door and the back. Others, seeking joyous simplicity after losing a set (or knowing that your wife, whom you walked out on for reasons other than what she might think, could have a set), would adapt both locks to the same key.

Monroe stuck the key into the lock. It fit. It turned. With his hand on the key he pushed the door open and was out of there into the comforting cold, stumbling forward down wooden stairs into a narrow alley. He looked right and saw that the alley dead-ended at a storefront on Pacific Avenue. He looked left, saw the alley open on to Jefferson Place, and heard a groaning, heaving, shredding explosion behind him that blew out that tiny kitchen window. The house raised up a few inches as if it were a big rocket making its slow climb off the launching pad, then came down, like the famous demolition film clip of the turreted Traymore Hotel crashing gracefully into rubble at the end of Louis Malle's movie, *Atlantic City*.

He was on Jefferson Place, his hand on a car, holding himself up, trying to catch his wind, when some kid on Nevada Avenue in a leather jacket spied him, yelled at him, called him a motherfucker, said he should stay right there or he'd blow him away.

Monroe didn't stay. He set off at a fast limp and he imagined that the kid behind him was the brother of the kid on the jitney. He imagined the gun coming up, he felt the fear burning into his spine, and he went faster, and something gave in his left leg and his left foot went up and down in front of him and he was *running*, taking off and flying with his heart beating wildly in his throat. The slumbering parked cars, the darkened doorways of Jefferson Place melted into a blur as Jefferson ended at California, where

155

everything had been torn down to make a parking lot that nobody used anymore.

His legs took him up California, toward Pacific Avenue, whose lights were slightly brighter than the Boardwalk's, and, as incredible as it could be, he saw that a jitney had stopped at California and Pacific to pick up a passenger. Jitneys were notorious for not waiting for people running to catch them, and Monroe was definitely running, running, running, not because behind him was a lethally armed urban adolescent menace pumped up on pills and action movies and music that glorified violence who probably was too lazy to chase him, but because Monroe's life suddenly depended on his being able to move, fast, and being able to reach that jitney, even though the jitney driver had closed the door and the jitney was inching forward into the flow of traffic on Pacific.

The rush of motion made him delirious, and, like a beginning ice skater drunk on newfound speed, Monroe discovered that he had no idea how to stop, and so he slammed against the jitney's closed doors and heard behind him the shout of "Motherfucker, I'm gonna kill you!" and the sound of expensive hiking boots slapping on broken pavement and realized that that lethal adolescent *was* chasing him after all.

The jitney stopped, the driver turned to him, opened the doors. He fell inward and pulled himself up, and the driver shut the doors behind him and moved into traffic.

Monroe hung there for a few seconds, panting, his heart beating wildly, his face warm from the exertion. He stood, turned around, saw the kid giving him the finger from the receding corner of California and Pacific, and then saw Nevada Avenue pass him and the brief, angry flash of orange flames from a house near the center of the block.

Then, bracing himself with his *left* hand, he pinched his wallet out of his pocket, gave two dollars to the driver, counted his change.

"You gave me back twenty-five cents too much," Monroe said.

"Gave you what I owe you," the driver said. He patted his baseball bat. "I found your quarter."

Chapter Eleven

◆ ◆ ◆ ◆ ◆

The Devil You Know

Ellie wasn't home when Monroe returned to his apartment. He had found both Sere and Mrs. Pasecki sleeping in a heap on the couch, with the television set still on.

He had tiptoed past them, pulled off his bloody clothes, thrown them in the garbage, slipped into his robe, and was about to go to sleep when he heard the television set. He quietly turned it off and Sere immediately began to scream.

Monroe had her in his arms.

"She needs a change," Mrs. Pasecki said.

"I'm going to do it," Monroe said. "You come near me, I swear I'll . . ."

"Be my guest," Mrs. Pasecki said, following him as he hoisted Sere onto the changing pad at the far end of the kitchen table. "You'd better not drop her."

"I can *do* this," Monroe said. He changed her diaper while Mrs. Pasecki told him that Ellie was spending the night at the Alcazar because something had come up about the Miracle Mile. Everything was on hold and she had to deal with it.

"What is she, running that place?" Monroe grumbled. "She say what had come up?"

"Who asks?" She gave him a sly look. "You had a woman visit you a few nights ago."

"She was looking for Ellie," Monroe said.

"Who asks?"

Monroe changed her diaper but Sere was still screaming.

He tried to calm her down but she kept screaming until Mrs. Pasecki turned the television set back on to MTV.

"She shouldn't be watching this," Monroe said. He turned off the set and Sere started up again.

Monroe yawned and noticed Sere's eyes were on him. He wiggled his fingers and she giggled. She looked at his left hand, which he'd used to hold her feet when he was changing her. He put her down on the rug and brought his left arm around, tried an improvised patty-cake.

She laughed.

He did it again and she reached for his face, touching the stubble. He laughed with her, thrilling as her soft, tentative hand move over his nose, his eye.

"You're not allowed to enjoy yourself too much," Mrs. Pasecki said. "God forbid you should want to spend all your time with her."

"This is too easy," Monroe said, wiggling his fingers. "She loves this."

"It gets harder, but it's always worth it." Mrs. Pasecki looked at her watch. "She'll probably need a feeding."

"I want to do that, too."

She got him a bottle from the refrigerator. As guitars squealed on the television set, Monroe propped his daughter against him and took the bottle in his right hand.

"Now, Daddy's left arm isn't working as good as it should, so you'll have to sit here like this."

"She don't understand what you say," Mrs. Pasecki told him. "What she feels is your voice and how you hold her. You should hold her now."

"But I can't—"

"Some father . . ."

Monroe opened his left arm and he had her then, the face fitting perfectly to him, the eyes open and full of wonder, her hand slowly coming up again to touch his face.

"Dah," she said. "Dah, dah."

"Yes," Monroe said. "Oh, God yes."

"Dah, dah."

Monroe sat down on the couch and held her closer than he'd ever held anyone in his life. Sere closed her eyes as he fed her. Then, while putting down the bottle to wipe her mouth, he found the remote control and turned off the set. Sere's eyes opened then and she put her hands on the bottle.

She fell asleep with the bottle in her mouth. Monroe wiped her chin, burped her, and waited until she fell back to sleep in his arms.

Her crib was stuck in the corner of the living room between the couch and the recliner. He lifted her over the armrests and gently placed her on her blanket.

He heard Mrs. Pasecki's shoes going down the stairs.

He closed the door, turned off the lights, lay down in his bed. Instead of feeling stiff and sore, his left leg hummed with power, and his left arm still glowed from the warmth of holding his daughter.

He experienced an incredible, wonderful, totally unforeseen moment of bliss.

Then the doorbell rang. Monroe fumbled for his robe, went down the stairs, opened the front door.

Marty Gant scowled at him in a lumpy trench coat, a black ten-gallon hat pulled low over his eyes. "Don't just open the door like that. I could've been somebody sent to kill you."

"But you weren't."

"How come you don't have a weapon?"

"You took my gun."

"Something else. A baseball bat. A knife. A can opener. Some damned thing."

"I didn't know I needed one."

Gant walked in, went up the stairs. "I want to see my girl."

"She's at work."

"The baby."

"She's sleeping. You'll wake her—"

"I had two daughters born to my wife, rest her soul. I know how to stare at a baby girl without waking her up."

Monroe followed Gant into the living room, where he stood over the crib, viewing the huddled form in the dim glow from the stairs. His hands were in his pockets, his hat still on his head.

"You look like a pervert," Monroe whispered.

"Perverts look like me," Gant whispered back.

Gant moved quietly to Monroe's bedroom. Monroe followed him. Gant shut the door, put on the light, threw his hat on the bed.

"You've been with her all night?"

Monroe sat on the bed. "Most of it."

"But not all of it. You were, instead, in the vicinity of Sixteen South Nevada Avenue."

"I was on Nevada Avenue for most of the afternoon."

"So I've heard. The question is, what time did you leave?"

Monroe smiled at him. "You told me I have this problem with time."

"You go into that house or not?"

"If you're referring to the house belonged to Detective Chou—"

"I'll lay it out for you. The boys down in the fire department have found some remarkable things in what's left of Sixteen South Nevada Avenue. Nothing usable, but it doesn't take much of an imagination to figure out how usable it might have been. And someone, I'm not saying who, has placed you near enough in that house."

"I didn't set fire to it, if that's what you're after."

"We don't need any explanations as to how it started. I have to ascertain if you took anything out of that house."

"Anything usable?"

"That would be the assumption."

"Harry the Toad put you up to this?"

"I volunteered to see you when your name came up." He

wandered to the closets, eyed Ellie's dresses. "Before you tell me anything, let me give you some background and inform you as to how the interested parties may react.

"It seems that Soladias was not aware of a surveillance operation directed against him, until about an hour ago. He has put the Toad on notice that he will not put the seed money into the Miracle Mile until he is sure that this operation does not involve additional persons in the police department."

"Ask Jack Chou."

Gant touched one of Ellie's gray wool skirts. "The Fu Man is recovering from surgery. The leg may have to come off. The Toad has tried to put a blanket on the Fu Man that's bigger and tighter than your own. I am proud to say he's failed. You'll find tomorrow's *Star* very interesting."

"Sir, is the Toad protecting him?"

"Depends on how you look at it. The good thing about a blanket is that it absolves you of all responsibility. If you're incompetent, you're incompetent, and that has a way of explaining away everything. The bad thing is that it can ruin you in more ways than one."

Monroe thought about that. "Tomorrow, what you're going to see in the *Star* is going to be wrong. Chou shot himself."

"If that were true, then putting the blanket on him would have been merciful, wouldn't it? If you had retired, it would have been merciful for you. But now, we have to reinstate you, so . . ."

Monroe was too shocked to say anything.

"Now hear me out. Inasmuch as you were the last person to be with Chou, and you were sighted in his house, and you happened to be on the scene when Chou tried to apprehend Soladias, the Toad is very, very interested in you."

"I'm not interested in him."

"You should be. Now, if I get a statement from you that you were not part of Chou's operation, were not in his house, and therefore took nothing that could be harmful to the Toad and his backer, the Toad has no reason to do anything for you. Your situation continues as it is."

"I don't want him to do anything for me."

"Hear me out. If you tell me you were part of Chou's operation, I will treat you as if you are still mentally incompetent and, presumably, experiencing delusions. Your situation will remain the same, but Soladias may be inspired to find out more directly how dangerous you can be to him. And you don't want that.

"Now if you tell me you were not part of Chou's operation, but you broke into the house and took something harmful to the Toad and his backer, I will have to take you and your family into protective custody. Such a statement *will* make you dangerous to Soladias, and though you have saved Soladias's neck, there's no kind of understanding we can come up with that will stop him from killing you if he feels threatened."

"But, sir, the truth is that—"

"*Hear me out.* If you tell me that you're not part of Chou's operation, that you broke into the house but that you didn't take anything, the Toad will not believe you. For him, intimidation, blackmail, and extortion are just different ways of shaking hands, and he could not conceive that you would be so stupid as to fall upon items that would nail him *and* Soladias, and just leave them to be burned down. In that case, I would still have to put you and your family into protective custody."

"Actually—"

Gant held up his hand. "I'm not finished. You have a fourth option. You can give me some reason to believe that you can't be trusted."

Monroe stood. "Sir, everything I've ever done has been based on earning the trust and respect—"

"Save it. You've backed into a situation where integrity could get you killed. If I can persuade the Toad that you can't be trusted, he'll let me reinstate you.

"I'll explain. As a fully reinstated member of this police department, you can and will be ordered by your division commander not to divulge any evidence or information whatsoever pertaining to the Toad, Soladias, or the Fu Man and his operation. If the information leaks out, you can be arrested for insubordination and, considering Harry the Toad's influence in the department, you *don't* want to be arrested."

Monroe scratched his head. "You're telling me that if the Toad can't trust me, he'll reinstate me so he can gag me."

"It's a variation on the concept of the devil you know. This time you would be the kind of untrustworthy, scheming individual that the Toad would understand. You control such individuals by putting them in a situation where they have everything to gain by following the rules."

"Like he did with Chou. . . ." Monroe said. "But I can be trusted, and I didn't take anything out of Chou's house because I didn't have time to think about it."

Gant sat heavily beside him. "I was afraid of that. I guess I screwed up again."

"Couldn't you just tell him I'm a liar?"

Gant shook his head. "I need proof."

"That I was in the house?"

"That you took something."

Monroe was sullen for a while. Then he said, "Why the hell didn't he do this the first time? Just order me gagged. Why did he have to throw a blanket on me?"

"Because you weren't a devil he knew. And you still aren't. You wouldn't steal a dime from a blind man."

Then Monroe had a hunch. It might have been due to the injuries he'd received. You get a bump on the head and you're supposed to look at life differently, right?

He had a hunch that something was in the garbage. Ellie called them tingles. Gamblers got them, or said they got them, after a slot machine or winning hand paid off.

Monroe had had something's-in-the-garbage hunches like this before and nothing had paid off beyond seeing how the discolored, soggy, stinking remains of meals, bills paid, baby paraphernalia, and other domestic detritus aroused memories of an unexamined life that should have stayed unexamined.

But he had nothing better to do, so he walked, awkwardly, his recently run-upon leg stiffening up, expressing its indignity at being forced to serve before its time. He tiptoed through the kitchen, put on the light over the stove, and dumped out the garbage.

In the pocket of his sweatpants was a key. Why had he held on to that key? He had no explanation. He gave it to Gant. "This'll fit the lock on Chou's front or back doors."

"He didn't give you this? If he gave you this that would mean that you were part of the operation."

"He didn't give it to me, but you can't trust me, right?"

"Correct." Gant closed his fist around the key. "Report to the department physician tomorrow at o-nine-hundred hours for a physical and a psych test. I'll make sure you pass. I'll sign a temporary weapons release form and you can get your gun. I'll find someone to qualify you at the range."

"I'd like Sergeant Almagro to do it."

"Almagro won't fake the results."

"I'll pass it, sir."

"Fine. You're being assigned to Traffic Safety so that Sir Isaac can keep an eye on you. He'll post you to Chou's old job at the tow lot." He clapped Monroe on the back. "You're back in, Lou."

Gant reached into his trench coat and gave Monroe his gun.

Monroe saw him out and had fallen asleep when the phone rang and he heard it this time, grabbing it with his left hand, bending his neck so he could bring it up to his ear.

A familiar female voice asked for his wife.

"This is Louis. We talked on the stairs. Ellie's at the casino tonight."

"Oh."

He thought he heard the ocean in the whispering silence of the line. "Can I take a message?"

"Tell her I was in the office, I heard this rumor, and I know Ellie used to work for the cops, so she'd be able to check on it."

"I'm a police detective," Monroe said proudly.

"She married a cop? How about that. The article didn't mention you."

"There was a lot the article didn't mention."

"I guess. Well, what I heard was, this cop got mad at all the drug dealers in his old neighborhood, and so he just went up to them, without having a gun on him, and he started taking their guns away, and one of them shot him in the leg, and now he's in the hospital. Did that really happen?"

"More or less," Monroe said.

"I thought it was true. I mean, I just knew, when I heard it, it was like a message to me. Everything became clear. Sometimes you have to risk everything for what you think is right. I mean, if he can stand up to those drug dealers who have guns, then what am I afraid of? So I called the lawyer. I'm filing the harassment and discrimination charges tomorrow. I wanted Ellie to know."

"I'll tell her," Monroe said.

"She used to tell me that you can't let fear stop you. You have to give your dreams the chance to come true. I wanted to tell her that I'd forgotten that. And then this happened, and I remembered."

The ocean was loud now. Monroe asked her where she was calling from.

"I'm subletting for the winter this condo that looks out on the beach. I just opened the windows and let it in."

"But it's freezing out."

"I'll close them soon. But right now, it doesn't feel cold to me. It's like it's blowing away everything that I was afraid of. You must think I'm crazy. Everybody thinks I'm crazy."

"You have to do crazy things sometimes," Monroe said.

"To stay sane, right?" She paused. "Well. Good night."

He said good night and he felt so close to her he couldn't hang up the phone.

She said, "You still there?"

Then she hung up.

Chapter Twelve

♦ ♦ ♦ ♦ ♦

On a Blanket with My Baby

"Consider hitting the target, grasshopper," Vinnie Almagro said, sounding as bored as he probably was. He stood behind Monroe, to his right, with his hands folded over the clipboard.

They were alone on the range except for the seagulls. Look up anywhere in Atlantic City, at any time of day, in any weather, and you'll find seagulls.

The nastiest, dingiest winter gulls haunted the police range, a tiny quarter acre bounded by swamps and an observation tower south of the municipal tow lot off Brigantine Boulevard. Gunshots did not scare them away. During the cold months, it was customary for police officers qualifying on their weapons to bring food for them, on the assumption that appeasing the birds would enhance their scores.

Monroe had brought along some leftovers that Ellie had taken home in an Alcazar Casino Hotel doggie bag. It was a Swiss-cheese bread hors d'oeuvre that Food and Beverage had whipped up for the Christmas week player party.

The birds didn't touch it.

The angle of the sun was wrong: the range faced west, and the afternoon sun was low and Monroe had to pull the visor on his police-issue baseball cap down over his eyes.

And then there were the clothes he had on. In an hour or so Ellie would pick him up and take him and Sere to the

Olde Salt restaurant for *Rolling Chair* magazine's Gals with Clout happy-hour party. Everybody who was anybody would be there, she had told him, and had forced him to put on his white, Italian-cut suit.

He wanted to wear his boring chocolate brown go-to-court suit, or his dark blue blazer and some gray pants.

The suit was five years old. Monroe had bought it when he was single and he thought Italian-cut suits were the thing to wear. It had since been ripped, stained, and forced to endure insults and abrasions its makers had not intended.

But, because Atlantic City still had a resident population of superb Italian tailors and dry cleaners, the rips had been mended, the abrasions rubbed out, and the stains reduced to ghostly shadows.

It fit him so tightly that his legs felt like sausages. When Vinnie Almagro saw the white, pressed pants peeking out from under Monroe's storm coat, he said, "Well." When Monroe unzipped the storm coat to free his shoulders, Almagro saw the painted, pink flamingo tie and pastel blue-and-red pinstripe shirt. He started singing the theme to *The Godfather.*

Monroe adjusted the noise-deadening earmuffs. He held his Smith & Wesson .38 chief's special in his right hand and squeezed off another round.

The gun jumped in his hand, made a high, dry popping sound, blew cordite fumes in his face.

The target, a paper, life-sized silhouette of a man's head, arms, and torso tacked to a wooden crossbar, rippled in the breeze.

Almagro made a note on the clipboard. "How much more you want to do this?"

Monroe saw a pair of seagulls fluttering on the earthen mound behind the target. At one end of the mound was the dessicated lump of Swiss-cheese bread. The birds gazed on him as if they were minor deities, blandly curious about what the mortals would do next to keep them entertained.

"I think it's the food," Monroe said. "I didn't bring the right food."

Monroe fired another round and tasted the wet, frosty wind. A small speck appeared at the lower left of the target, far from the printed torso.

"It's a humid day," Monroe said. "They told us in the academy humidity affects trajectory, right?"

"It helps if you want to hit the target."

Monroe lowered his arm. Almagro called for a time-out. Monroe unloaded the gun, packed up the rounds, and followed Almagro to his cramped, immaculate silver-gray Toyota sedan, where the other poured a cup of hot wonton soup from a Thermos jar he'd filled at a Chinese take-out near city hall.

"This is what I look forward to," Almagro said. "I test so many out here, they're always complaining about the shot or the sun or the windchill factor. The soup washes it all away."

Almagro passed Monroe a cup. He sipped the broth and said, "You should be happier. You got your job back."

Monroe inhaled the luscious aroma of chicken and scallions. "Not if you don't qualify me on the handgun."

"You can get a temporary medical suspension on the gun and come back in a month, but I don't think that'll matter much in your case. It's the old story. If they want you, you can't do anything wrong. If they don't want you, no matter how qualified you are, no matter how much better you are than everybody else, you're out. The important thing is the urine test. I hope you didn't eat any poppy-seed bagels, or you'll come up an opium fiend and I can't help you with that."

"I haven't eaten a bagel in months."

Almagro pulled a poppy-seed bagel out of a lunch box, dipped it in the soup like a doughnut, bit off a hunk.

Monroe let the soup warm him. "You see the paper this

morning about what happened on Nevada Avenue?"

"The media always gets it wrong, grasshopper."

"He shot himself and I don't think it was an accident."

"It can't be accidental," Almagro said. "Accidents can be attributed to negligence. If an off-duty officer is injured due to personal negligence, the department can deny him his pension and disability benefits."

"He wasn't thinking about them at the time."

"What he was thinking about isn't important. What motivates a heroic act is rarely heroic."

"Was Chou working undercover for anyone in the department?"

"I wouldn't know." Almagro's attention wandered to the cars and buses rushing past on Brigantine Boulevard. "But you remember what we teach in the academy. Number one, trust yourself to know what you're doing. Number two, if you can't trust yourself, then cover your ass."

Monroe sighed. "You got another poppy-seed bagel?"

Almagro gave him a plain. "You and Ellie celebrate your reinstatement last night?"

"She stayed at the casino. They're going nuts trying to come up with a holiday marketing event. She said Christmas in the Alps isn't going to work out."

Almagro shook his head. "I *am* crushed."

"I had a chance to play with the kid. I even changed her diaper."

Almagro dunked his bagel again and said, "Wow."

"I used my left hand to hold her legs. I felt so good, I decided never to put my arm in a sling anymore. I felt so good, I wanted to go up to these assholes we got all over this town, I wanted to tell them that all this scheming and scamming and carrying on is all unnecessary, that life is *only* about having kids and keeping the good stuff going. The rest is all bullshit."

Almagro said, "Bullshit can get you killed."

Monroe watched a seagull hover overhead. It could see

them eating and it screamed at them. Monroe got angry at the bird. What gives this bird the right to scream at me? he fumed to himself.

Almagro sensed his mood. "Pissed off, grasshopper?"

"Absolutely. All this stuff, from getting beaten up to getting the blanket, it had nothing to do with me. It's all somebody else's game. Yet I had to pay for it. I had to get hurt. And they fake my physical as much as they want, but I'm still hurting."

Almagro ate quietly, the soup dripping down his chin, acquainting itself with darker stains on his leather bomber jacket.

"You can look at it differently," he said. "You can look at it as if it has *everything* to do with you."

"Thanks a lot, Vinnie," Monroe snapped. "Make me feel like an even bigger piece of shit."

Almagro shook his head. "Think of your daughter. Now think of yourself. Now think of what happened to you. They call it throwing a blanket on a baby; like they're covering up something."

"That's it exactly," Monroe said. "They fix it so you're stuck. You can't do anything. You can't win."

"I don't know about that," Almagro said. "From the point of view of the baby, who was out in the light and suddenly it's all dark and she can't see anything, that can be true. Look from another point of view, from above, and you know that if the baby keeps moving in any direction, sooner or later she's going to come back into the light."

"Like what could be a direction right now?"

"Deciding if you're going to qualify on your handgun."

"No way." Monroe shook his head. "My hand-eye coordination is gone, I'm not dressed for it, and the birds wouldn't eat my offering. I'm doomed."

Almagro put the cup on the Toyota's black dashboard, lifted up the clipboard, and filled in the rest of the weapons qualifying form.

Monroe popped one of the wontons into his mouth. It was too salty. "You want these things?"

Almagro signed his name on the form. "When they make 'em too salty, I toss 'em outside."

"That's littering."

Almagro signed another form. "Not if you're a bird."

Monroe saw the two seagulls on the mound and said, "Wait a minute."

He opened the door, walked across the range, and put the cup of wontons on the mound. The birds didn't wait for him to step back. The wontons vanished in seconds.

He took his position in front of the target, loaded, put on the earmuffs, and squeezed off six rounds. Five hit the target, three were in the vital organ zone.

"Sergeant Almagro," Monroe called back to the car. "Let's take it from the top."

♦

"You had a call last night from that woman you counseled," Monroe said.

"I *don't* want to hear about it."

"She said nice things about you."

"Everybody says nice things about me. Except you."

As he sat in the front seat of the Mercedes, Monroe told his wife that he had passed his qualifying test. She checked her reflection in the rearview mirror and told him that that was nice.

"So I'm back in," Monroe said.

"So am I," she said, "When I saw the paper this morning, it just clicked."

She told him that the marketing exec who wanted Christmas in Switzerland was pushing the theme to edge into her territory, and that it seemed, for a while, that she'd be cut out of running special events, but that when she saw the newspaper that morning, she'd called Darrell Pratt and Pratt said it would go.

"The day before Christmas Eve, we're going to honor Detective Jack Chou at a public ceremony on the Boardwalk in front of the Alcazar. He's that guy who got wounded taking all those guns away—"

Monroe said, "I heard about that."

"It's so perfect!" she went on. "I used to work at the department. I know cops. They love attention and validation and feeling like they're heroes as much as anyone."

"The last thing Jack Chou needs right now is attention and validation," Monroe said, remembering how Chou had looked at him when he'd taken the last gun, when he had the attention of the entire street on him, when he lowered the gun.

He told her what happened.

"Sounds like you have some kind of psychological problem about him, Louis. If you were there, with all those people, how come nobody else saw that?"

"Because Jack Chou is a hero in the department and everybody, from the crime-scene investigators on down, wanted him to stay that way. Sometimes, you see things you don't want to believe. If you had seen how he looked, before he did it, and you had seen him, bleeding and in pain after he did it, you wouldn't want to believe it, either."

"Sounds like jealousy to me. A public ceremony on the Boardwalk, right out in front of the Alcazar, honoring Jack Chou, with the mayor attending—we might even be able to get the governor—would positively empty out every Chinatown within a five-hour drive of here. Jack Chou would get a medal, and, when it was over, they'd come right into our casino."

"But it's wrong." Monroe struggled not to raise his voice in front of Sere.

"Honestly, Louis, get your head on straight for once. What's wrong or right in this town has never amounted to a hill of beans as long as people feel good and *somebody* makes money off it. It's my job to make sure that that somebody making the money is the Alcazar Casino Hotel, and I'm going to do it. Soon as I got the idea I ran it by Carl Cayleen, and he went for it immediately. Then I called up Darrell Pratt, and he thought it was fantastic and he said not to worry about Councilman Todesco mouthing off about police violence in the streets. He said Councilman Todesco's on his way out."

"He say how?"

"Oh, you know the rumor mill. Darrell just said that, when it happens, we'll feel real good."

He turned around and saw Sere bundled up in her car seat, wearing a one-piece, red Santa's-elf suit with bells on her booties. "How's my little girl?" He waved his finger at Sere the way he had last night and she kicked her feet as she giggled at him.

"What are you doing to her?"

"Being silly. Daddy's being very, very silly."

When he said Daddy, he heard Ellie take a short, sharp breath. But she said nothing, so he kept playing. The car moved effortlessly over the cracked and potholed winter roads in the poor, forlorn Northside neighborhood.

"This car really rides smooth," Monroe said.

"Thank you," Ellie said. "Does this mean I can keep it?"

"Sure. Why not?"

"I suppose this means you want something from me, some kind of concession."

"No concession," Monroe said.

"I can't get over this change in you," Ellie said. She stopped the car at a light and scrutinized him, as if she could smell traces of perfume beneath the odors of cordite. "There must be another woman."

Monroe hesitated a fraction of a second too long before denying it, and he was in the doghouse again.

Chapter Thirteen

◆ ◆ ◆ ◆ ◆

Bad Enemy

Every city on the Jersey Shore has one surf-and-turf house where nobody tells you that you have to dress up—you just know. Named for a popular menu item that features seafood (which originates from the sea, i.e., surf) and beef (which was raised on the land, i.e., turf), these dimly lit, horribly decorated surf-and-turf restaurants are gathering places for the affluent, old-guard types who are old enough to remember the Depression or World War II, when the ability to have meat, butter, and a lobster tail on the same plate symbolized the fulfillment of the American dream.

Though the restaurants have added grilled chicken breasts, poached salmon, salad bars, and steamed vegetables to appease the victims of quadruple bypass surgery, their vision of the rich, buttery, salty good life remains for those with the audacity or insouciance to believe, in their cholesterol-encrusted heart of hearts, that money really can buy happiness.

For more than half a century, the Olde Salt Public House, perched in the middle of the New Mexico Avenue beach block, was Atlantic City's premier surf-and-turf purveyor. It had been a speakeasy during Prohibition. The heavy, dark Tudor beams and slathered stucco had been installed after Repeal.

Monroe had only eaten there once, when he was in his early twenties, on the night before the day his father was sentenced to jail for taking a bribe. It had been his father's last great indulgence before an event that, he knew, would mark him forever as someone who did what everyone did, but had the bad luck to get caught.

Monroe hadn't heard from his father in years. Though if he had, he would tell him that the place hadn't changed a bit. Inside was the same assortment of thick, dowdy sack-suited men and conservatively draped women, and, here and there, a young Turk eyeing the mysteries of the rich, the powerful, and the politically significant. Above them hung antiques, photographs, peculiar relics, odd objects from the city's past.

Monroe took in the scene as he sat at the intricately carved black walnut bar, surrounded by people who didn't know him, didn't notice him, didn't talk to him. Pinned to his lapel was a tiny plastic hammer with a rose entwined around it. Those who wore it were guests of *Rolling Chair* magazine and could get unlimited drinks at the bar.

Monroe didn't care that the hors-d'oeuvre trays seemed to miss him, and that the aromatic bowls of fresh roasted mixed nuts at the bar were just out of his reach. He was drinking the third in what would be a series of margaritas that, he suspected, just might lead him into oblivion.

He caught bits of conversation, of deals to be made and deals that had fallen apart. Once or twice he heard the Miracle Mile mentioned. And he heard his wife's name, once.

Beth Todesco never showed. Darrell Pratt, officially representing the police department, would wander back to the bar with his arm around someone he was schmoozing and order drinks. This time Pratt positioned himself between Monroe and his schmoozee, Atlantic City *Star* reporter Kevin Urlenmeyer.

Urlenmeyer's sandy hair fell off his head in bangs that curled in above his eyes. His mustache had curled into his mouth. A glob of seafood cocktail sauce hung off his goatee.

Monroe knew that Darrell Pratt was the kind of guy who

would tell you, loudly, when you had food on your face that was making you look stupid. Monroe waited for Pratt to lower the boom. Pratt didn't.

"Now what's this sex thing you promised me?" Urlenmeyer said to Pratt.

"You keep it down, boy," breathed Pratt, who was very, very drunk. "Suffice it to say somebody tall's going to have a great fall, and you're catching the ball."

"I should be grateful, but I'm not. What's in it for Big D?"

Pratt hid his annoyance by picking up a scotch and soda for Urlenmeyer and a bourbon and water for himself. "Big D is pleased to take care of the people who should be taken care of."

Urlenmeyer sucked on his scotch. "Well, it wasn't because of me it got on the front page. The editor liked it."

"But you wrote it," Pratt said. "It wouldn't've been on the front page unless it had somebody to do the right job."

"Well." Urlenmeyer chewed his ice. "I try."

"Soon you'll be able to try again."

"Going to be that big, eh? We're about due for something trashy. A few months ago I thought we were going to get the mayor on that state corruption probe, but that went south."

Pratt nudged Monroe as he put his hand on Urlenmeyer's shoulder, "Now, we better be going on."

Monroe said to Urlenmeyer, "Uh, excuse me. I'm Louis Monroe. I'm a detective with the police department. I made some busts in vice a while back and we spoke on the phone."

Pratt was furious, but Monroe ignored him.

"Yeah," Urlenmeyer said, not remembering him. "I remember you."

"I'm curious about something. You wrote a story that was in the papers today, about what happened on Nevada Avenue? You go down there and talk to anybody?"

Urlenmeyer glanced at Pratt, as if to ask, *Is this guy for real?* "I did what we always do with a story like that."

"Lou," Pratt began, "Kevin is a professional. He knows what needs to be done—"

"You mean you got it over the phone from somebody at the department," Monroe said. "Like Captain Newton?"

"Yeah," Urlenmeyer nodded. "He was a source."

"But you must have checked it with somebody else?"

Pratt said, "Lou, the man works for his newspaper. He doesn't work for you."

"I know that," Monroe said. "It's just that—" He paused when Pratt jabbed the point of his cane on Monroe's toe.

"You gotta problem," Urlenmeyer said, "write a letter to the editor. Make sure you sign your name and put in a daytime and evening phone number. It may take a few weeks before it appears. They've got a backlog."

Pratt came like a wall between him and Urlenmeyer. He said, "*Later,* Lou."

Monroe went back to his drink and saw, in the mirror, his wife working the room with Sere hanging from her waist and shoulders in a knitted pouch. Beside her was Carl Cayleen, tall, gallant, always good with a joke. Both of them were working the room, but Ellie was getting all the attention, having her hand shaken and her cheek kissed by the magazine's staff as well as the well-dressed, suited-and-tied people who supposedly ran the town.

It was the first time he had seen her around these people and he was proud of her. She had a way of making people feel special to be in her presence.

"You have such a lovely, lovely wife," Councilman Todesco said.

Monroe turned, saw Harry the Toad sweating happily beside him. He snapped his fingers. "Another one for Lou Monroe here. Lou Monroe." He put a hand on the bar and gazed at Ellie. "Look at her, would you? She's so popular."

"I guess she is," Monroe said.

"And so are you."

"Not in the same way," Monroe said.

"We understand each other so well."

Monroe was confused. "We do?"

Todesco seemed pleased. "I'm a little bit more experienced at this game than you are. In my circles, you have to be very careful to treat everyone with respect and consideration. You never know when you might need them."

Monroe pulled the margarita toward him. "You put a blanket on me."

"And I took it off."

Monroe thought about it. "I guess you did."

"And I'm looking out for you."

"Like your son-in-law?"

"Not in the same way," Todesco said, indicating that he was being clever. "He has a way of surprising my associate and myself, but we are all very proud of him."

"Soladias?"

Todesco held his finger over his lips.

Monroe thought for a moment, waiting for the questions to bubble up from the booze that was sloshing in his brain. "Why didn't your associate figure that Chou was surveilling him?"

Todesco became jocular. "It's the most amazing thing, how you can know somebody and then know you don't know them. We both had assumed that he would simply play by the rules. He and our associate have been familiar with each other over the years."

"Familiar enough to get street money for the mayor?"

"I had asked my son-in-law to procure it. I also had a prior relation with our associate through his activities with vehicles."

"Stolen?" Monroe said.

"I believe the industry euphemism 'previously owned' still applies. For a while I had a distribution network operating in my garage. The cars went in and the parts went out.

But I didn't have direct contact with my associate—he was just one of a number of suppliers. My son-in-law had contact with him."

"With the associate."

"When he informed me that we had someone in common, I told him that if he maintained this contact and kept his head down, he would find himself promoted rather rapidly in the department. And he was."

"For one bag of cash?"

"Several. Our associate understood that the need for funds is constant in the circles in which I move, and that, as chairman of the Public Safety Commission, I could obtain privileges for his contributions. Such privileges helped our associate grow to dominate his field. It was then I decided to involve myself more closely in his affairs and relieve my son-in-law."

"You edged him out."

"The situation had grown beyond a few bags of cash. I felt a more experienced hand was required."

"Your own."

"These very mitts."

"But Chou didn't like that."

"He became erratic. His relationship with my daughter deteriorated. He began a series of silly actions that, I think, were attempts to annoy me and my associate. I tried to protect him as best I could. I thought a few judicious suspensions would slow him down. They almost did, when, in retrospect, I made an error. That low-income housing project had to go up at Surf and Island Avenues. Our associate had to go somewhere. I looked at the map and there just aren't that many streets where he can operate without offending someone. I picked Nevada Avenue, on the condition that he buy up the abandoned properties and pay taxes on them. I had forgotten that my son-in-law had been born on the street and was living there. How were we to know that he used it as an opportunity to observe my associate's place of business? Then there was that silly raid that cost me one of my favorite Jaguars and yesterday's display, and that brings us up to date."

"Does your associate like that Chou's getting all this attention?"

"He loves it."

"He loves getting his office trashed, losing those guns and his car?"

"My associate is surprisingly mature for his age. He understands the price of publicity. What he lost yesterday is just a fraction of what the casinos pay in advertising."

"Wait a minute. You said advertising."

"Promotion, publicity. My associate had been complaining to me that he really wasn't doing the level of business he had had in the Inlet, that many of his out-of-town customers had not been informed of his new location. Well, now they know."

"That's not why Chou did that."

"No, but the cause is not as important as the effect."

Monroe took a deep gulp. "And Chou enjoyed being the go-between, until you relieved him?"

"I assume so. He never said anything and did whatever I asked without question. Which brings me to *my* question. Are you happy with the way things are going so far?"

Monroe closed his eyes. "Sure. Why not?"

"Then this can only make you happier. My associate wants to express his gratitude to you personally. Now, I know it might seem somewhat intimidating to you—"

"He tried to kill me once."

"But he didn't succeed, did he? Now, the situation I'd like to set up is, well, being that my son-in-law has put himself out of the picture—"

"He shot himself to escape!" Monroe said. It had just clicked.

Todesco put his finger over his lips. "I want you to come in and take his place, that is, the place he used to have."

"Bag man?"

"That's one way of looking at it. My associate, as you may be aware, has decided to go legit. He's going on to bigger and better things. The Miracle Mile is back on track, I'm happy to say.

"But we still want to keep those bags of cash coming. So we'll need someone to work with my associate's successor. I must admit, it's a toss-up between you and someone else, but my daughter has strong feelings about you."

"Beth's in on this?"

"She's as far from it as is possible. But she's aware of the situation and I trust her judgment."

"She says she doesn't talk to you."

"She doesn't talk, but I pick up on things." He gave Monroe a fatherly nudge. "Of course, my associate will make the final decision as to who maintains the street contact, so he needs to see you personally."

Monroe looked him in the eye. "You wearing a wire?"

"Are you?"

"No."

He was so relieved his face almost liquified. "You don't know how *pleased* you make me. Believe me, my associate can't wait to meet you."

Monroe looked at Todesco's round, sweating face, the eyes, so kind and open under the sagging brows. "You're going to rip him off, aren't you?"

Todesco's tone became conspiratorial and chummy, as if he was letting Monroe in on a secret Monroe already knew.

"Absolutely not. I'm doing exactly what the casinos do, but on a grander scale."

"You're taking his money."

"I'm exacting a fee for providing him with an experience that he could not get otherwise. My associate is very secure on his own turf, but when he contemplates other situations, he is not so secure. Mr. Lindberg and I are providing him with the illusion of that security. Within a few days a paper trail will be in place that will make it appear that all of his business activities are legitimate. Of course, the taxes and the fees to be paid for this service *are* enormous, but it is only the first step. In a few weeks the word will be out that a youthful, entrepreneurial real estate speculator, the scion of a wealthy Panamanian banking family, is contributing seed money for the Miracle Mile. In a few months it will be discovered that the Miracle Mile lacks some approvals. There will be environmental issues raised, and so on. Naturally, his investment will be returned, less fees for acquisitions, promotional expenses, professional consultations, land use and environmental studies, permit applications, and other charges that will improve the lot of some of my other associates, who have been suffering, absolutely suffering, from the lack of major development in this city. By then I will have introduced him to those whose society he craves. He'll be invited to sit on the boards of charities, museums, orchestras, the ballet! He'll be photographed on the society page in a tuxedo, and he will be so grateful."

"But he's still a drug dealer. To a drug dealer, only two things count: money and the ability to kill anybody he doesn't like. He might not be able to read a contract, but he can count every penny and he knows in his head exactly where his money is."

Todesco dismissed that. "They've said the same about every first-generation immigrant success story. You might have to break a few necks on your way up, but once you're at the top, it all seems so inevitable."

Todesco cuffed him affectionately on his shoulder. "Now, I admit, I was somewhat short with you. But now that we understand each other . . ."

He beamed a smile so warm that Monroe almost backed off from its heat. Then Todesco moved off to work the room, and for the first time in a long time Monroe blacked out completely. The ocean came up and the blows came down and the men were laughing at him again.

He wasn't sure how long he had been out when a voice was asking him if he was okay.

Monroe looked up at a dignified man with short, frosty cropped hair, his face showing concern. "Uh, hi."

"Do you need anything? Some coffee?"

"Lou don't need coffee, Earl," Darrell Pratt boomed. "Needs a good kick in the ass."

"I'm Hamilton Earl," the man said. "This is my restaurant."

Before Monroe could introduce himself, Pratt slapped his bourbon glass on the table. "What you say, Ham Hocks? Ham Hocks, we used to call him, and Earl the Curl, when he had that processed hair and was bugging all the ladies and was stealing cars off the beach block. Where you been hidin', Hocks?"

"Here," Earl said. He asked Monroe again if he could get him anything.

Monroe shook his head. "I just hit my limit."

"I'll be happy to call you a taxi."

Monroe was about to say that his wife was driving when Pratt cut him off. "Ham Hocks, how come I wasn't *informed* you owned this joint? No bank in this town ever gave a nickel to a Black man. Where you get the change?" Pratt pushed his glass toward the bartender for a refill.

Earl scanned the crowd as he absently swished the brandy in his glass. "I worked my way up, Darrell. From the kitchen."

"What you get into the kitchen for, when you was running cars in to Harry the Toad?"

Earl smiled in such a way that Pratt became aware that his voice was too loud. "I got a job washing pots because Lysell Richards was prep cook here."

Pratt snorted. "Man, oh man, all these years you was after Lysell. We *all* were after her. Her folks didn't want her to marry a car jockey," he added for Monroe's benefit.

Pratt took a gulp of bourbon. "You went legit for her,

and she went off and married me. Tough luck, Hocks."

"Not at all," Earl said. "I own the most respected restaurant in Atlantic City. My wife is an English professor at Atlantic County Community College. Our children are attending Lawrenceville and Princeton."

Pratt whistled. "You can put the respect into the man, but can you put the man into the respect?" Pratt slapped his thigh. "Earl, how many of these White folks know they're eating off your dishes? How much you had to scrape and bow to get them in?"

"I didn't have to, Darrell. I just made this place better than everything else. Service, food, prices, wine list. And I paid attention to what my customers wanted and I gave it to them. It's not impossible to beat the casinos—they're in the business of attracting losers. I went after the people who had the money and loved it too much to want to let it go."

"You just shitting me," Pratt said. "You're pissed I stole your girl, now you ranking me out by being Mr. Better. Lou, you should've seen Earl when he was in his prime. Ladies lined up for it. Must be half the kids in the Inlet don't know they got him for a dad. And, the word was, old Paulie Marandola, the old Eye-talian Mob boss? Whenever he had a body he wanted to get rid of, he'd call old Earl the Curl."

"Darrell," Monroe said.

"Yeah, Lou boy?"

"It's time for you to apologize."

Pratt jabbed his cane into Monroe's toe again. "You seem to forget, now you're back in the department, I outrank your ass. I can fucking bust you down for disrespecting a superior."

"Don't apologize to me. To Mr. Earl here."

"I say nothing to him he ain't heard in the neighborhood."

"But you're not in the neighborhood anymore," Monroe said. "You have no right to get on him because he's successful. And you have no right to get on me, because I knew

186

you when you weren't kissing the assholes of people like Urlenmeyer over there."

"I maintain relationships with the media to *represent* this department," Pratt sputtered.

"You're representing yourself," Monroe fired back.

Earl picked up his brandy. "You gentlemen have so much to discuss. Both of you are welcome to return with your wives and have dinner on me."

"Police officers are not allowed to accept gifts of service," Monroe said.

"I suppose I should be giving you a bill for the drinks, then," Earl said. "All this excitement has made the exact amount slip my mind."

Pratt watched him go. Monroe got up to leave but Pratt pinned him to the chair.

"I can be a bad enemy," Pratt said. He moved off the stool. "You remember that, Lou boy. You remember it good."

Monroe was drunk so it was easy for him to sit back and watch Pratt put on a happy face as he returned to the crowd.

He sat and he listened and he heard, over the conversation, a song on the restaurant's music track. It was a syrupy instrumental arrangement of a song that he and Ellie had danced to at their wedding.

He repeated the lyrics in his mind.

> *Under the Boardwalk*
> *Down by the sea*
> *On a blanket with my baby*
> *That's where I'll be.*

His mind slipped away then until he made out a name being paged. Telephone call for Mr. Urlenmeyer.

Monroe looked up from the bar, saw Harry the Toad standing a few bodies away, in a group, laughing at some-

body's joke. Somewhere at the back of the bar, Kevin Urlenmeyer moved through the throng toward a telephone at
the corner of the bar. Urlenmeyer picked up the receiver,
whipped out a notepad and pen, and began to scribble
things down. Then he hung up, finished his drink, wiped
his mouth on his handkerchief, went up to Harry the Toad,
and said, "Excuse me, Mr. Todesco. Do you have any comment about a Ms. Cynthia Verheull, an administrative
assistant in the Public Safety Commission, filing sexual
harassment and discrimination charges against you?"

Conversation ceased and the background music became
unbearably loud. Harry the Toad was flush with drinks and
humor and he froze when he became aware that the only
human sound was his own laughing. It took him about a
second to realize that he was the absolute center of attention.

He said, "What?"

"Sexual harassment and discrimination. The charges say
you fondled her and repeatedly asked her if she wanted to
see pornographic videos and, when she refused, submitted
an unfavorable employment review that effectively denied
her promotion—"

"Now, this is all nonsense. Anybody who knows me
knows that that's nonsense. I love cars, not people. I mean,
I love people, that is, I like people but—" He stopped. He
was *still* the center of attention.

"Councilman Todesco, is a Ms. Verheull employed by
the Public Safety Commission, of which you are chairman?"

"Yes, but, you're not giving any credence to this, this
thing. I am an *elected* official and . . ."

Urlenmeyer was scribbling furiously. "I'm afraid it's
news, Councilman."

Then it dawned on Todesco that he was *still* the center of
attention, at a party that was celebrating the power and influence of women in Atlantic City.

188

"You'll excuse me," Todesco said, "I have to make some phone calls." Monroe saw Hamilton Earl appear at Todesco's side and lead the flushed and flustered man through a door behind the bar.

Chapter Fourteen

♦ ♦ ♦ ♦ ♦

Chou Visited

The next morning Monroe changed Sere's diaper, put her in her plastic tub in the bathroom, and gave her a quick bath, fed her, burped her, let her sit on the cushion on the living room rug and wiggle a rattle while he called the Alcazar and informed them that Mrs. Monroe was ill and would not be working today.

"That party was a little too much for her?" the guy who answered the marketing department's phone said.

"I guess so," Monroe said. He promised to have Ellie call in when she woke.

Then he went to the kitchen, improvised a breakfast of fried eggs, toast, and orange juice, and managed to carry it down the hall on a tray, one-handed. He passed the bathroom and saw his wife on her knees in front of the toilet.

"I am so . . ." she said.

"Hungover?"

She smelled the toast. "If that's food, I can't look at it. I can't—"

"It'll be on the bed if you want it," Monroe said. "I'll be with Sere in the living room."

He checked on his daughter, gave her a ball that jingled as it rolled, went downstairs, and got the newspaper.

Kevin Urlenmeyer was on the front page of the Atlantic City *Star* again. His byline appeared under two large photos, one a grinning campaign portrait of Councilman Todesco, the other a shot of a determined Cynthia Verheull.

Monroe put the paper on the kitchen table. Ellie staggered in, saw it, and staggered back to the bathroom. "I called in sick for you," Monroe said.

She stopped. She went back to the bathroom. She returned with her face wet, eyes puffy, head hanging low. "Remind me never to drink like that again."

"I will," Monroe said. "What brought it on? You hadn't touched a drop until Urlenmeyer got on Councilman Todesco."

She glanced at the newspaper. "She the one's been calling me?"

Monroe nodded.

"You could've told me."

"I did."

"Could've told me her name."

"She didn't give me her name."

"She used to call herself C.V. You could've told me what she wanted."

"She wanted to talk to you. She was afraid to do this."

"And you told her not to be."

"Actually, she told me."

She gazed at the paper sadly. "Not to be afraid?" Then she bent double. "Oh, Lou, there's so much to be afraid of. They're going to want to know about her."

"Nobody has to tell them."

"They're going to find out. They'll threaten her to expose her."

"I don't think she'll back down."

"Then she'll threaten them. Oh God, Lou, she'll expose me."

"She admires you."

"But admiration can turn around so quickly into something else."

He put his hand on hers. She held it tightly. He put his arms around her and she began to laugh. "I remember somebody breaking the law last night."

191

"If you're going to drive drunk," Monroe said, "a Mercedes is the car to have."

Sere made some noise with the rattle and they stared at her.

"Oh, Lou," she said, "we're so vulnerable. Somebody finds out I was what she was, all of this could go at any moment."

"You don't have to work for a casino."

"What else is there?"

"You were very good with people like her."

She pointed to Councilman Todesco. "But I'm better with people like him."

"Does he gamble?"

"Doesn't everybody?"

"I thought there was some rule about politicians not gambling."

"They can gamble. We just can't comp them or give them credit."

"Does he owe the casino money?"

"A lot. We'd like to write it off but you can't do that and keep it quiet anymore."

"He can pay it off. He's got that car dealership."

"His dealership isn't doing well. People didn't buy luxury cars during the recession and they're not buying that many now."

"He's got other sources."

"I don't want to hear about them."

"You've already heard about them. And forget about the Miracle Mile. It's not going to get built."

She released him, went to the kitchen sink and threw cold water on her face, then looked out of the rain-streaked kitchen window. "She'll expose me after they expose her. She'll think it'll be a good thing, getting the truth out in the open."

"Sometimes it is," Monroe said.

"That's what I told her when Darrell arrested her and

handed her over to me. I told her, never be afraid of anything. God, I used to believe that. It's so easy, when you're on the bottom and you have nothing, to believe that. But we have so much to lose now."

"You won't lose me," he said.

She went back to the bathroom and shut the door. When he followed her a few minutes later, he heard her crying inside.

♦

He discovered his car wouldn't start because there wasn't any gas in it. After two minutes of wondering if he was sane, he siphoned some out of the Mercedes, started the thing, filled it up, and spent the morning in the dusty record room in the back of city hall, going through personnel files.

Then he drove to Atlantic City General. He still didn't like hospitals, and he liked visiting the wing where his room had been even less. He tried not to favor his left leg too much as he went into the Atlantic City General's Ascher Pavillion, walked down the bright beige corridor, where he could see, through open doors, men and women in their pajamas, slumped on elaborate hospital beds, watching television, punching the little button for the nurse.

A police guard sat on a swivel chair on a desk blocking the doors to the rooms of Detective Chou and Pepe Medina. The guard, a short, wide, flat-faced woman named Addick, asked him why he had a gun under his sweatshirt.

Monroe showed her his detective badge.

Officer Addick rolled the swivel chair into the open door of Chou's room, asked him if he wanted visitors. Then she rolled the chair out, took Monroe's ID and his weapon, and pointed to the place for him to sign Chou's visitors' log.

Monroe saw Darrell Pratt's signature on the log. Beth Todesco had not come by.

Chou looked like a marionette in his bed. His right leg was encased in a variety of bandages, most of them clustered around his thigh. Wires held it above the sheets. Tubes leaked down below the bed. He also had a tube going into his arm.

He had an extravagantly hideous flower arrangement on his desk in a purple and green Alcazar Casino Hotel vase. Beside that was a small bowl with a water lily floating in it. The bowl had a card beside it. Monroe saw the words *Because you did so much.* It was signed with the initials C.V.

Chou had a newspaper open on his lap. Monroe had read it earlier. Under the article about Councilman Todesco calling his sexual harassment charges an attack on the Miracle Mile was a larger one about the hero of Nevada Avenue.

"Look a' this," Chou said sluggishly. "Urlenmeyer dug up my neighbor Mrs. Savitsky. And Mrs. Morello. They're saying I'm such a great guy. A regular fucking hero."

Then his eyes wandered to the television. Chou waited for a commercial before he noticed Monroe. He spoke slowly, sluggishly. "How you like your old room?"

Monroe shook his head. "I was next door, in the room they have Medina in."

"So now they want to throw a party for me." He gestured at the vase. "Mayor wants to give me a medal." His eyes turned back to the set. "Make a big Chinese party out of it."

"Will you be all right to leave?"

"As long as I get painkillers. Love the suckers. You don't get mad. You don't get down. You don't get scared. They put me on these suckers, I said, 'Where you been all my life?' "

With his eyes on the set, Chou reached for a pill in a small cup on his bed table. He swallowed it without water. "What're you waiting for? You got my job. Go out there, sit on your ass, watch some tube with MacReedy."

"I didn't take your job. It was given to me. I start tonight, but before that, you're going to tell me why you shot yourself."

He increased the volume on the TV set.

"I figured most of it out," Monroe said.

"Sure you did. Well, maybe I didn't shoot myself. Maybe that bastard Pepe—"

"You had the gun in your hands when it went off," Monroe said.

"Says you."

"You did it because you reached that point where everything was going your way, and you didn't like it," Monroe said. "You realized you were trying to escape from something that you can't escape from."

Chou increased the volume on the TV set.

"I got in your house before Soladias destroyed it. I saw what you had up there in the front bedroom. First I thought you were working undercover. Took me a while to figure out that you didn't have that surveillance setup to get Soladias. You were using it to cover your ass in case somebody connected you with him. If anybody found out you were committing extortion and indulging in criminal conspiracy, you could drag him down, too."

Chou fumbled with the remote control and dropped it. Monroe picked it up and turned off the set.

"Go fuck yourself, okay? I'm a goddamn hero. I get the bad guys."

"You got one yesterday," Monroe said. "Right in the leg."

Monroe closed the door, sat in a chair. "Let me tell you about how I ran up against Reuben Claymore."

♦

"So you had to kill him," Chou said. "He was a bad guy and you got him."

Monroe shook his head. "He wasn't a bad guy. Not completely."

"He was trying to kill you. That's bad enough for me."

"He was trying to kill himself," Monroe said. "The part

195

of himself that he felt was evil and wrong."

"What else could you do but kill him? Turn the other cheek? You were in handcuffs, hung up there. You didn't have much of a choice."

"No," Monroe said. "There's always a choice. What bothers me is that I still don't know what I *could* have done. And that's why, whenever I feel I'm up against something I can't handle, I hear that ocean, I feel those cuffs going around my wrists."

"You're telling me you'll never recover," Chou said.

"I'm telling you that anytime I want to feel sick, I can feel it. Anytime I want to feel like I can't win, that it's too much for me, that ocean just comes up around me, and I hear them laughing at me, and I'm right there."

"That's the worst, when they laugh," Jack Chou said haltingly, as if the parts inside him that had been patched together were rapidly breaking apart again. "I can't let nobody laugh at me."

"Who's laughing now, Jack?"

He said, "Let me tell you about me and Soladias."

♦

It had started before he met Soladias, when his parents were working in his uncle's restaurant. "First of every month, like it was the rent, the cops would come around and take money from my uncle, who was legal, so they wouldn't turn in his cook and my parents as illegals and have them deported. Watching that, I figured, if I'm going to get anywhere in this town, I'm going to be the cop."

When his parents finally became legal and bought their liquor store, they learned to keep making the payments. "My mom called it playing the rules. I tried to get my mother to say playing *by* the rules, but that was too much for her. Some things, you get too old, they don't sink in anymore, and the thing I could never get to sink in to her was that, by playing by the rules, by making the payments and not complaining, they were just keeping the scumbags in power. By then, I'd come back from the army—I'd got drafted but as close I got to Vietnam was a supply base in Texas—and I joined the department. I was at the academy, where I met Beth, who was also at the academy, and she filled me with all this piss and vinegar about how you could really make a difference and clean up the town."

His first mistake was infecting his parents with the same spirit. "I told them to stop making the payments. It was right around the time they were talking about legal casinos, and some casino company wanted to buy the land the store was on, but they weren't sure about selling. So they stopped making the payments. A month goes by, nothing. Then this juvenile delinquent prick junkie they had working for them kills them both for twenty-seven dollars in the register."

"And the department threw a blanket on you," Monroe said. He would have told Chou that he had found the incompetency judgments in his file if Chou had asked. But Chou went on as if every bad moment of his life were common knowledge.

"They threw it on me because I was going around saying the reason my parents were killed was they stopped making the payments. Now, I admit, it's crazy to blow people away because they don't kick back a few hundred bucks, but by then I was a patrolman and you see crazy things all the time on patrol. You see so much shit, it's in your face all the time, that it's the thing you believe first."

He said there had been an incident in his commander's office and he had to be subdued. From there he was confined to a mental hospital near Newark for observation. "I think I spent three years there, but I can't remember any of it. Beth says the second-to-last time she spoke to Harry it was to get me out, and then we got married and he didn't come to the wedding, and the last time she spoke to him was to get me back in the department."

"They put you on after three years in a mental hospital?"

"You didn't see that in the file, did you? If you got somebody like Harry behind you, pieces of paper can fall out of files.

"I came back, saw that the old liquor store had been condemned and torn down, and there was a lien against the property, but that nothing got built because the big wave of casino construction was over."

He was back on patrol when he ran into the junkie that killed his parents. "But it wasn't him that went after me. It was me going after him. You'd think some junkie piece of shit, half dead the way they are, couldn't run faster than me when I wasn't so fat, but he did. I chased him around, lost him, and that's when Soladias said he'd kill him. I gave him seven dollars, just like that, and I said, 'You show me results, I'll give you twenty.' "

Soladias had tried to bargain him up, but Chou stayed firm. When Soladias showed him the results, Chou said, he vomited up his lunch. It was when he'd given him the money that Soladias laughed at him. "He said it was so much fun that he would've done it for free. I just took off, tried to forget about it. But how do you forget about it? I didn't know how deep I was into the shit until Sir Isaac—he was a sergeant then, and trying to make it as a nightclub comedian—busted Soladias on possession of a stolen vehicle. The charges were dropped, not because of anything Sir Isaac did, or didn't do, but because Soladias let it be known that he had something on me, the guy who was married to Councilman Todesco's daughter, and who, even if she and him weren't speaking, was under his protection.

"I had no idea I was under Harry's protection. I had no idea that Soladias had anything on me. But he did, and it was like I could hear him laughing at me again.

"And then, then I was collecting overtime on a narco sweep in the Inlet, and Darrell Pratt, on one of his first busts, jumped on some kid, turned out to be Soladias's bodyguard. We didn't get Soladias, but we got the kid and Soladias filed all these brutality citations against Pratt, and I figured, as long as I was as bad as Soladias, I'd *be* as bad as Soladias. I drove my car right up on the sidewalk and through the window of the grocery store Soladias was selling his shit out of, and I told him I had something on him that would get him killed, and I started laughing at him, and Soladias dropped those brutality citations, and the kid was convicted and sent to jail and he never came back."

"What did you have on Soladias?"

"I found out who the father was of the junkie that killed my parents. See, during the trial, he had one of the best criminal lawyers. At the time, I just thought that the guy was appointed by the court. I asked around, found out he was appointed because somebody who had money paid money. The money was coming, real quiet, from the junkie's father. Funny thing was, the junkie never knew who his real father was. He never wanted to find out. But me asking around, after a while I figured it out."

"And?"

"I laughed at Soladias. And it became a challenge, you know, to get things on him. I figured, why not get him on bribery? Soladias was getting big on his corner and I wanted to be the cop who took his money, like the cops that took my parents' money. I didn't need the money. So I asked Harry what we could do with all this cash, and we were on a roll. Where the cops that would take from my parents got two hundred dollars, I got from Soladias two *thousand* dollars, then three thousand and five thousand every month. It went from me to Harry, and each penny I kept track of. I felt I was undercover, the department's token gook, being nice to everybody, following the rules because that was how you do the job, all the while knowing that there were no rules, only what you could get on people, and what you could get away with. I had a partner in those days who I clicked with, because we were both covering our asses, trying to put on the best face we could. Guy named Ray Deegan. Made sergeant and killed himself last summer."

"I knew him," Monroe said.

"Deegan was corrupt and proud of it. I didn't think I was corrupt, just smart to the way things were. I figured it was only a matter of time before I made a big bust or brought down some really big bad guy. Then I'd be the guy that Beth thought I was."

The opportunity had come when Harry Todesco decided to accept payments from Soladias personally. "Happened the day I made detective, two years ago. Soladias suddenly didn't want to know me, and Beth was on one of her tirades about what a rotten bastard her father is, and I said, 'Let's get him.' And I showed her all I'd written down, of how much was taken, of where and when I took it and how I passed it on, who might have seen it get passed on— everything. And Beth got real quiet. She waited until I clocked on, then she took it all and went out to one of those toxic waste dumps they have in the Pine Barrens and burned them. I clocked off and she told me what she did, and it was like Soladias was laughing at me again. When the morning came, I was in my parents' place on Nevada Avenue, running my model cars up and down my old room, like I was six years old again, waiting for the cops to come, so I could give them the payoff money in a little take-out bag from my uncle's restaurant."

A few days later, when Harry Todesco stole a load of turkeys, Jack Chou became the Fu Man.

"And I just didn't care what anybody had on me. I didn't care about rules and procedures, or getting suspended. I got away with it because you can get away with just about anything when your father-in-law is Harry the Toad. And suddenly I was getting attention. I was becoming a hero. I loved that. It was when I saw Soladias opening up shop on Nevada Avenue that I heard him laughing at me again.

That's when I bought the cameras and the phone taps. I was going to nail him this time. I wanted to prove to myself that I could do it."

"You didn't want to prove it to yourself," Monroe said. "You wanted to prove it to your wife."

Chou closed his eyes. After a while he said, "You just got the bad guy. Was it that obvious, that the only person the Fu Man wanted to be a hero to was his wife?"

Only if you were a cop who couldn't tell his wife how much he hated how things had changed between them. He wanted to deny it, suppress it, escape it—anything *but* confront it head-on and do something about it.

At that moment, he felt the blanket slip off him. He was finally moving toward the light.

◆

"But I fucked up again," Chou said. "Everything I had on Soladias, on Harry, burnt up. . . ."

Then Monroe remembered. "If all that stuff was so important, why didn't you have an alarm system on the house? Or a fire prevention system?"

"Because you don't put something like that in unless you want to announce to the neighborhood that you got something worth protecting."

"Nobody would know."

"*Everybody* would know. The whole thing about living in a neighborhood is that you can't keep secrets. Everybody knows everybody else's business. They just don't talk about it to your face."

"Harry told me that Soladias didn't know."

"That's because Soladias doesn't live there and doesn't talk to anybody but his people, who also don't live there. Everybody commutes. Soladias himself has this apartment upstairs of his club on New York Avenue. He just comes to Nevada Avenue with his punks and trashes it."

"Why didn't you leave?"

"I had no other place to go."

"You could have sold the place and left town."

Chou shook his head. "No way. That place, and the land where my parents had their store, is all there is of me. I don't have any roots in China. It's the neighborhood thing. The lifeguards call it having sand in your shoes. Once it's in, you can never shake all of it out."

"My house got torn down," Monroe said. "It's now a strip shopping center. But there was never a neighborhood. We were on this big lot, and you had to go through all these weeds and trees to get to the neighbors."

"It was different on Nevada Avenue," Chou said, his face relaxing. "When you're right up close to people, what you don't see and hear, you don't need much imagination to figure out. For some people, I guess, that's hell. But for me, it was something you could have faith in. No matter how bad things got, there was always a place to come home to, where people wouldn't care about how bad you'd been, or what mistakes you'd made. Even though it would flood there, and the cops took money off my parents, and so much other stuff happened that was just plain terrible, there was a feeling of closeness, of tightness, that things would work themselves out, that I didn't have to be anything different from anybody else."

"What happened to that feeling?"

"I lost it the day I paid Soladias twenty bucks to kill that kid."

◆

What little light had passed through the drawn curtains had faded to a starless black, something rare in Atlantic City, where the floodlit reflections of the casino hotels turned the evening sky a murky pink on all but cloudless evenings.

"Tell me how to get rid of Soladias," Monroe said.

"Kill him."

"That's not an option."

"That's your only option. Anything else, he's too big, too important, too rich."

"How rich?"

"Twenty-one, maybe twenty-two million. It's all over the place, in all kinds of different accounts. And there's the land. He's got more land than any single person in the city. He was just about the only one buying here during the recession. There might be somebody in the Fed, wants to make a name for himself, come down here, listen to me, and launch something to screw the city. But that's all it would do. Tie up his land, tie up his money, and screw the city. This is still my town. I don't want it screwed."

"He's screwing it every day," Monroe said.

"Don't I know it. I thought, If you can't beat him, exploit him, like Reagan did with the Colombian drug cartels, getting them to pay for guns for the really dirty CIA jobs. I remember how everybody was so surprised that that would happen. I wasn't. You're allowed to exploit people that move in but don't fit in. They did that to my parents. My parents let them." His eyes became wet. "They were so happy to be in a place they thought nobody would kill them."

"You should have tried to get him on tax evasion," Monroe said.

"He pays taxes. His returns used to list him as a housepainter. Now he's an investor. He's got every goddamn thing covered. Even me. You'll see, good old reliable Kevin Urlenmeyer will get a call about me taking all that money, or some of the shit I pulled with Ray Deegan and Bigfish and Jerry Lad, and I'll be shit. Or maybe Soladias has a customer—he's got customers all over this town—who works in this hospital, can come in here, give me the kind of medicine that'll end it right there."

"Harry says Soladias isn't holding a grudge," Monroe said. "Besides, you're equal now. You trashed his place and got his car shot up, he did the same back to you."

He brightened. "So it's really going to happen? They're going to pin that medal on me?"

"It might," Monroe said.

"I want Beth to be there. It won't count if she isn't there."

"Why don't you ask her?"

He closed his eyes.

"Why did she burn what you had on Harry and Soladias?"

"Because she's a neighborhood kid, too."

"I thought her folks came out of the Pine Barrens."

"Harry moved to the island to get into politics. They lived down in Chelsea. Beth's as much a neighborhood kid as me."

"Which means?"

"You can go after people in another neighborhood, you can be a pain in the ass if you want, but you don't turn in anybody from your own. Least of all your flesh and blood." He smiled wistfully. "She and me, we used to fit real close."

Monroe thought of his wife and how close they used to fit. What had come between them? Was it just that job? Or was it the fact that she saw him get hurt, and that he was still hurting?

"And now," Chou says, "if I just lie here and do nothing, they'll pin a medal on me."

Monroe stood. "I'm going to get rid of Pieto Soladias."

"Don't even try it. He can kill you, your wife, your kid. He can burn down your house, he can trash your car. He can take everything away from you. How you going to get rid of him?"

"Wasn't it you who said not to worry about how?" Monroe replied.

"Yeah, but I'm nuts. And I'm a bad guy."

"I don't think so," Monroe said. He left and opened the other door. The curtains had been drawn. The face of the figure on the bed was covered in bandages. Both legs were in casts suspended by wires. The white casts and bandages around the figure on the bed rendered him anonymous.

Monroe listened to the rasping sound of drugged sleep. Then he closed the door, picked up his gun, signed out, and went home to see his daughter.

Chapter Fifteen

♦ ♦ ♦ ♦ ♦

Show Cop

Call it beginner's luck. On his first night as a show cop at the municipal tow lot, Monroe got what he needed to bring Soladias down.

He didn't expect it, and, in retrospect, it was too easy. He had gone over the procedural manuals on narcotics arrests. He knew the recipe of a successful bust. He just didn't have any of the ingredients, which were not, unfortunately, available at your neighborhood grocery store.

He put on his uniform and decided that it fit okay. Though he was a detective, and had earned the right to wear whatever clothes he wanted, the show cop's position required that he resemble a cop. You could be a sergeant, a lieutenant, or a captain, and you had to wear the uniform.

That's what Sir Isaac had told him on the phone. "Nothing much you have to learn about the job, except you defer to MacReedy, the lot superintendent. He's the boss there. Very honest. Very upright. Wants things done to the letter of the law."

"I respect people like that," Monroe said.

"I hope so. You don't do what he says, he can have you in for insubordination."

"I follow orders, sir."

"Good. Beyond that, you just have to look the part and act the part."

"Like being on the Boardwalk," Monroe said.

"Except that people are going to be pissed off. You're

there to make them not want to take it any further than that."

"How far can it go?"

"You know why they call Connor MacReedy No-Nose?"

Monroe didn't.

And so Sir Isaac told him of a thin, shriveled relic from the days when the Irish ran city hall who was given the run of the lot when the town was dying and every penny squeezed off a tourist counted for blood.

It was back when Brigantine Boulevard was a narrow strip of asphalt through the marshy no-man's-land between the jumbled suburban housing along the city's west side, and the noisy clam boats in the city marina. The impound lot's office was a wooden shack that, according to legend, had been a duckblind that an associate of an Atlantic County state senator sold to the city for $30,000.

During the first, fabulous summer of legalized casino gambling, when hordes of people lined up to play slot machines, the sudden, unbelievable flood of illegally parked cars provided the funds to pave the impound lot and lace it with a decorative perimeter of milky green concrete blocks. By the time the second casino opened, the lot expanded to two acres. Seeing the need for a more weatherproof facility, an office large enough to hide the expanded safe to hold the cash payments, the city leased a temporary office trailer for the site.

Connor MacReedy was notorious for taking a hard line at the impound lot. No car was released until the towing charge and fine were paid, in cash, no excuses, no exceptions. Once the car was on the lot (and not hidden in the swamps beyond the motor pool) the politically connected, the criminally organized, even members of the clergy had to pay or walk away.

Within days, the trailer's collection window, where MacReedy slithered up to take the money, had to be replaced with reinforced glass because of the harder objects thrown at it. The corrugated aluminum exterior walls of the trailer became pitted and pocked.

When one irate motorist set fire to the trailer's tires, MacReedy proudly extinguished it with the remnants of his coffee Thermos. When that wasn't enough, he unzipped his fly and used "nature's own."

MacReedy distinguished himself among city employees for his ability to withstand such abuse without ever calling for assistance.

But, just as the storm of 1962 nearly removed Atlantic City from God's creation, so did one motorist, many years later, almost send MacReedy to the gates of heaven.

The motorist, an accountant for a Mob-linked amusement-arcade company, decided to vent his disgust by paying his fine with sacks of pennies.

MacReedy didn't blink when he looked down from the reinforced glass collections window at the canvas bank sacks lying in the dirt. Instead, he demanded that the pennies be fed through the window, one at a time. MacReedy announced to the motorist that there would be a delay while he counted every penny, reminding the man that "we don't take Canadian."

MacReedy had counted $8.43 when the accountant, who was also a heavy user of methamphetamine, whipped out an SIG Sauer P230 .32-caliber automatic pistol and started shooting up the office. The bullets tore holes in the trailer's aluminum skin. An aluminum shard caught MacReedy in the face and ripped off most of his nose.

MacReedy didn't even touch his face. He picked himself up off the yellow linoleum on the floor, went to the collections window, the blood, skin, and cartilage hanging down, and glared at the accountant, who had his gun up and aimed to deliver one more shot.

The accountant covered his mouth and went to the bushes, where he vomited up the dinner he had just had with his boss, Paulie "Socks" Marandola.

The man was still retching when MacReedy unlocked the office door and slowly walked down to meet his assailant. He smashed his portable TV set on the guy's head.

Traffic Safety Officer Elizabeth Todesco, the city's first and only female police wrecker driver, was coming in with a car when she saw the TV set come down. She stopped her truck, jumped out of the cab, and, as an Atlantic City Police Officer, made the first and only arrest of her life. She used a tie-down rope from her wrecker to secure her suspect. Then, only after she promised to run the impound lot office in his absence did MacReedy let her drive him to the emergency room of Atlantic City General.

While in the emergency room, MacReedy demanded that what was left of his nose be sewn up. He was back on the lot in two hours.

The accountant was charged with attempted murder, destruction of municipal property, and possession of an unlicensed handgun. MacReedy refused to grant interviews to the media. When a lawyer arrived at the lot with a pot of chrysanthemums and informed him that he could sue the city, and win at least one million in damages, he ordered the lawyer to leave.

Both the mayor and Paulie Marandola visited Mac-Reedy's office. Ironically, they arrived within minutes of each other, the mayor bearing a parchment proclamation, the Mob boss holding a basket of fruit.

They both promised that what had happened would never happen again.

The mayor made good on his promise by having bulletproof steel panels installed around and beneath the office. Inside the office, next to the cash register, was a new color TV, with a cable hookup, paid for by the city.

The mayor further insisted that the police department post an officer, a "show cop," at the impound lot at all times, to keep the peace.

Paulie Marandola also made good. After being released on bail, the accountant who tried to kill MacReedy was discovered in a steamer trunk in the underground parking lot beneath Philadelphia's Liberty Bell Pavillion. He had been shot several times through the nose, and his mouth was stuffed with Canadian pennies.

"Did Beth Todesco get anything out of it?" Monroe asked Sir Isaac.

"Got the blanket taken off some guy."

"Would that be Jack Chou when he was in a mental hospital?"

"Not our Fu Man. Our Fu Man has nothing in his past that would *ever* suggest he was anything more than the great guy he is."

"What if it came out?"

"That *somebody* in the department went mental? He'd be useless. A lawyer would get ahold of it, and no matter how much the judge instructs the jury to ignore aspects of the arresting officer's background that do not pertain to the case, he wouldn't get a single conviction. Newton's Law of the Insanity Offense: 'In a court of law, you can never be a little bit crazy.' "

"So that means, once somebody is declared mentally incompetent, even if they pass all the tests that say they're okay—"

"They're junk. Useless. Unless they can get it expunged from their record, and that takes time and money and more time and money, and even then, people remember. If there's a reason that our Fu Man never signed his name to an arrest report, that's it. Once his name goes on the report, the defense attorney only has to ask if he's ever been declared mentally incompetent, and the ball game's over."

"But the prosecutor will object and the judge will order it stricken from the record," Monroe said.

"But the jury will have heard, and when the defense attorney talks about reasonable doubt, the person the jury will be doubting is you. So give up any fantasy you might have of doing significant police work. Give it up for the rest of your life. On dipshit misdemeanor cases where it's just the judge deciding, you'll win some, lose some. But if it's a major felony, like larceny, grand theft auto, narcotics, or murder, and your name is on the arrest report, it might not even get to trial."

◆

He kissed Sere's sleeping head good night, waved good-bye to Mrs. Pasecki (Ellie had gone to work), and drove to the office trailer sitting in front of four acres of paved, flood-lit, razor-wire-and-chain-link-fenced-in automotive purgatory just off Brigantine Boulevard.

He parked behind the trailer, stepped out slowly, lifting out his left leg, which, despite a few yards of running, was still stiff and uncooperative.

Inside, the gaunt, stooped-shouldered shadow of Lot Superintendent Connor "No Nose" MacReedy perched like a gargoyle, on the edge of a rusting metal folding chair, his blunted beak aimed at a portable TV set. He was watching a *Star Trek* rerun.

Monroe looked around the narrow, boxy trailer, took in the bulky cash register on the desk beside the TV set, the flickering fluorescent lights, the police scanner, a mildewed street map of Atlantic City, a filthy coffee maker resting on a buzzing refrigerator, the oddly tilted water cooler, the grimy metal door leading to the toilet. His eyes were drawn, not to the TV set, but to the heavy hands and big, black numbers of the time clock bolted on the top of the cash register like a stuffed owl.

Monroe introduced himself. He asked MacReedy if there was any system by which he could signal Monroe if the situation outside was getting out of hand. He asked MacReedy if he'd want him to make patrols of the lot's perimeter. He asked MacReedy if he had any specific instructions for him. He asked MacReedy if he gave a shit if he lived or died.

The minute hand on the clock by the cash register hesitated, trembled, jerked forward a notch on the clock, then seemed to hang back, afraid to move forward until it shuddered and jerked again.

At the end of the rerun came another rerun. MacReedy watched it fixedly, pausing only to take money from a woman paying her fine at the bullet-proof window. Mac-Reedy recorded the ticket paid in a ledger on his desk, made change from the register, then pressed a button on his desk that automatically opened the gate on the lot.

He also pressed the button when a city wrecker came by with a car. He'd record the time the gate was opened and wait for radio confirmation of the make, model, and plate number from the driver. Monroe heard Beth Todesco call in a Mercedes. He noted that it was the fifth car she'd towed that night.

Her cars were coming from New York and Nevada Avenues.

"That Beth," MacReedy grunted. "She's hitting 'em."

"Hitting who?"

MacReedy turned his attention to a rerun of *Gilligan's Island.*

Monroe felt stupid standing there. The office contained only one other chair, shoved against a wall. He took it.

He heard the clock tick and already he wanted the shift to end. His neck was still tight. He had to move his body to turn his head to the left and look east, all the way down to the twisted, charred hulks of wrecks that had been removed from city roads, and the dark, unruly swamps beyond. He saw a dark hulk that resembled Soladias's Porsche.

From his chair he could also look west, through the bulletproof collections window, at the lonely pay-phone booth, its door stuck half open and its shredded phone book dangling from a chain, whipping about in the wind, and beyond it the potholed entrance to the lot. In the distance, about two miles away, the red signs on the casino hotel towers beckoned in the cold.

The police scanner, with its cries of urgency and sudden distress, performed a rasping, percussive counterpoint to the bubbly inanity from *Gilligan's Island.*

Beneath the crackle of the laugh track, Monroe heard the cold sighing through old bullet holes whose putty filling had cracked and fallen out. He saw, beside MacReedy's legs, the thin blue line of flame lurking in a kerosene heater.

MacReedy cackled at something on the set.

"Is it really that funny?"

"You never know what to expect," MacReedy said.

Monroe was startled to hear the man's voice. "But it's a rerun."

MacReedy raised his chipped purple-and-green Alcazar Casino Hotel Luck-E Star coffee mug. "Each time it's different. You notice things you didn't see before."

"But it's just a TV show."

MacReedy laughed so hard that the pale, three-sugared, four-creamed coffee jumped out of the mug and darkened the stains on his ripped midnight blue, city-issue storm parka.

Monroe dragged the chair closer and looked over MacReedy's shoulder. The phone, a jangly thing that still had bells in it, rang every few minutes. MacReedy always took the call. He'd check the lot ledger beside his TV set, run his finger down the list of plate numbers, and confirm that a car "matching the description" was towed to the city impound lot.

MacReedy never hid his glee if the car was on the lot. He'd tell the caller that for the city to release the car he'd need a valid license plate, valid registration proving ownership, and a proof-of-insurance card (if he's a New Jersey driver) *as well as* seventy-five dollars for the tow, twenty-five dollars for the fine, and a fifteen-dollar daily lot storage fee, which would double at midnight.

"In cash," MacReedy would add. "We do not accept personal checks, money orders, bank checks, traveler's checks, credit cards, or casino chips."

Monroe couldn't make out what the caller said, but the tinny, painful shriek of rage was obvious and disturbing.

MacReedy replied, "Have a nice day," hung up, turned his shredded face to Monroe, and said, "Heh."

♦

Monroe was losing himself in the question of how people who were shipwrecked on an uncharted island could shave, style their hair, put on makeup, and iron their clothes when he saw, through the collection window, a small group of motorists leaving cabs at the entrance to the lot. Monroe looked for any sign of trouble but they seemed resigned to the misery of paying their fines in the freezing wind, announcing to MacReedy that they hadn't deserved this and that they would never, ever return to Atlantic City.

MacReedy would tell them, "Have a nice day," turn to Monroe, and say, "Heh."

"You do this when Jack Chou was here?"

"I never do nothing else." He turned back to his set.

It was about forty-five minutes to midnight, and a line had already formed outside the payment window. Monroe's lungs had just about collapsed from the kerosene fumes. He stood, zipped up his storm coat, and announced to MacReedy that he was going to work the line "just to keep things quiet."

MacReedy sucked on his coffee, watching *Hogan's Heroes*.

Monroe opened the door and felt the wind hit his face. He stepped down the rickety wooden stairs. The clear, crisp chill in the air, the distant scent of ocean brine, and motorists' sour, defeated gloom reminded him of the stretch he'd pulled as a rookie cop on the Boardwalk beat. You want to know what it feels like to be a loser, go blow a fortune in a casino and then go out and try to walk the Boardwalk. During those long, cold months, Monroe would feel that he had been put on the Boardwalk beat for the reason of assuring losers that *somebody* was worse off than they were.

So what is it about getting your car taken that made these people act as if no one was worse off than they were?

Monroe saw a jumpy guy in the line, maybe a little older, heavier, and happier than he was, bundled up and shivering, telling a shorter, stouter woman in a white down jacket something about pulling down a bundle. As Monroe drew closer to the line, he heard the man's words tumble toward him on the wind.

"—I couldn't believe it. I actually won something. I've been coming here six years and the first time in my life I hit a decent jackpot, they tow my car."

"Shoulda parked in the casina," the woman beside him said.

"You gotta be crazy to park in the casinos," the guy said. "It's unlucky. That's the only reason they got those garages. Because it's unlucky."

"So look at where you are, Mr. Lucky," the woman muttered.

The man trembled in the cold, his round, fleshy face flush with the certainty and confidence that new winners have. "You get what you pay for in this life. Soon as I get my car back, I'm buying me a good time. And I'm feeding the meter."

You go ahead, Monroe said to himself. He had to smile.

His smile faded when he saw the creep in the black leather greatcoat, matching flat-brimmed leather hat, huge black hiking boots. He was either part of Soladias's crowd or wished he was.

The creep was swaggering around the front of the trailer, too impatient to keep still. Sure it was cold, and MacReedy, inside the slightly warmer trailer, liked to take his time processing the citations. But this creep guy couldn't wait.

Monroe figured he'd slow him down. He opened his parka wide enough to reveal his uniform. He stepped up to the creep and flashed his all-purpose Boardwalk smile.

"Uh, hi," he said, knowing that the creep would ignore him.

The creep was young, probably in his early twenties, with thick, brown hair hanging down from his hat. He had makeup around his brown eyes, and some goop on his pocked cheeks that made him appear as if he had a tan.

"Hey buddy, we have a line here," Monroe continued. "These people were here first. Things'll go smoother if you wait on the line."

The creep rolled his lips forward, as if he was about to spit, stepped forward, and banged a black gloved fist on the collection window, where the woman in the white down jacket and pink ski pants was waiting for MacReedy to run a check on her license.

"Hey, you!" he yelled. "I'm ripping your face off if you don't give me the fucking car!"

Monroe dropped his Boardwalk smile. He put his hands around the creep's left hand, twisted the wrist a few inches up and around, causing an excruciating pain to rip through the creep's arm.

The creep's eyes opened almost as fast as his mouth. He said "Gaaah," and bent over. Monroe had to pull him back so that the creep didn't bash his forehead on the trailer.

He let the creep worm his way out of the joint lock. The creep pushed back his hat, put both hands on his waist, and announced, "You fucking touched me."

"I asked you to get back on the line and be patient," Monroe said.

"Fuck you and your fucking patient," the creep said,

skipping back on his heels, aware that everyone was looking at him. He was enjoying the attention. "I don't got the patience to be patient. I want Mr. Soladias's car and I want it now and you're going to get it for me or you're going to get messed up."

Soladias's car?

"Nobody's going to get messed up," Monroe lowered his voice, remembering from his Boardwalk days that you could calm an explosive situation just by taking the level of energy down a notch. "In a few minutes these people will have their turn—"

The creep narrowed his eyes at the woman in the pink ski pants. "I'm done, I'm done," she said, moving away from the window.

"You're *not* done," MacReedy squeaked from inside the trailer. He sneered at the creep. "Get the smelly fuck off my lot, you stinking spic scum."

"Oh, I stink? Would you look at him, tellin' me I stink? No fucking nose on his face and he says I stink," the creep yelled. "A city truck boosted the car, right in front of the Demimonde, Mr. Soladias's restaurant." He pronounced it *ree-stow-ran-tay*. "The bitch hooked it," he insisted. "I have witnesses."

Monroe stepped forward. "Tell me what kind of car you're looking for, and I'll do a double-check."

"Ain't no need—" MacReedy began, a slight quaver in his voice.

"You're not going to check nothing, you shit," the creep said, pointing a long, gloved finger at Monroe's chest. "You're going to get Mr. Soladias's car. Now."

Monroe counted to ten. "You'll have to tell me—"

The creep put his hands on his head, as if Monroe's ignorance were causing him the intense mental anguish that inspires lawyers to sue. "I don't have to tell you nothing. You boosted it. You get it back. Everybody knows Mr. Soladias's car."

"Black Porsche 928GT, New Jersey vanity license plate M-R-K-R-A-K, or, 'Mr. Crack,' " MacReedy said from the window.

"Not that one," the creep yelled. "The other one. The Mercedes. The lawyer's car."

"Wouldn't put it past old Cheez," MacReedy snickered. "Let's see a license and registration, shithead."

"Back up a minute," Monroe said. "You have to tell us what kind of car it is."

The creep clenched his fists and spit. "It's a Mercedes, asshole!"

Monroe remembered seeing a half dozen Mercedes on the lot. And he didn't like being called an asshole. "Talk decent and we'll handle this."

"Asshole up there call me a shithead."

That's because he's an asshole, Monroe was about to say.

"He don't have no right to call me a shithead."

Monroe looked up at MacReedy. "Mr. MacReedy was just about to apologize."

"I was certainly *not!*" MacReedy shrieked. "That . . . that deesgusting dirt ball there can kiss my nuts before I'd say a civil word to him."

"You wanna talk about *deesgusting*?" the creep shouted back. "See this nose what I got on my face? It don't look like no asshole. What you got is an asshole. Right in the middle of your fucking face."

"About this Mercedes," Monroe said. "I need a license, registration—"

"And pay the fine," MacReedy added, "paid, in cash, in full."

The creep rushed Monroe, stopping short of grabbing him. "Mr. Soladias don't pay no fines. Beside. The car was legal parked. You don't give it back, I kill your ass."

"That's it!" MacReedy barked. "You're off my goddamn lot. Fuck you and your goddamn car." He glared down at

Monroe. "Get the shithead out of here."

The creep reached for something under his coat and Monroe came in, trapped the hand with his right, and swept the creep's front foot with his right leg. The creep went down, hard, on his ass. Monroe spun him around, drove the hand into his back, pinned the hand with his right knee, and, when the creep didn't struggle, began to pat him down. Monroe pulled out a gleaming silver balisong knife in an inlaid leather case.

"Bring the bitch!" the creep shouted. "Bring the bitch. Bring her here. She took the car. It was legal."

Monroe found the creep's wallet. He forced his left hand to pull out the expired New Jersey learner's permit inside that identified the bearer as Akembe Augustino of five South Constitution Avenue, Atlantic City.

The wallet was stuffed with one-hundred-dollar bills.

Monroe put the learner's permit back into the wallet and handed it back to him, and helped him to his feet.

"Mr. Augustino, I hope you took a cab here."

"Mr. Soladias going to kill all you for this."

"Mr. Augustino, your learner's permit is expired," Monroe said.

"I want the car, man!" He began to cry.

"Not tonight," Monroe said. He glanced at the other people on line, who turned around, as if they hadn't been watching the show, and busied themselves with their purses and wallets.

The creep blotted his eyes with leather gloves and kicked the gravel with his feet. "Gimme the knife back."

"I'm keeping that," Monroe said.

"Mr. Soladias gave it to me personally. I lose it, I have to pay for it. Mr. Soladias charges a lot for his knives."

"From what I saw in your wallet, you can cover the loss."

"You take the money, man."

"I don't take money," Monroe said.

"*Everybody* take money. Asshole in the window say he want it. You give it."

"We can only release vehicles to licensed drivers," Monroe said.

Augustino rubbed his face and looked at the luxurious leather gloves on his hands, which had been ripped when he fell. "What the fuck is this? I parked that car right, man. I put fucking money in the meter. Mr. Soladias told me, he say, from now on, we do everything legal, and I did it, man. I did it."

"Whatever happened, I wasn't there to see it," Monroe said, helping him up. "Mr. Soladias can come out and get his car, or his lawyer, or whoever owns it."

"That's the thing, man, Mr. Soladias don't know it's missing," the creep said. "I'm his driver tonight. I drive him and I put him right out front like he want and . . ." He looked at Monroe. "Mr. Soladias have a lot of car trouble already. You should hear him talking about it. He'll kill me if I don't have his car back."

"He won't kill you," Monroe said. "Criminals who are going legit don't kill people."

"Shit, man, where you been? Long as I been with Mr. Soladias, he don't do nothing himself no more. He just say the word, and Lukee or Jesus do it. Just today, I driving him to the ree-stow-ran-tay, I heard him say, 'Pepe going to die of natural causes.' They have a somebody, inside the hospital, who sells drugs to Mr. Soladias. He going to do it."

Monroe saw the fear in Augustino's pitted face. "Can you get a name and description of this person in the hospital?"

"What you thinking, man?"

"I'm thinking that if you can come up with a name and description, I can put you into protective custody, you tell your story to . . . you tell your story to somebody . . . I can't make any promises or any deals. But if we get Soladias on what you tell us, you will never, ever have to worry about him again."

"You don't know Mr. Soladias. You can't get him on what I say."

"It can start the ball rolling," Monroe said. "Wait with me in the office over there until I go on my break. We'll go someplace we can talk, you tell it all to me. Then I'll get somebody from the department to listen to you, and then you're in."

"Sergeant Pratt. I saw him on the TV, making the speech. I tell him, okay?"

Monroe agreed and led him past the line, up the rickety steps, and into the trailer.

MacReedy stood and pointed and said, "This facility is not open to the public."

"He's with me," Monroe said. "He's going to wait for me until my break and then—"

"That filthy shithead goes outside," MacReedy roared.

"You ain't calling me no filthy shithead!" Augustino snapped back.

Monroe stepped between them. "It's freezing outside," he said. "He's only going to be here until I go on break."

"He's going outside because it's the *law*!" MacReedy shouted. "We en*force* the *law*. Out he goes."

"In that case, I'm going on my break right now, okay?"

MacReedy shook his head. "Not now. Not at midnight. This is the busiest goddamn time here. You're leaving at o-one-hundred hours, or when I have determined I no longer require your presence, whichever comes first."

Monroe took his car keys from his pocket. "Okay. You'll wait in my car downstairs. Put the heater on—"

MacReedy sneered. "This shithead don't look old enough to operate a vehicle. Let's see a license. He have a license on him?"

Augustino pointed for him. "I don't need no fucking license to rip your fucking face off."

"Listen," Monroe said. "I'll turn on the car. You sit in the front seat. Put the heater on when you need it. . . ." Then he remembered. He barely had enough gasoline to make it here. He had planned to get more on his break.

"The environmental protection statute prohibits the idling of vehicles on municipal property in coastal zones!" MacReedy said.

"What's he going to do," Monroe said, exasperated, "freeze?"

"Hope so." MacReedy glared. "Shit don't stink when it's frozen."

Augustino took a swing at MacReedy but Monroe pulled him back. "Do this for me," Monroe said. "Meet me at this deli on Atlantic Avenue. It's called Schneckle's, you know where it is?"

"Shit, man, I know where everything is," Augustino said. "And I can see Mr. Soladias's motherfucking car right out to his window here. It's that Mercedes sitting right there."

"The cream-colored one?"

"The green one. That's his lawyer's car."

"*I said out!*" MacReedy screamed.

Monroe walked Augustino to the door. "Take a cab. Go somewhere. Hang out. At one A.M., I'll be there."

Augustino pointed at MacReedy. "You are a fucking liar, you asshole-face! That car is right there. It was parked legal—"

MacReedy had a joyous expression as he pulled out a Mossberg 500 Security shotgun from under the desk, pumped it, and aimed it.

"You're not going to fire that in here," Monroe said. "It would come right back in your face."

"Risk I gotta take." MacReedy grinned.

"Call a cab," Monroe told Augustino. To MacReedy: "I don't suppose he can use the phone?"

"Personal calls are not to be made on the municipal telephone system, at any time, by any individual. There's a pay telephone sitting outside for your convenience."

"I don't got no quarter," Augustino said, his eyes on the shotgun. "I put the last one in the meter."

Monroe gave him one and opened the door. "Schneckle's at one, okay? If I'm late, wait for me."

Augustino turned to MacReedy. "When I get famous, I come back, I do to you what Mr. Soladias do. I cut your fucking head off, man."

MacReedy said to Monroe, "I order you to arrest this shithead for creating a public nuisance, making terroristic threats, defiling public property, extortion of municipal services."

Monroe said, "No way, Jose." He went out with Augustino. A cab was unloading more disgruntled motorists, this time what appeared to be a group of nightclub revelers. Augustino ducked into the cab and said, "You got a shitty job, man. When I'm famous, I'll take you with me."

"That's okay," Monroe said. "I'd rather say I knew you when."

♦ ♦ ♦ ♦ ♦

Chapter Sixteen

Santa Claus

As the minute hand drew closer to toward 1 A.M., Monroe decided to let MacReedy have it.

"You didn't have to antagonize him," Monroe said.

MacReedy's face was inches from the TV set.

"I mean, what the hell are you doing to people here?" Monroe said. "Okay, some of them are a pain in the ass. They're stupid, they're loud, they act like assholes sometimes. But why do we have to rub their faces in it? They've made a mistake. They're here to pay for it. So why can't we just be decent to them?"

MacReedy turned up the volume of the set.

"Go ahead and pretend you can't hear me," Monroe said. "I'm sick of it. This town went belly-up because it dumped on tourists and it'll go belly-up again, and casinos and fancy building projects won't save it."

MacReedy made the set louder. Then he lowered the volume. "Sir Isaac send you down?"

"Yes."

"He's gonna send you right back."

Monroe was about to leave when the phone rang. MacReedy listened, handed it to Monroe. "This one's for you."

Monroe heard pulsing dance music. "Impound Lot, Detective Monroe."

Soladias laughed at him. "Hey, man, how's it going? Got something for you. In the bag, you know? You supposed to come to my place. Maybe you pick it up."

"I don't want anything from you," Monroe said.

"Shit, man, sometimes, you know, what is it, a horse that's a gift, you look in the mouth. I'd go see you, look in your mouth, but I'm having car trouble." He laughed again. "Very American. Car trouble. Look it in the mouth."

"I can't understand you," Monroe said.

"It's okay, man. When you rich, everybody understand you, and you sing real good too, you know? But, everybody pissed, about the car trouble. Everybody in the city. I send some boys out. They fix you right."

He cut the connection and Monroe told MacReedy who it was on the phone and that they'd better call for backup.

"We ain't calling for help," MacReedy said.

Monroe had his radio up but got nothing but static.

"There ain't no radio that works right in here," MacReedy said. "All the metal they put around us. This here," he pointed at the TV set, "is on the cable."

He saw the police scanner's antenna wire going up and through the trailer. Beside it was a transmitter. He went to pick it up and MacReedy yanked away the transmitter microphone.

The phone rang again. MacReedy took the call. He held the phone for about five seconds, keeping his attention on the Professor and Mary Ann. "Yes, Sergeant. I'll tell him." He hung up and said, "Sergeant Pratt's coming down."

Monroe went for the door. "I'm going on break."

"You ain't going nowhere until I release you and that is an order."

"I have to go on break now," Monroe said. "You have no idea how important this is."

MacReedy went to the door, locked it inside with a key, and put the key in his pocket. "It ain't that important, then."

They came three minutes later, three enormous, dark limousines, a black Jaguar and the dark blue official business car, some other cars, one with the Atlantic City *Star*'s logo on it, and two television news vans.

When MacReedy saw the television vans he backed away from the collection windows.

Pratt, in a heavy black wool chesterfield coat, swung his legs out of the official business car, poking the uneven gravel of the lot's driveway with his cane as he came to the collection window.

"Now you let me handle this, Mr. MacReedy, and everything's going to be cool."

MacReedy fearfully motioned Monroe to sit in his chair in front of the window. Monroe hesitated, then complied, looking through the grimy glass as the television-van lights came on, blinding him.

He looked down, hiding his eyes, and saw Pratt standing beneath the window with Councilman Todesco in a similar black chesterfield.

"That you up there, Louis?" Todesco said. "Good to see you, son."

Pratt said, "How many cars you got on the lot?"

Monroe turned to MacReedy. "Fifty-seven in violation, four seizures due to improper documentation, seventeen abandoned vehicles, twenty-one wrecks or stripped vehicles that cannot be driven, for a total of ninety-nine," Monroe told him.

"How much owed on the ones you can drive away?"

MacReedy recited the figure. "Fourteen thousand one hundred and sixteen and ninety-two cents, payable in cash, with proper documentation."

Monroe relayed the figure. Pratt mentioned it to Todesco, who said, "No problem."

The lights dimmed and Monroe felt every second leaking away as the television sound technicians fussed with volume levels. Monroe saw a female reporter from the Atlantic City *Star* joking with Pratt.

Behind the vans, a group of Soladias's men were shuffling in the cold.

Finally the lights came back on and Darrell Pratt said, "I think everybody's heard of the councilman, here. When he told me what he was going to pull, I just about fell out of my bed. This just doesn't happen in our town. Well, thanks to the councilman, it does. It's Christmastime, ladies and gentlemen, and the man I'd like you to meet is Santa Claus."

Todesco took the microphone and said, "Thank you, Sergeant Pratt. I think I'll grow a beard, get all the pretty girls to sit on my lap." He winked at the female reporter, who waved her hand and said, "About that sex harassment . . ."

"We'll get to that. No. Let me deal with that now. I said when those charges were filed that they were false, malicious, and that they represented an attack on everything I've held dear. Since then, we've discovered, thanks to the diligence of our police department"—he nodded at Pratt—"that the individual bringing those charges is a former prostitute, and, no doubt, something of a shakedown artist. This revelation puts the charges against me in the right perspective. I don't think we have to concern ourselves about them any longer.

"Now, on to more important things. I want to tell you that I can't reveal, as yet, the name of the individual who is providing seed money for the Miracle Mile project. But I can tell you that he, and not myself, is the real Santa Claus. I've been meeting with him rather steadily for some time, and Mr. Salazar—"

It was a calculated slip.

"Spell that, Councilman?" The reporters hefted their portable tape recorders higher.

Todesco appeared to be embarrassed. "I'll ask all of you to disregard that. It's late and my tongue can wag. As

I was saying, I've been meeting rather steadily with"—he smiled—"and I mentioned to him that some people, through no fault of their own, can make a mistake about parking in this city, and that, being that it's Christmastime and that people need their cars, he's agreed to pay every fine, in full, for every vehicle on the lot, as a Christmas present to the people who visit our wonderful World's Playground."

"In cash," MacReedy whispered. "Make sure."

But Todesco had a signed check in his hand. He entered the figure *$15,000* and handed it to Darrell Pratt, who held it up so the cameras could photograph it.

A reporter asked Pratt to move his thumb. Pratt obliged.

Another said, "Who's Peter Salazar?"

"That will be revealed, in time," Todesco said.

Pratt said, "On behalf of the police department, I just want to remind individuals that this procedure does not excuse or condone motor-vehicle violations. But if you got a car on our lot, well, come and get it!"

He passed the check in the window to Monroe. "Open the gate, Lou," Pratt said.

Monroe gave the check to MacReedy. "But this ain't cash," MacReedy said. "We can't do nothing, this ain't cash. And we got to see documentation and identification and—"

"I said, *open it*, Lou. And that's an order."

According to police procedure, orders from ranking officers are to be obeyed over civilian requests. Monroe hit the worn, chipped lever beneath the window and heard the electric motor whine and watched the floodlights shift to capture Soladias's people rushing forward to take the cars.

MacReedy watched it from the far window. "Ain't no way in hell half those boys is old enough to drive. How they going to know what cars is theirs?"

"They don't have to," Monroe said. "They're going to steal them all."

♦

It was nearly two A.M. when he filled his car's tank at an all-night gas station at the foot of the expressway, then shot up Atlantic Avenue to the deli, noticing that Beth Todesco's wrecker wasn't anywhere on the street.

Augustino hadn't arrived. He took a booth in the back, ordered coffee, and waited.

At 0222 hours, Beth Todesco came in, saw him, took a booth in the front, facing away from him.

At 0237 hours, she got up from her booth and said, "Lunch?"

She had the drawn, weary expression of someone who had just surrendered an entire empire.

"I'm expecting someone," Monroe said.

"Me, too." She sat across from him.

On cue Babe brought more coffee.

She waited until their food came.

"So who's the new girl?" she began.

"There's no girl," he said.

"But you wish there was," she said. "I can pick up on that."

"What you should pick up on is that the only person I want is my wife."

"But you don't want her as she is."

"You should talk."

"That's why I'm talking."

He took a bite and was conquered by the sweet, cheesy, greasy explosion of calories, cholesterol, and everything else that was bad for him.

"He needs you," he said.

"He put you up to telling me."

"He didn't have to. It's pretty obvious."

She chewed her sandwich. "I thought he'd be different. And he turned out to be just like my father."

"I don't think so," Monroe said. "I think your father

knows what he's doing. Jack just got caught up in it."

"But he enjoyed it. You have to admit that. He enjoyed breaking the law, pulling shit, making a total menace out of himself."

She licked her fingers. "I got better things to do. Tonight was harass Pieto Soladias night. I towed every expensive car parked on Nevada Avenue and New York Avenue near his club."

"There were that many violations?"

"None. I towed them whether the meters were filled or not. Municipal agencies are allowed to make mistakes. Somebody has proof that the meter was pumped, or it was defective, they take it to traffic court and they get their money back." She stretched her arms and yawned, like a cat curling up on a hot radiator.

Monroe lost his appetite. Augustino had been telling the truth. "You checked in with MacReedy recently? Or your father?" he asked her.

"Why should I?"

Monroe told her.

She tried to hide her frustration. She failed. Finally, she asked him who he had been waiting for.

But all Monroe heard was the ratcheting sound of the handcuffs and felt himself hanging under a pier, the ocean swirling around his feet, feeling the impact in his face and his gut, a baseball bat on his left knee and collarbone, the garden hose on his ribs, his legs and his arms and the laughter. Why were they laughing? Why were they doing this to him? Why was it, when you try so hard not to give up, not to give in . . .

"Lou? Are you okay?"

He felt himself sinking deeper into the scene, the blows bringing dull grunts to his mouth. He wanted to escape, but he also wanted the scene to play out. He had to stay to the end because he had to know, he had to hear the shots from his gun, he *wanted* to kill someone.

She showed concern. "I say something or what?"

He felt himself on the edge of death and feeling helpless, and hating himself for being so helpless as Claymore told him that he was going to kill him, and he said, "No," and it made him smile and the smile brought his right leg up and it kicked at Reuben Claymore's face, kicked him in the mouth, hit him in his big, open, laughing face. He watched Reuben Claymore go back, smash the back of his head against a wooden pier, and fall down as the ocean rose up to take him and pull him under.

And then it was over.

"What happened to you?"

"I . . ." he paused. "I saw it through."

"Saw what through?"

"The memory. This thing that keeps replaying in my head. I saw it to the end."

"And what happened?"

He asked himself if he should tell her that he had killed a man, and that the memory had informed him what he had been refusing to face all along: that he hadn't acted in self-defense, that it wasn't pain or fear for his life or his loved ones that had motivated him to put his foot in that mouth. He'd *wanted* to kill Reuben Claymore. It wasn't a choice based on logic, necessity, or moral wisdom as much as it was a desire born in self-hatred.

He asked himself if he should tell her that when he understood he was capable of evil, it was as if the blanket slipped off and he had finally come completely into the light.

"Nothing happened," Monroe said. "I'm still here. You're still here. We're still looking at each other, wondering why it is we ended up with the people we ended up with."

She sighed again. "You got that right."

"Because what we don't want to admit is that you're with Jack and I'm with Ellie because we wanted to be with them."

"We made a mistake."

"We didn't make a mistake," Monroe said. "We stopped trusting ourselves."

"Trust has nothing to do with it—"

"It has everything to do with it. Things turned out the way we didn't expect, so, instead of accepting the situation, or doing something to make it better, we blamed ourselves for making a mistake."

"And look where it got us?"

They were quiet for a while, the rasping, broken, abbreviated tales of crime and crises of Monroe's police radio filling the void.

"Can I ask you something?"

She said, "Anything."

"How can you eat that all the time and not gain weight?"

"Did Jack tell you to ask me that? Or is it 'you show me your problems, I show you mine'?"

He wanted to tell her that he admired the way her skin was so thin as to be almost translucent. She certainly didn't make his heart beat faster, but he found that he was comfortable with her. One of the things you learn when you're married is that it's important to be comfortable with a person.

He wanted to be comfortable again with his wife.

"I go into the bathroom and vomit it up," she told him. She gobbled a french fry. "There. Now you can despise me."

"I don't despise you."

"Jack is the only man I ever met who didn't give a crap about me being fat or thin."

"See? Maybe you made the right decision in marrying him."

"But he wanted to have kids. You get fat when you have kids. That's one of the reasons we split up. He wanted to have kids and I was sure that as soon as I got pregnant I'd get fat and he'd leave me for another woman who was thin. I was sure of it."

"That's the real reason you broke up? It didn't have to do with him having something on your father?"

"You can't bring down Harry Todesco with a column of figures in a loose-leaf notebook. And that sexual harassment thing? No way."

"She has a right to get justice."

"And she'll get it," Beth said. "He's been pinched for cash lately, but he'll chop half those cars Soladias's boys stole off the tow lots. That'll bring in some cash. Then he'll just buy her off."

"But if he's harassing her, he should stop."

"He'll stop if it costs him enough money. And the whore will get hers. That's all that whore wants, money."

"Beth, you can't possibly say that. So many of those women just get caught up in a situation that they can't control—"

But a wall had gone up between them.

She said, "Go fuck yourself," grabbed her purse, and went to the lavatory.

♦

Monroe had a french fry in his hand and was thinking about eating it when he heard on the radio Officer Jerry "Lad" Ladzinsky calling in an eighty-six—body found—at Nevada Avenue and Jefferson Place. "He's a male, missing some parts."

"Roger, Ladzinski," said the dispatcher. "What parts?"

"The head and whatever's on it."

"Say again, Ladzinski."

"Victim is male, late fifties, maybe older, decapitated at the throat below the jawline. Flesh is still warm. Well dressed. Nice suit. Looks like he was dumped from a moving vehicle."

"Roger, Lad. You see the head anywhere?"

Bigfish came on. "Negatory. But we don't got his pants off yet. Maybe it's there."

Monroe put down the french fry and lowered the volume on the radio until the voices were whispers. He could no longer eat.

He thought of Beth Todesco and wanted to ask her if she understood that he was trying to help her and that he respected her and valued her friendship.

Tell that to your wife, he said to himself.

She emerged from the lavatory, bright, cheery, as if no bad words had been said. They paid the bill and walked out into the cold, dark, empty quiet of the street. Her truck, *Whiskey Alpha Five*, slumbered, parked in front of the fire hydrant. A black, plastic garbage bag had been hung from the boom.

"Oh, my God," she said, "something's in there."

Chapter Seventeen

♦ ♦ ♦ ♦ ♦

On the Boardwalk with My Baby

Homicide Detectives Dousmanis and Phelps were amazingly brief. In a large banquette in the back of Schneckle's, Dousmanis sat facing the front of the deli so he could look up and see who was coming. When he wasn't looking up, he wrote down Monroe's and Todesco's answers to his questions.

He asked Monroe and Todesco when they'd left the lot, how long they'd been at the deli. He finished by asking Monroe to describe what had happened when they saw the wrecker and pulled Akembe Augustino's head out of the garbage bag.

"Aren't you going to ask me who might have done this?" Monroe asked.

Detective Sergeant Dousmanis, his dark, swarthy, mole-pocked face decorated with shaving cuts, checked what he'd written on his pad and said, "No."

Phelps, a slim, balding, Black man with a crew cut who moved as if at any second the floor would fall out from under him, returned from supervising the crime-scene crew around the wrecker. "How many people might've been awake and not under the influence of alcohol, tobacco, or firearms and still walking on the avenue way down here at two A.M. and saw the fuckers that put the bag on the truck?"

"Zero," Dousmanis said, making a note.

"He came on the lot to get a car that was towed—"

Todesco banged her foot against his.

Phelps picked up a coffee cup that had been left on the table by the medical examiner and drank. He stopped, put down the cup, picked out a cigarette, dropped the soggy cigarette in front of Monroe, paused as if it required effort to remember what Monroe had said. "We talked to Mac-Reedy. When we need a show cop that gives blow jobs to drug dealers and hangs off the mayor's asshole," Phelps said calmly, "we know where to find him."

"I feel *responsible*," Monroe said, struggling to hold back his rage.

Todesco kicked him again, harder.

Phelps asked Dousmanis, "How many people you think are going to be pissed off about this kid getting scratched?"

Dousmanis let out a sigh as if he'd just dropped a load. "Family, if he's got one."

"Family?" Phelps put down the cup and then picked out the cigarette with two fingers.

"They should never've locked up Paulie Marandola. You never saw this shit when he was around."

"Or you saw." Phelps smiled. "But you didn't look."

Dousmanis closed his notebook and Phelps did his nervous strut to the front of the deli. "You're done. Both of you."

"There are some leads you might want to check out," Monroe said.

"I'm sure," Dousmanis groaned as he stood.

"You're not going to ask me about them?"

Dousmanis shook his head.

"Why?"

Under the table, Monroe felt Beth Todesco's hand clamp down on his.

Dousmanis yawned again. "You're not important," he said and walked to the front.

Monroe waited for Todesco to move out of the banquette. She was making short, sniffing sounds. When she didn't move he turned and saw her holding herself rigid, tears on her face. Her hand was still on his, under the table, but it felt cold. Monroe turned over his hand and held hers, meshing his fingers with hers. They didn't respond.

"It's not your fault," Monroe said to her.

"It is," she said, removing her hand from his. "We let Soladias live."

He heard Todesco's sniffles grow louder as she walked out of the deli and onto the street. The crime-scene squad still hadn't finished with the wrecker so a patrolman offered to drive her back to the lot. He held the car door open for her, bowed as she got in, and slammed the door shut when he saw Monroe.

Monroe experienced one of those moments when a man falls in love with his car. He put his key into his Z and the engine started as if to say, "Where've you been?"

♦

Mrs. Pasecki was feeding Sere when he returned to the apartment.

Ellie was still at the casino.

"Another big meeting?" Monroe went into the kitchen, picked up the phone, dialed his wife's extension, and got her answering machine. "Hi, there. This is Elle Monroe. You've reached my voice mail—"

Elle Monroe? She was calling herself Elle now? She always called herself Ellie around him. He hung up and dialed the casino's main switchboard.

The Alcazar's operator answered and he demanded that she page Mrs. Ellen Monroe.

"Sir, it's four in the morning—"

"I know what time it is. I'm her husband. I want to know where the hell she is."

He was transferred into the marketing department. "Good evening. You've reached the voice mail of the Alcazar Marketing Department. To speak to a casino host, press number one on a Touch-Tone telephone, or, if you want to leave a message—"

Monroe stabbed the number one. The host desk, located on the casino floor, picked up, and Monroe heard the distant noise and clatter of the casino behind a vivacious female voice. "Hi, this is Margory and I hope you're having a terrific time at the Alcazar. What can I do to make it even better?"

"I'm not at the Alcazar and I want to speak to Mrs. Ellen Monroe. I want to know if she's on the property."

"Mrs. Monroe is . . . on the property, sir, but, it really *is* late—"

"I'm her husband. Either I speak to her now or I'm coming over there and I'm going to find her."

"I'm sorry, sir, I didn't catch your name. . . ."

Monroe told her. She told him to wait and he heard a syrupy sea of up-tempo pop music, with a refrain of "Be a Luck-ee Star at the Al-ca-zar."

He became aware that Mrs. Pasecki was standing beside him, holding Sere in her arms. Monroe saw his wife in the baby's face and his anger drained from him. He held out a finger and watched her tiny hand wrap around it.

She said, "Gahh."

"Gahh gahh to you, too," Monroe said.

"This is what you got to be happy for," Mrs. Pasecki said.

Monroe said, "Did Ellie tell you why she wasn't coming back?"

"Did she tell *you*?" Mrs. Pasecki asked him.

"No, she didn't tell me." He felt Sere's hand touch his face. "That's Daddy's beard. That's Daddy's mouth. That's Daddy's neck—"

He remembered the head he'd found in the garbage bag and grimaced. Sere pulled back her hand. He tickled her foot.

Then the music gave way and Margory came back on.

"Mrs. Monroe is a guest at the hotel tonight. I've located her room, sir. Please hold."

He held his hand up and his heart began to thud in his chest as he heard the first ring.

Sere reached for his hand on the second ring. By the third ring he was hoping that there may not be an answer, that he would have the good sense to hang up and acknowledge that—

On the fifth ring a man's voice said a very weary, "This is Carl."

Monroe heard a sleepy female sigh in the background. He'd heard that sigh before.

The voice on the phone repeated, "This is Carl."

"It's probably a mistake," Ellie said. "Hang up."

Monroe brought the phone down with a crash. Sere's eyes went round, her chin wrinkled, and then she cried. Mrs. Pasecki moved her away, patting her back as she tried to calm her down. "Daddy's upset tonight, dear."

"My wife should be *here*."

"It's okay, Sere girl, it's okay."

"It's not okay," Monroe said.

Mrs. Pasecki paused, sighed, and agreed. "Your father's right. It's not okay. But sometimes, if we want to stop crying, we have to pretend that things are different. So pretend, girl. That's it. Everything's going to work out. Your Daddy's not going to leave you. What's out there that's so important for him to leave you?"

"She really thinks I'm going to leave her?" He came near her and she turned her head away. "I'm not going anywhere, Sere. I—I just got mad, that's all. Not at you. Mad at . . . mad because I can't be sure about some things."

◆

She was naked, her skin cold, on top of him, waking him up, telling him in a voice that cut into him, "This is what you want, isn't it?"

239

His wife.

The lights were off, a trace of predawn blue was spilling into the bedroom. They hadn't made love since before he'd gone into the hospital. Ellie had been pregnant then, her breasts tremendous, her belly falling between them, the skin tight and warm and moving with the child inside. They had been careful, then, quiet and gentle and unhurried.

There was nothing gentle in her now as she clawed at him, her anger obvious and intimidating as she grabbed him and forced him, and herself, into arousal. The room was too cold and Monroe wondered if the heater had gone on the blink. He was about to say that he didn't think he could do this when he discovered that he could.

But unlike the awkward, arrhythmic steps that proved to him that he could run again, or the words Sere had uttered, Monroe shared no joy in this discovery. His body's strength and heat were being pulled from him, taken from him into the coldness of the room and the woman above him, who had brought with her the casino hotel aromas of tobacco smoke and alcohol.

He put his hands on her thighs to stop her, or at least slow her, but felt how strong and smooth they were, the muscles dancing under the skin. Monroe was surprised; the voluptuous softness that had attended her pregnancy had been burned off in the casino's spa. Her legs held him like claws, imprisoning him until he could do nothing but surrender to the force that made him arch his back and rise on his legs and push up as she descended until he became almost an extension of her, reminded of his otherness when cramps appeared in his uncooperative left arm and leg. He kept moving and the cramps faded.

He let his hands glide up until they brushed the ridges of her chest, his left slower until she bent low and her breast fell into the hand, the nipple raking his palm. He held the other breast and looked up into her face, now glistening from the effort. He felt the hot breath from her open mouth, saw her eyes wide, bearing down and *through* him, fixed on some deep destination that her rage and lust was pushing them toward.

There was no love in this, he realized, none of the gentle, caring regard that had made him feel, in the days when she was pregnant and he could run miles and miles, that it was her soul wrapped around him.

As soon as the realization surfaced in his mind, it was lost, drowned in a torrential flood of need for her that he had repressed. That need made him halt, shudder, slide himself against her, slowing her relentless progress until he was poised, as if on the edge.

She stopped, put her scalding hands over his, pushing her breasts flatter, the nipples burning him. She trembled and the rage that had been driving her abruptly ceased. He sensed it leaving her and she became lighter on him, almost weightless.

In the luminous blue of morning he saw her face gleaming with sweat. Droplets hung on her nose, on her chin, on her eyes. She bent her head and it looked as though she could have been crying. He couldn't tell. For a minute or so, her eyes were shut tight, and first one, then two drops fell on him.

The drops were warm on his face, and so were her hands, still holding his hands to her breasts, and Monroe was again overwhelmed by the shock of how beautiful she was and how *much* he had wanted her, and that desire, rising like a wave, rushed him into her. She let go of his hands, rocking back, her eyes open and surprised.

Then, balancing, she laughed and bore down on him, recklessly, violently, not caring about his injured limbs, and it was in that careless moment that the wave crested and Monroe felt his mind and his heart and his seed leap up into her.

She kept going, urged on by his pleasure. Then he heard her breath go deeper, stronger, slower, as she pushed herself down on him and threw her head back, her body becoming rigid, her breasts suddenly motionless before him, her hands on his chest gripping him, the nails scratching his skin.

Then she took off, her voice making soft, murmuring sounds as she found her pleasure, savored it, and then lay gently on him, her face wet against his neck, her lips on his shoulder, her breath slowing to the rhythm of sleep.

Monroe knew she wasn't sleeping. But to say anything would disturb the calm, rosy peace, this wonderful feeling of closeness that, for all the things that seemed to be tearing them apart, had, for once, kept them together.

Disturbing the peace—that was against the law, wasn't it?

◆

Sere slept late again. Both Ellie and Monroe were awake and ready when she stirred in her crib in the living room. Working in tandem, they changed her, prepared her morning bottle, fed her, sharing the newspaper.

Monroe read that Akembe Augustino had been raised by his mother, a former prostitute, in various Atlantic City low-income housing projects. He had been part of the Make the Grade program at Atlantic City Regional High School, where an anonymous donor had agreed to provide funds for disadvantaged Atlantic City students that would pay all their college expenses as long as they graduated from school with a B average.

"Something wrong, Louis?" Ellie asked him carefully.

He mentioned what had happened with Cynthia Verheull.

"We can't have her jeopardizing the Miracle Mile. She's going to be bought out," Ellie said. "As long as she keeps her mouth shut, she'll be okay."

"Does Harry Todesco have that much money?"

"No," Ellie said, looking away. "But others do."

Then he saw that Pepe Medina, the assailant charged with wounding Traffic Safety Detective Jack Chou, had died last night when an inadvertently high dosage of pain-killers was administered.

Then they went, as a family, for a stroll along the northern edge of the Boardwalk, the winter wind rubbing their faces pink as it added a light, high chop to the water in Absecon Channel.

The Boardwalk was narrow along the northern edge of the Inlet. He looked to his left, across the channel to the sand dunes of Brigantine and the jumble of angular summer palaces and boxy condos crowding the beach. To his right, Monroe gazed into the Inlet and imagined, amid the new low-income housing projects and vacant lots, a house that he would design and build for his wife and child. It wouldn't be a large, pretentious seashore palazzo, like the oversized mansions a few miles to the south, in Ventnor, Margate, and Longport.

But it would have some things. He imagined a sundeck on the roof, and plenty of glass on the third floor to fill the house, and Sere's playroom, with warmth and light. On the second floor he'd want a wide room with a ceiling high enough so he could have a mat and practice his jumps and falls. The ground floor would be mostly a garage for the cars, with enough room for him to work on them. Monroe didn't have any hobbies, but, if he picked something to fill his time, it would be restoring old cars—not antiques, but cars that he personally liked. He saw himself slowly re-storing his 280Z until it gleamed.

Of course, the Inlet would have to change for him to want to build a house in it. A mix of markets, shops, and small restaurants would have to occupy the street corners where the kids sold drugs. And the city itself would have to change: the rip-off mentality that characterized all seashore communities but reached an untoward intensity in Atlantic City, would have to mellow. People would have to realize that there's more to making a living at the shore than getting rich by exploiting tourists and gamblers who, though they could be so foolish as to hope their dreams would come true here, deserved more from a visit to the Jersey Shore than being turned into victims.

He looked down at his daughter's hooded head poking up in the stroller. Having spent a little more than eight months on the planet, what did she see?

She pointed to a group of old people fly-fishing into the waves that had eroded so much of the sands beneath the Boardwalk that they crashed over the seawall and spilled onto the street.

"Those are fishermen," Monroe said, suddenly embarrassed when one of them turned out to be a woman.

"And over there, that's a lighthouse," Monroe said to her, pointing out the Absecon Lighthouse, a nineteenth-century landmark now landlocked and rendered useless by the small navigation beacon at the northeast corner of the Boardwalk. "And that's an amusement pier, where they have rides and crazy things that you'll like when you're older. You see that pier? That's where Daddy stood, for five years, when he was on the Boardwalk beat. He stood in front of that pier and told old ladies where the public toilets were. Daddy was helping people."

Ellie held Monroe's left arm and helped pushed the stroller. She stopped in front of an oceanfront condo where she had lived when she was working as a call girl. "Helping people," she repeated absently.

As Sere stared at the large, gray, nasty winter gulls soaring overhead, Ellie said, "I have to get out of here."

"To work."

"The Oriental marketing party. There are a million and one details."

"They can wait," Monroe said.

"They can't."

244

Monroe saw the beach stretching out, a wild, strange, empty place ending in crashing, slate-colored surf. They passed joggers and people on bicycles, bundled up in bright jackets and pants, a few bus people getting pushed in rolling chairs, and some older folks from the senior citizens' housing projects. Just about everyone smiled warmly when they saw Sere. What was it about kids, Monroe asked himself, that brought out deep feelings in people?

"We have to get out the invitations," Ellie said. "We have to get some Asian American organizations involved. We have to put out press releases."

She let go of his arm and Monroe saw the tower of the Alcazar Casino Hotel rising high above them, one among the other casino hotels looming above the Boardwalk, arrogantly lording it over the ocean like the imposing, enigmatic stone statues of Easter Island.

"What? Carl will be mad?" Monroe snapped. "Who's more important in your life, him or me?"

She stared at him for what must have been an entire minute, her face stretched out and down, distorted by shock that rapidly gave way to disgust.

"After all that's gone on, you have to ask?"

And she turned away from him and began walking toward the casino.

Monroe didn't follow her. Sere was watching the birds. She hadn't seen her mother leave.

He turned the stroller around. "Sere, your mother and I have had a disagreement."

Sere pointed to a bird and said, "Gahh."

"That's a bird, girl. Say bird."

She pointed to him and said, "Gahh, gahh."

He thought of his wife going to the big tower on the Boardwalk, where she could park her casino car in the casino garage, get her meals in the casino, work off the meals in the casino health club, buy her clothes in the casino shops, get her hair done in the casino salon, sleep in a casino hotel room and maybe find the boss of the casino share the *room*, if not the bed, with her.

She also got money, money that bought the stroller Sere was sitting in. She got that for making people come to Atlantic City and gamble.

His job was supposed to be . . . what?

He was passing New York Avenue. He paused, looked down toward the pink-and-green awning of the Demimonde Nightclub. Parked in front was the official business car.

Harry the Toad had said it was a toss-up between him and someone else. As if to answer his unvoiced question, Darrell Pratt emerged from the club with a large black plastic garbage bag filled with what resembled, from a distance, bundles of cash.

He thought he heard the ocean move closer to him, the sound rising to take him and drag him down.

◆

Cynthia Verheull was waiting for them on the porch when they came back.

He introduced them. "Ms. Verheull, this is Serendipity Monroe."

She had been crying but she brightened when she bent forward and shook Sere's little hand.

Sere said, "Hool."

"There, you're on a first-name basis," Monroe said.

"Ellie's—?"

"At the casino," Monroe said, hoping his face would hide any feelings.

"You're going to need help with that." They lifted the stroller onto the porch. He unlocked the door and she lifted a surprisingly uncomplaining Sere into her arms and up the stairs.

Together they unwrapped Sere and changed her. Cynthia

246

got the bottle from the refrigerator and Monroe fed her on the couch. Cynthia sat on the recliner and watched Sere close her eyes and fall asleep in Monroe's arms.

They put her in the crib. Monroe kissed her forehead, letting his lips linger on the warm, soft skin.

Then they sat on the stairs. "You saw the paper?" she asked him.

"I saw what they wrote. They don't always get it right."

"They said he found out from the police department."

"It wasn't me," Monroe said.

She sat with her knees against her chest, her arms wrapped tightly around her legs. "I've been offered fifty thousand dollars," she said.

"As a settlement?"

"Go-away money."

"You have to go away?"

She folded her arms. "There isn't much point in staying. It doesn't matter if I take it or not. My job's gone."

"If it's government it's almost impossible for them to fire you."

"I didn't tell them what I did before I went to secretarial school. They can fire you for not telling them some things. Besides . . ."

"You've lost your taste for it?"

"For a lot of things." She looked back into the apartment. "I can't understand how some people can be so lucky. The kind that just walks right into the casino and hits the jackpot. I look at what Ellie's got. . . . This is all I ever wanted. A place to come home to. A little baby to love me. A husband I can depend on. If I had to spend two years turning tricks to get a real sense of what I want out life, why can't I get it? Why can't it just happen for me?"

"I don't have an answer for that," Monroe said.

"I thought Ellie would. What if I just call her?"

"She's hard to get ahold of. I told her about you, though."

247

"I hope she . . . I hope she understood."

"She did."

"I just don't know what to do."

"About the money?"

"About everything. I wanted to ask Ellie. I thought she could tell me."

Monroe thought about it. "You get to a place, sometimes, when you can't ask anybody. You have to trust yourself."

"I trusted myself and look what happened. I've never been offered so much money that I didn't want."

"Then don't take it," Monroe said.

"And do what? Tell the media that they're trying to buy me off?"

"You tell the media, and you can't be sure how they'll play it. Don't say anything. Just take Todesco to court."

"But a jury isn't going to look at me like a person who was abused and intimidated and wants to see the laws work for a change. They'll see cheap trash."

"They're not supposed to. They're supposed to see what's in front of them."

"Do they ever?"

"You have to hope they will."

She straightened her legs. "Part of me says, To hell with it, take the money and move somewhere and try to forget about it."

"But you won't forget about it."

She shook her head.

"Do you know who made the offer?"

"No. If I find out who, will you arrest him?"

Monroe couldn't look at her. "It's not a crime to pay someone to do nothing," he said.

She said, "Cops." She went down the stairs and never came back again.

Chapter Eighteen

♦ ♦ ♦ ♦ ♦

Tell Her About It

The call from the casino came as Monroe had finished feeding Sere dinner.

"Our marriage is over, Lou."

Monroe looked at Sere on the carpet, moving around a rubber ball. "Sere's staying here," he said.

"She's staying there until I get a full-time caregiving situation set up here. Then I'm coming to get her."

"She's my daughter," Monroe said, hearing the ocean roar around him.

"She's never been your daughter. There isn't a court in the land that won't give her to me."

"We're not going to court." He tried to say that he couldn't imagine fighting her, but he felt himself choking up.

"How did this happen?" he said finally.

"It doesn't matter how," Ellie said. "What matters is what we're doing about it."

"Ellie, we should put things back together."

"I'm not sure I want them back together. I don't want to stay with a man that hates what I do for a living."

"I don't. . . . I just feel that . . ."

"I *know* what you feel, and I'm tired of it. Get it through your banged-up skull, Lou, it's not me and not the industry that's doing something bad. It's self-serving assholes like you who demand that we be what you want us to be. If you'd just let me be what I am, you might understand that

249

there's nothing wrong with what I do, and that I have every right to be as successful as I can because, like it or not, the casino industry *is* this town and it's not going away and we'd all better be on the same side or the town'll go right back down the tubes again."

"Ellie, you can . . . you can be anything you want. Just, don't ruin what we have together."

"We don't have anything left to ruin," Ellie said.

"We have . . . we do have something."

"What? Each other?"

"No. We have hope."

"Speak for yourself."

He heard the line go dead and wondered if it would be okay for Sere to see him like this.

◆

MacReedy ignored him for the entire night.

Ellie arrived in a limousine the next morning to take Sere with her. She came with a woman from the casino's day-care center and a pair of casino security guards to help her move out some of Sere's things.

Monroe sat at the kitchen table, watching it happen, watching Sere's amused expression: another fun ride in the big car, Ellie promised her. He said nothing and did nothing until she was nearly finished.

Then he went to his wife and put his hands on her hands and said, "Don't go."

"I am. We're just incapable of being together."

"I'm capable," he said.

"You're not interested in me or my career."

"So," Monroe began. "How's your Oriental marketing event?"

She sighed. "The guest of honor wants to make a speech and he won't let us approve it in advance."

"What's wrong with that?"

"He is to be seen and not heard. He could make some

stray remark and the media could go to town on him, on the casino, everybody."

"Why can't you trust him?"

"Because he's a bitter, hateful individual and you were having an affair with his wife."

He was almost grateful when she said it, because he had been expecting it, waiting for it, not knowing what he would do when it came.

"Ellie, we just talked, that's all. I needed someone to talk to and you were at the casino all the time."

"Well, *I* needed someone who was on my side, who didn't look at me and my job as a crime against humanity, and I found him, and I've done a little more than talk."

She was trying to hurt him and he let her. Then he said, "Ellie, I'm still on your side."

"Lou, we've been through this. We're just not right for each other."

"Ellie . . ." He tried to take her hands again but she wouldn't let him. "We need to start over again. We need to open up to each other. We need to have faith in each other, to trust each other. I promise you, I'll go see the casino. I'll accept what you do. I'll try to enjoy it."

"I don't believe you anymore, Lou, and now that I have my daughter, I don't care. But I do trust you. I trust you to stay out of my life."

She went out, leaving the door open. He was shivering in the cold before he turned and closed it.

♦

As sober as a funeral director at an Irish wake, tall, distinguished, stoop-shouldered Carl Cayleen, chairman and CEO of the Alcazar Casino Hotel, Inc., began by telling the thousand or so people huddled in the rain on the Boardwalk two days before Christmas Eve how honored, and lucky, he and his casino were to host this important event.

"The truth of the matter is that the people who come to

this city, which, when I look at our demographics, is still justified in calling itself the World's Playground though I would like to see more customers from the Antarctica market—Ellie? Can you get on that? Where's the great gal who pulled off this shebang? Ellie? She must be inside waiting for me to shut up so we can all go to the reception."

In your goddamn casino with my daughter, Monroe wanted to shout. But he kept quiet. Cayleen said his piece, and moved back.

A wet wind laden with rain, brine, and decay tumbled in from the ocean, blasting the modern, postcasino Atlantic City reek of diesel fumes off the Boardwalk. Monroe was part of a crowd of well over 1,000 Chinese people in dark raincoats and umbrellas, mixed with police officers from all over the state in their dress blues, black rain slickers, caps riding high on their heads, their faces turned toward the dais erected just to the side of the red-and-gold light-spangled Boardwalk entrance to the Alcazar Casino Hotel. He looked for Beth Todesco and didn't see her.

A woman in an eye-searingly bright red down coat from some international federation of Asian Americans stepped to the rostrum, thanked Cayleen, and introduced the Honorable Bernard Tilton, the mayor of Atlantic City, who had been standing uncomfortably on the edge of the dais beside Darrell Pratt and the short, potato-shaped frame of Atlantic City Police Chief Manuel Navarra, whose face gazed past the crowd at the dismal gray chop on the ocean.

Navarra had his hands on a wheelchair in which an even grayer Corporal Chou sat, frowning uncomfortably as the wind raked his face, his dress blues exposed under a new, police-issue storm coat, his leg thrust forward in a cast.

"Nee how ma!" Tilton boomed into the microphone.

The woman from the Asian federation seemed confused. Then she responded to the traditional Chinese greeting, *"Ding ho!"*

Tilton smiled. "Friends, visitors, Americans, we're here

252

to honor a hero among us. We're also here to honor the hero that is in all of us, the spirit that doesn't stop, doesn't hesitate to defend his city. The people of this city, as well as Asian Americans everywhere, have been through tough times. I'm pleased to say that due to the effort, determination, and cooperation of our people here, we have the manpower, and the money, to reinvent our city as what *we* want it to be. And, through the efforts of people like Detective Ying Luck 'Jack' Chou, we are living in that city now."

More applause followed, and the woman from the Asian federation came out. Chief Navarra wheeled Chou forward. The mayor held up a tiny blue Distinguished Public Service Medal and, as the woman translated, announced that he was giving the medal to "one who was willing to give everything for all of us."

The crowd applauded. The mayor and the woman from the Asian federation applauded. Carl Cayleen applauded. Photographers took pictures and their flash bulbs made the rain sparkle. Then Chou reached for the microphone.

"He wants to say something!" the woman from the Asian federation cried as she handed Chou the microphone.

A strange, eerie tension rippled through the crowd. No one really wanted to hear Chou talk. The ceremony was over. It was time to go into the casino, dry off, grab some food at the party, and gamble.

Chou put the microphone to his lips and Monroe tried to read his face. He saw fear on it, and Monroe believed that, in an odd but not unusual way, Chou's fear was the same as his.

"I WANT TO SAY," Chou's voice roared out at such a volume that people plugged their ears. The mayor pulled the microphone a few inches from his face, and Chou said, "I want to say that . . . I was born here and . . ."

He stared at the expectant faces and, for a moment, seemed spellbound by their attention.

"I was born here, on Nevada Avenue and, I want to say

that I grew up with the feeling that people will hate us, that they will do whatever possible to prevent us from being what we are, and who we want to be and . . . and . . .''

He faltered. The mayor moved to grab the microphone but Chou held on to it. "Sitting in that hospital, being awake and aware as I heard the doctors cutting off my leg because, because, to you, maybe, I was in the right place at the right time, I came to an understanding. I've learned that . . .''

He faltered again, aware, Monroe guessed, that to these people and the city his experience was insignificant. His fame had been engineered. He was just another draw, a pull, an excuse to bring people to the Boardwalk where the temptations would work on them and take their money.

And yet, Monroe sensed, Chou's microdot of fame had given him an audience, and with that audience he had a few seconds of power and Monroe hung on the question of how Chou would use that power. Would he inflict upon them the bitterness he deserved to feel? Or what he said just might outlast this dreary day, and change, even in the smallest way, the forlorn city and the numerous visitors and inhabitants.

"I've learned that," Chou repeated, "I've learned that as bad as life can get—"

The mayor reached for the microphone again.

"In a moment, it can all be different. Our luck can turn, our lives can change. A person as unworthy as myself can be up here, in front of you, for no reason other than that I survived."

He let go of the microphone, shocked at what had come out of his mouth. The mayor took it, said, "Let's get the hell inside!"

Monroe tried to catch Chou's eye but the man had slipped into a daze. A group of Atlantic City police officers surrounded the wheelchair, and, like pallbearers, slowly lowered it to the wet Boardwalk, where it was rolled into the Alcazar.

Pieto Soladias was in a group at the far end, laughing with his bodyguards, who were holding umbrellas over his head. Monroe watched as Soladias started a shambling walk from the casino toward Nevada Avenue.

Monroe followed him, hearing snatches of conversation, and more laughter. The man was so proud, so assured of his own importance, that Monroe thought he felt as Chou had, helpless and angry and darkly convinced that if we could only get rid of the Soladiases, our streets would be safe, or children would never try to destroy themselves, there would be no murder, poverty, or despair.

This feeling, this furious hatred, was wrong, Monroe reminded himself. It was wrong and it was stupid because it distracted from the complex social forces that permit vicious, brutal, selfish individuals, in legitimate or illegitimate enterprises, from looting the resources, perverting the trust, and distorting the values that keep America from sliding into tyranny.

Monroe knew it was wrong but he found himself enjoying it. Hatred was such a vast organizing principle. How simple, he decided, just to kill the man. Make the world a better place.

He passed a patrol car that was idling on the Boardwalk, theoretically as a crowd-control device, but actually on the boards because it was a hell of a lot of fun to exercise the perk of law enforcement and put your big, fat, rumbling patrol car in a place that had been sanctified for human feet.

Bigfish and Jerry Lad were in the car, eating pizza, watching Soladias and his crew lope past them. Monroe heard Bigfish mutter to Jerry Lad, "I still think I can take that half-pint son of a bitch."

Monroe turned.

Jerry Lad said, "I think he heard you."

255

Monroe put his hand on the driver's-side door where Bigfish sat. Bigfish made a show of keeping calm. He opened his mouth, stuck in his fingers to extract a sliver of pepperoni that had failed to take the long slide down to his stomach.

"Try," Monroe said.

"You talking to me?" Bigfish said.

"Get out of the car."

Bigfish smiled, took his time putting down his pizza, pulling his raincoat around him, slowly, slowly opening the door, putting one big boot on the wet boards, and then another, then rising like a colossus to glare down at Monroe.

But Monroe wasn't under him. He had slipped behind Bigfish, into the driver's seat, slammed the door, put the car in gear, and started moving forward.

Bigfish said, "Hey—"

Inside the car, Jerry Lad said, "You really shouldn't be driving, somebody in your condition—"

Monroe stopped the car and Jerry Lad's face went into the dashboard. "Get out," Monroe said.

Bigfish came around to Jerry Lad's door, which was unlocked. He opened it, thinking to reach past Jerry Lad for the keys.

But Monroe, because of his small stature, had no difficulty lifting his right foot off the gas pedal, pulling his right leg into his chest, shifting slightly, and planting a side kick into Jerry Lad's hip that sent him sliding out of the car into Bigfish, pushing them both onto the boards.

He reached over, closed the door and locked it.

"Payback time," Monroe said.

♦

Soladias and his crew were strutting down the broad ramp at Nevada Avenue. The ramp was wide enough to permit Boardwalk access to patrol cars, repair trucks, and vehicles in the Miss America parade.

256

Monroe let the patrol car glide up behind them. He saw the remains of the building that Chou had destroyed, and beside it, what looked like a little grocery store. Light shone from the windows above the store, and a new, stubby, bug-like black Porsche 911 was parked in front.

Monroe checked the rearview mirror, saw Bigfish and Jerry Lad arguing with each other as to who would radio in the loss of a patrol car. Then he turned on the cherry light and floored the gas pedal and aimed the car at Soladias, who must have heard the engine race, because he glanced over his shoulder and veered away as the patrol car shot by him into the wet street.

Soladias's largest bodyguard pulled out a handgun but Soladias laughed and motioned him to follow him into the grocery store.

Monroe stopped the car, threw it into reverse, swept around until he was facing the grocery store. Then he tapped the gas and the patrol car's V-8 surged, kicking the car up the curb, over the sidewalk, splintering cheap ply-wood and shattering glass until Monroe saw Soladias's face go sheet white and the bodyguard bring up a Ruger .44.

The windshield in front of Monroe shattered but held. He didn't know what to do next. He didn't care. He couldn't stop the car, which plowed into aisles of cellophane-wrapped cookies and pies and newspapers and cans of cream of tomato soup.

Pieto skipped through the back door. It was like hide-and-seek. Monroe wondered if the grocery store would hold. It did. He crashed through the back of the store, bursting into an alley.

Soladias ran between one of the bungalows, back toward Nevada Avenue. Monroe put the car in reverse, backed through the grocery store, hitting something with plumbing that shot water over everything before the car waddled onto Nevada Avenue, pulling the store down with it.

Soladias dove into the black Porsche. For a moment it

seemed as if his bodyguard was too big to fit. But he did, and the Porsche's headlights winked on. Its wheels were spinning when Monroe slammed into its rear end. The Porsche shot ahead, scuttling up Nevada Avenue like a black insect. Monroe kept on its tail, smashing into it again as the Porsche spun around and headed toward him.

At the last second both cars veered away. Monroe hit the brakes, spun the patrol car around, and was four car lengths away as the Porsche left the street for the sidewalk and the ramp that took it up onto the Boardwalk.

Somewhere in Monroe's brain was a sign flashing that it was illegal for privately owned vehicles to drive on the Boardwalk. People could get hurt.

Soladias drove fast enough to indicate to the few guys with the plastic-wrapped rolling chairs and the people walking with umbrellas that he didn't care if anybody got hurt.

Monroe gripped the steering wheel lightly. It was time to get the bad guy.

They were soon past the casinos, screeching around the bend at the opening of Absecon Channel, coming down on the big, wide ramp leading to Atlantic Avenue. This was the last ramp big enough to take a car before the Boardwalk ended, about a quarter mile to the north.

The Porsche revved toward the ramp and Monroe hit the gas. At the last second the Porsche tried to turn aside, but slipped and snagged a fender on the steel railing. The fender tore itself off the car and the car bounced off the opposite railing, coming to rest in the center of the ramp.

Monroe pumped his brakes and skidded into the Porsche, spinning around and around until he heard something grinding and he saw it was the Porsche, groaning into first gear, heading down the Boardwalk, toward the very end. Monroe gave chase. He floored the gas pedal and kissed the Porsche's crumpled back bumper.

He used to run this part of the Boardwalk. He knew the

last-chance ramp at the very end that led down to the vacant stretch that once was Captain Starn's Pier.

If only he knew the patrol car as well. Unlike human legs and running shoes, which can stop and start on a dime, the patrol car had accumulated a surprising factor of inertia on the wet boards. When the Porsche slowed to make a quick swerve toward the down-ramp, and Monroe pumped the patrol car's brakes, the patrol car was going too fast to stop. He hit the Porsche, spun it around, and veered to the right as a railing appeared in front of him. The railing broke apart as the car pushed through. Monroe heard metal scream and break and the dark face of the water come up and push in the shattered section of the windshield as the car went down, flipped, and hit the water on its back.

At that point Monroe wondered if he'd buckled his safety belt.

◆

Nobody tells you what to do when you drive a police car into eight feet of freezing ocean water.

It took some doing. Monroe had to remember where he was. He had to figure out why the engine was racing overhead, and why it suddenly gurgled and died, and why he was upside down with his head bent against the dome light.

Where the hell was the water coming from? The ocean was swirling around him and it was real this time.

He gulped air and tried to open a door. It wouldn't budge. Water was pressing it closed. He tried to open a window and cursed the fact that patrol cars have power windows. He was certain that power windows don't operate when a car is underwater.

The key was still in the steering wheel column. Monroe said, *What the hell*, twisted the key back to accessory (heard the ping of the key-is-in-the-ignition-asshole gadget), and hit the power-window switch and nothing happened.

He did it again and got mad, then realized that part of the problem of being upside down is being upside down, and that he was pressing the damned lever in the wrong direction because he was sitting in an upside-down car.

So he pressed the lever the other way and got a numbing blast of salt water in his face, in his mouth, up his nose, down his back, in his throat—which made him cough bubbles that blurred the lights on the dashboard that were still on as if it was perfectly normal to be upside down in eight feet of water that was really, *really* cold.

He reached out of the window and put his hand in briny goop. He had to grab something. He grabbed the window and noticed how small the windows were on these new-model patrol cars. You'd think there'd be more room, you'd think Detroit would assume that sooner or later some hot-rod cop would shove his car off the Boardwalk into Absecon Channel and have to pull a medium-sized human body out of a window.

Sometimes you can be happy, and even thank God that you were born short and slight of build. The window edges scraped against his skin and he had the unpleasant sensation of pulling himself into the dark water (glowing oddly from the cherry bar that was still flickering somewhere in the murk) and *still* being upside down as even more water worked itself into his eyes, ears, nose, and throat.

And then he was up, out, his head bursting into cold, windy air, mouth opening, coughing up half the channel while the water threw him against the patrol car's rear tire. The rubber was still hot.

Before he could grab the tire, he was out and over it. The tide was coming in and the channel was swollen with ocean water rushing into Clam Creek. Monroe went under, flapped his arms, and went under again, turned over onto his stomach and heard someone shouting at him.

Soladias's bodyguard jumped off the Boardwalk, landed heavily on the beach rubble. He took off his long leather jacket and marched into the surf, twirling the jacket over-head like a lasso. He flung it at Monroe.

Monroe thought, This guy wants to save my life. He tried to tell the bodyguard to fuck himself, but the freezing water was throwing him into shock. He was sinking and he gagged on water.

Later he would say he had a vision of his daughter in his arms, turning to him, opening her mouth, saying, in Chou's voice, "Get the bad guy."

He pushed down with his arms, stuck his head above the water, and grabbed the jacket.

Jesus pulled him in, then fished out his gun and threw it in the ocean, then hoisted him up and carried him to the edge of the Boardwalk and shoved him under the railing.

Monroe lay on his side, feeling the hard, wet boards beneath him. He coughed up water and saw Pieto Soladias standing over him.

"Okay," he said. "We're even now. I save you. You save me."

"I'm . . . not . . . done . . . yet," Monroe said, coughing pitifully.

"You done. You well done," Soladias laughed. "You try to fight me, you lose. Everybody who fight me lose, because Pieto Soladias is what it's all about. You have to lose because you go up against somebody that never lose. It's not in the plan, man. Now, you tell me, what I do to get you mad, hey?"

He extended a hand. Monroe grabbed it and let Soladias pull him to his feet.

"Get with the program, man. I give you a ride home."

He glanced at the bodyguard, who had pulled himself up from the beach and now stood beside Monroe. "Jesus, baby, that Porsche don't seat three. I take Monroe home. You go back to base. I meet you, okay?"

He pulled a wad of cash from his pocket. "Here, for this, the jitney, or a taxi."

Jesus seemed astonished, and then hurt, not that Soladias would abandon him, wet and freezing, but that he would spend any time out of his protection.

"It's okay, Jesus," Soladias said. "He can't do anything to me I need you to save me from."

Jesus didn't move as Soladias went back to the Porsche.

♦

"I want to tell you, it wasn't against you personal that I tried to kill you, when you were up on that building spying on me. I had to make a statement. Sometimes you gotta make a statement."

Monroe said nothing.

"It would have been good I was wrong about you, that you really could have killed me," Soladias said as the car oozed into gear. "But I was right. I'm always right."

Monroe was dripping wet, his teeth chattering, as he said, "Wrong."

"Opposite, eh? I'm right, you're wrong. You get tired of being wrong, sometimes? Me, I'm never tired of being right. Being right is what it's all about."

Monroe asked himself what he was going to do. He couldn't punch the guy out in a speeding car.

And then Monroe saw it. He finally knew how to get this bad guy.

"Have you ever been to a casino?"

"Whaddayou mean, been to a casino?" Soladias said as he eased the Porsche through the Inlet streets. "Someday maybe I buy one. But the shows they got there? Boring, most of them. And I don't gamble. I'm not that stupid."

"I hate casinos," Monroe said carefully.

"Shit, you can't just tell me you hate where your wife works and makes all that money."

"Casinos take money from people. They turn ordinary people into losers. It's a rip-off and everybody knows it and yet the people keep coming and keep losing."

"That's because everybody want to be a winner. You want to know the secret to winning, man, it's not giving a shit. I don't give a shit whatever I do, and look at me. You go in a casino, there, you put your money down, and you don't give a shit, they can't get you."

"You're wrong," Monroe said, hearing the first nail hammering itself into Soladias's coffin.

♦

She had to be paged.

"I'm not talking to you," she said.

"I'm bringing you a customer, a very, very rich customer who wants to clean the casino out," Monroe said on Soladias's car phone. "He wants his own table." To Soladias: "What kind of table?"

"A table to play on, man. Something with felt on it, I don't give a shit."

"What kind of game do you want to play? Blackjack? Roulette? Baccarat? Poker? Craps?"

"Something with a dealer in it, man. I don't like dice. Too easy to fuck with them. Make it cards, the twenty-one thing."

"He wants his own blackjack table," Monroe told Ellie.

"How much is he coming in with?"

"He's the guy backing the Miracle Mile," Monroe said.

"Lou, if you're bullshitting me . . ." she began. "We can't do anything for him unless he's rated."

"What does he have to do to get rated?"

"He'll have to come in, apply for credit, which means we'll need a financial statement or some verification of available funds on deposit."

Monroe held the phone away from his mouth so his wife could hear. He asked Soladias. "You got any money in a bank?"

Soladias opened his mouth and savored the words. "Twenty-two-point-five-five-two-million dollars. It's in banks and stocks and land and all kinds of shit, man."

"You know where it all is?"

Soladias tapped his head. "All of it. You think I'm stupid or something?"

"You know the account numbers?"

"You don't do business unless you got a head for numbers."

Monroe said to his wife. "We'll be at the casino in five minutes."

"We'll be ready," she said.

♦ ♦ ♦ ♦ ♦

Chapter Nineteen

The Right Place

Under the rules established in New Jersey for granting casino credit, a gambler has to provide the number of a bank, stock, bond, or money-market account before the casino could advance him a chip to play with.

As Soladias provided one number to an unusually flustered credit manager, Monroe tried to go off and find a phone to call in an all-points bulletin on a blue Mercedes, New Jersey tags.

"You staying with me," Soladias said. "You going to bring me luck."

The credit manager was flustered by the fact that Soladias had recognized him as a former customer. "You want to know what I do with your fucking money, Charlie," Soladias announced, seated in a fake but luxurious Louis XIV chair in front of the VIP credit desk, situated just close enough to the casino to hear the jangling of the slot machines and smell the chilly mixture of booze, cigarette smoke, and adrenalized greed.

Monroe stood, dripping, at Soladias's right. At his left, Ellie Monroe in a smart, gray hound's-tooth suit with her casino ID badge prominently displayed. She wore the most astonishingly unrevealing poker face.

She blinked when Soladias gave more account numbers. The credit manager tapped them into a keyboard. Out of the corner of his eye, Monroe saw Ellie close her eyes and begin to pray.

"Bingo," the credit manager said.

Ellie opened her eyes, looked up, past the casino's gilded, glittering ceiling vaults, beyond the hidden catwalks and their unblinking surveillance cameras, through the restaurants and the hotel tower with its garish, uncomfortable rooms designed to make gamblers spend as little time in them as possible, through the roof, past the reddish, infernal halo that shrouded the casinos at night, to the starry firmament beyond and whatever gods, goddesses, deities, or demons presided over the acts of fate.

She mouthed the words, *Thank you.*

◆

After a half hour Louis Monroe managed to pursuade Soladias that Monroe was better off showering and changing into dry clothes instead of dripping and stinking beside him in a blackjack pit.

Soladias, who was slightly drunk on Coco Locos, down two million, and beginning to give a little more than a shit, said, "Sure, anything you want."

Monroe went off and called in an all-points bulletin on the Mercedes. Ellie wrote him a comp to the spa and the pro shop. He took a shower in the spa and put on an Alcazar green-and-purple warm-up suit, matching socks, and court shoes. He looked at himself in the mirror and decided the colors were a bit much, but he could get used to them.

He went down, saw a crowd had formed around Soladias that consisted of patrons as well as representatives of the New Jersey Division of Gaming Enforcement, the FBI, DEA, and IRS gaping at the mountain of square, platinum $10,000 plates Soladias was moving across the felt.

"He's down another eight hundred and fifty thousand," Ellie had told him. "This could be the biggest week of the year!"

Monroe said, "Great."

She added, "I hope you don't think this will have any effect on our marriage."

"I want to see my daughter," Monroe said.

"She's not your—"

"She *is*," Monroe said.

Ellie took him up to her room in the hotel. Sere was taking her nap in a portable crib. They watched her sleep for a while and Monroe put his arm around his wife.

She let him keep it there.

◆

It took the casino twenty hours and forty-two minutes, at the rate of about one million dollars an hour, to clean out Soladias. During that time Soladias ate and drank at his table, leaving it only to take bathroom breaks where, hidden cameras revealed, he ingested massive quantities of methamphetamine.

Monroe had been sleeping with his wife in his arms when the call came in. It was late morning. Soladias wanted to see him, now.

"Are you still in the casino?"

"You meet me outside, under the Boardwalk. You think I want those bastards watching me to try to get their hands on me?"

"How're you going to get out?"

"Through the kitchen, man. My customers remember me."

Monroe found him alone, squatting in the garbage without his coat, his eyes swollen into slits. He looked like a corpse. "Get me out of here," he said.

Monroe saw a few nails that hadn't been put in Soladias's coffin. "I'll call a cab," he said.

◆

"Having no money is nothing, man. You know those rich fucks in the restaurants and the hotels and the fancy shops in the casinos? They don't pay for nothing. Some of them, they're so important, the places they give it to them so they can say, Look at the rich fucks that come in here and eat."

Monroe nodded. Anthony Andropopolous, with his former police dog Patrocles in the front seat of his cab, came in a hurry.

"That Olde Salt place," Soladias said as he shut the door. He chewed on his knuckle. "What I've always wanted to do is go in that Olde Salt and have all those fat-assed fucks that think they're so big and powerful look up to me with the respect I deserve. Because I deserve it, man."

They left the cab in front of the Olde Salt. The lunch crowd was filing in and Soladias, his eyes sagging, his face marred with stubble, his breath foul and clothing soiled by spilled drinks and food, shoved past them and banged his hand on the maître d's podium and demanded a table by the fireplace.

Earl appeared immediately. He made a show of checking the list. "Mr. Soladias, I have something for you at the bar while your table is being prepared."

"Who the hell are you?"

"I'm the man who is going to buy you a free meal," Earl said, put his arm around Soladias, and gently pushed him toward the bar. "I've heard much about you." He caught Monroe's eye and beckoned him to follow.

"I'm having brandy," Earl said. To the bartender, "Mr. Soladias is having—?"

The bartender flinched at Soladias's name.

"A Coco Loco," Soladias breathed. "With the strongest rum you got."

"Mr. Monroe?"

Monroe declined.

Soladias curled his lip. "That one tending the bar, he must be one of my customers." He threw a leg over a stool. "Hey, man, what's your poison? Speed? Crack? What you

268

spend all your money on so you can put up with a job in a place like this?"

He turned to Earl. "You hear about me from him?"

Earl shook his head. "It's my business to be informed about important people in this city. I don't just feed people here. I serve the community."

"You own this joint?"

"Lock, stock, and barrel."

Soladias leered at Monroe. "Listen to him, the proud owner. You listen to me, man. You don't know what it means to own something until you lose it. I'll get it back, no problem, but it has to be gone for you to . . ."

His drink appeared and Earl lifted his. "I'm well aware of loss, Mr. Soladias." He waited until Soladias was swallowing when he said, "Akembe Augustino was my son."

Soladias continued drinking, his eyes rolling away, as if he'd caught the strains of a familiar tune playing in the room and was trying to remember the song's title. The alcohol made him shudder, so he put down the drink, wiped his arm on his sleeve, chewed on his knuckle, and said, "I never heard nobody with that name."

"Oh, he could have used a different name with you." Earl made a show of taking a deep breath and letting it out in a protracted sigh. "He wasn't the Boy Scout type and I am to blame for that. Akembe was never sure that I was his father. He's one of a . . . number of children of mine that I have had out of wedlock."

"Who needs kids? Who needs bitches, man? You fuck them and they think they own you," Soladias said.

"His mother died of a drug overdose when he was young," Earl went on, his words paced and calm. "I would occasionally arrange for him to have money, until I saw what he spent it on."

"I gotta say he was a fucking loser from the day he come to me. Only reason I kept him around was, you get days, you know, when you need to have somebody around who is worse off than you. Kids like him, they're born in the ghetto and they die in the ghetto."

"Yes," Earl said emotionlessly, watching tensely, like a praying mantis about to strike, as Soladias finished his drink.

Soladias set the glass down hard on the tabletop. "Where's my fucking table, man?"

"It's being prepared," Earl said. "I was wondering, though, this is your first time with us, isn't it?"

"First of many, man. Those fat-asses out there, they think people like me don't deserve to be in the same room with them, but, let me tell you, they're just like me. We're made of the same shit, them and me. They gotta get used to seeing me in the right places. Like this one, here."

"Yes, Mr. Soladias, this is the place for you. I wonder if you'd be interested in seeing our kitchen?"

"I want to eat the food, man. I don't want to see no fat-fuck cook spit in my soup. Make me lose my appetite."

"I thought that you'd be interested because the kitchen, unlike the dining room, is all new. About five years ago, we had a flood and I was forced to remodel. The insurance wasn't enough to pay for the damages and the new equipment I wanted, so Councilman Todesco arranged a cash loan for me."

"And he got the money from me," Soladias said.

"Councilman Todesco always treated me the best he was capable. That's all we can ask." He touched his brandy to his lips.

Soladias raised his glass. "I want another one of these, and with the *good* fucking rum, this time. You think I don't know cheap shit?"

The bartender glanced at Earl. Earl's eyes said *no*. "I'm aware that the money came from you, Mr. Soladias. Among the people who dine here, secrets are commodities that are traded, bought, or sold. Everyone in this room is aware of what happened to you last night. You're probably a topic of conversation. I'm sure many of my diners would love to meet you after—"

Soladias slid off his stool. "Let me at 'em, man."

"*After,*" Earl said, "I show you the kitchen you helped me buy."

Now it was Soladias's turn to take a breath and let it out in a slow, expansive, magnanimous mutter. "I'll see your kitchen, man, but I ain't paying for the lunch, man."

"Mr. Soladias, you've put in a lot to this community. It's payback time," Earl said, pushing away from the bar. He paused and caught Monroe's eye.

"I hope there are no objections from you, Mr. Monroe?"

Monroe said, "None from me."

"I gotta go hungry while I see a fucking kitchen," Soladias muttered. "Man, there's no such thing as a free lunch."

Monroe said, "If you don't mind, I'll sit it out here."

"Anything Mr. Monroe wants," Earl said to the bartender, "is on me."

"Sure," Monroe said.

Earl put his arm around Soladias's back and nudged him toward a side door behind the bar. "As I told you, Mr. Soladias, I don't feed people here. I serve my community."

Monroe drank a glass of water, put down a tip, and left after five minutes. He never saw Pieto Soladias again.

271

Epilogue

♦ ♦ ♦ ♦ ♦

While representatives of the Federal Drug Enforcement Agency, the FBI, the New Jersey Division of Gaming Enforcement, the Atlantic City Division of Taxation, and the Alcazar Casino Hotel, as well as several reporters for the Atlantic City *Star*, attempted to locate Pieto Soladias, Police Reporter Kevin Urlenmeyer, who was also Mr. Epicure, the newspaper's anonymous restaurant critic, wrote a rave in his "Moveable Feast" column about the "distinctively delicious" rib roast and creamed sweatbreads specials at the Olde Salt.

Patrolmen Anthony Filmont and Jerome Ladzinski claimed that they contracted food poisoning from rancid pepperonis, and that this caused them to black out while on duty. They had no further explanation as to why their assigned patrol car ended up in Absecon Channel.

While in Atlantic City General, Detective Jack Chou sold a piece of property on Pacific Avenue to K-Zar Resorts, parent company of the Alcazar Casino Hotel, Inc., for two-point-three million. He then announced his retirement from the Atlantic City Police Department. He has not yet reconciled with his wife, Traffic Safety Officer Elizabeth Todesco, though her signature appears more frequently on his visitor log.

Hamilton Earl, owner of the Olde Salt restaurant, has identified himself as the principal donor to the Make the Grade scholarship fund. He was recently profiled in *Roll-*

ing Chair magazine as one of the "Ten Guys with Clout." The Atlantic City *Star* has reported that the Miracle Mile project was shelved due to lack of significant financial commitment. A check signed by Peter Salazar, drawn on the account of Miracle Mile Associates, for $15,000 made payable to the City of Atlantic City, was returned for insufficient funds.

In addition to his duties as public information officer, Sergeant Darrell Pratt has become the host of *Walk the Walk*, a local public-access cable TV show highlighting the personalities behind law enforcement. Captain Dennis "Sir Isaac" Newton, billed as the Comedy Cop, was the first guest.

Carl Cayleen resigned from the Alcazar to accept the chairmanship of a casino management company that is currently entertaining elected officials in Baltimore, Philadelphia, and Washington, D.C., with visions of new jobs, increased tourist spending, higher tax revenues, and the "whole new level of excitement" that legalized gambling can bring.

Former Alcazar marketing vice president Dan Raleigh has returned as the casino hotel's new chief executive officer.

A jury eventually found Councilman Harry Todesco guilty of sexual harassment and discrimination against Ms. Cynthia Verheull. The foreman of the jury said that it was Ms. Verheull's honesty, in describing both her former and current occupation, that impressed upon them the seriousness of her allegations. In addition to ordering Ms. Verheull to receive the promotion and salary increase, retroactive to the date she filed charges, the jury awarded her $200,000 in punitive damages. Councilman Todesco has appealed the verdict.

Marty Gant, commander of Internal Affairs, was promoted to the rank of inspector. A widower, Gant has been seen in the company of Dangerous Delores LiPatti.

Mrs. Ellen Monroe was made a full-time director of marketing at the Alcazar Casino Hotel. She is supervising the collection of Pieto Soladias's twenty-point-one million dollar gambling debt.

During the spring, the Monroe family traveled to Philadelphia, where they boarded a cruise to Bermuda. Before leaving, Louis Monroe was told that he had been transferred into the Internal Affairs Division to serve under Marty Gant.

Resplendent in a matching ensemble of Alcazar Casino Hotel pool wear, Monroe relaxed with his wife and daughter on the pink, carefully tended sand of Horseshoe Bay. Aware that he owed his visit to the fragile island paradise to the casino at which his wife labored, he decided that legalized gambling did have a place in the scheme of things, and that he could, after all, accept his wife and the success she worked so hard to achieve.

He became confident that he would finally be able to appreciate Atlantic City, not as a morally conflicted morass of schemes and scams, but as a place of strange contrasts and sudden reversals, of high drama and low humor, of elite sophistication and hideous bad taste, and, most significantly, a city of people who, however much they fight and stumble on the straight and narrow path, remain capable of doing the right thing.

Sure. Why not?